Jasper's Cafe On The Boulevard

Tracey Fagan Danzey

ISBN-13: 978-1508483250
ISBN-10: 1508483256

*Written for my beloved mother and dearly missed friend,
Mrs. Dana E. Fagan, and my grandmother, whom was shared by
many and affectionately named "Nonnie," Mrs. Evelyn Elizabeth Ray
Gaitwood, my rock, my hero and my inspiration.*

*This book is dedicated to an amazing, likeable, valiant individual. He is
a gentleman that I remain in admiration of while having the privilege of
calling him my son . . . Tanner Ryan Fagan.*

You are your mother's joy.

Gratitude

At the very end of each and every day, I fall on my knees and begin to pray.
I ask the Lord to be my guide and to make my wisdom broad and wide.
Help me to accept the trials of living then sincerely thank Him for all He's
giving.
Walk with me each and every day, as He looks over me and my family every
step of the way.
I ask Him to take us in His arms and to protect us all from any great harm.
As for each newborn, whether boy or girl; teach them to spread joy all over the
world.
Then after I've put in all my requests, I rest peacefully knowing how much
I've been blessed.

Dana E. Fagan

ACKNOWLEDGEMENTS

Thank you for the continued encouragement through the years of this project resting on dusty shelves when life borrowed me time and time again. My mother's lingering words would have me remove it from the shelves as an incomplete manuscript, and only to return as a published novel.

I offer my heartfelt gratitude to my Life Coach, Erika Foster, and to my Editor and biggest supporter, Jamie (a.k.a. "Slash"), for each continuing to see the vision on the days and nights when I couldn't. Additional gratitude to those I've had the pleasure of working with at the Westport Writers' Workshop for critiquing, celebrating, and inspiring my work while validating me as a storyteller.

To my dear, dear, dear beta readers and friends. Thank you for believing in me as a writer, respecting my developing craft while not treating it as such. You allowed me to exhaust you with endless queries and concerns about this story. Please know that it was your feedback and relationship with each of the characters, along with those immeasurable words of encouragement that has made this project viable. Thank you Tosha Schmidt, Christine Conti, Marisa O'Doherty, Scottenia Williams, Almarie Barge, Kay Woodard, Pamela R. Hardy, Erika Foster and Lisa Harewood, my very first beta reader. Each of you will always be VIP Patrons of Jasper's Cafe with your names written on the walls and a place card in my heart. Thank you! And to Brenda Taylor Wright, thank you for being my Simone.

Simply stated, I am the luckiest girl to have the steadfast support from my very best friend, cheerleader, and husband, Tony Danzey, who often reminds me, "You can do it, baby!" When someone else believes in you more than you believe in yourself and tells you often enough, it becomes magic! Thank you for always making me believe, Mr. Danzey, and for believing in me. To my sister and BFF Tosha— thanks for running the race with me! To Tanya—you are absolutely perfect! And smooches to my Baby Girl (a.k.a. Nikki). To Joseph Fagan—thank you for allowing me to be a daddy's girl. To the other men in my life, Thomas Fagan, Brett and Vance Gibson (a.k.a. my brothers), thank you for loving me and always supporting me.

Thank you, Father God, for without you, I am nothing and none of this would be possible. The glory belongs to you.

JASPER'S CAFE

Sometimes I don't even know who I am anymore. I can't help but wonder who they believe me to be. I feel emotionally dwarfed, always showing up on the outside looking like one person and feeling so completely like another inside. Really, who am I? I sit in my car and scrutinize each patron as they walk in and out of Jasper's Cafe, over and over again, doing my best to identify anyone displaying behaviors worthy of me hijacking, and then I go all in, trying to capture their slightest mannerisms to later assimilate. That probably sounds pretty crazy and may explain some of my confusion. Oh, but the truth in all of this is, it's not crazy, and I'm certainly not crazy. I'm just beginning to do the work on myself to better answer everyone's question, now forcing a confronting reality for me . . . who is Torie Lynn Harper? They should probably be very careful of what they've asked for because they may just get to know me!

These feelings of confusion began soon after moving from my home in New Canaan, Connecticut, a small affluent New England town where the Black population is less than one percent, to the nearby inner city of Stamford. I quickly learned that being Black, educated and gorgeous would not prove to be a key into their community. My being polished and privileged seems to only make my acceptance by the masses further out of reach. To understand me is to understand that I have now been forced to master the ability to speak fluently in urban dialogue, often supporting it with the sometimes necessary facial expressions and body language that inherently makes one think twice before trying me. I can even apply a delicate wag to the neck when warranted—all of this in my efforts to simply fit in. I have learned that being a social hybrid isn't necessarily a bad thing; there are many advantages to being able to speak in a softer tone with methodically paced inflections, crisp enunciation of specific syllables, and always sealing it with the appropriate formality. For some, it suggests that I am a pedigree; sadly for others, it lends to the idea that I think I'm White. Now that's a notion that isn't even possible, nor desired. It's kind of like having had voice lessons all of my life; I'm constantly prepared to be called for a performance in a moment's notice. I switch as often as needed from a primary language to a secondary and from the secondary back to the primary, each dictated by the company that I am in at the time. Now that probably sounds crazy, but it's become my life.

Millie will be here any second now, and she'll talk me out of this funk. Lately this seems to be her reoccurring role. Well, ever since Mother and Nanna Bess passed away, particularly because I hadn't been given enough time to process Granddaddy's sudden death 13 months prior. While cancer is extremely unkind, heart attacks are particularly cold and cruel because they often don't allow you to say goodbye. That part about Millie's new role isn't true. Millie has been taking care of me, or as I prefer to say, "has had my back," since we were five years old. I can recall it so vividly, Mother holding my hand while walking me through the doors of Mrs. Palmer's kindergarten classroom. All of the children were seated in rows of four, each of the boys and girls were completely uniformed, and by that I mean White! There wasn't one child who went beyond cream on the color wheel—not even beige, a color that resembled my mother and grandparents at least. Requesting someone to be as brown as me would be a far reach. Certainly that was my very first time feeling . . . different. I would never have that feeling again until moving to the city. That day was monumental for many reasons; it was my very first day of kindergarten, the first time that I would meet my new best friend, and the first of many days in my life when I'd be putting on my big-girl panties. Five-year-old Mildred Kravitz saw my uneasiness as I buried my face in my mother's coat. She immediately abandoned her seat to greet me with huge welcoming eyes and brownish-red spirals falling across her face, only moving those that obstructed her view. She stood and waited patiently with her hand extended offering, "Come on, you can sit with me and we can be best friends." We have been just that every day since. We even methodically planned our acceptance to Penn State where she earned her law degree and I earned my Masters of Finance degree, which we both have used to facilitate launching our careers at Klein-Matheson Corporation.

Jasper's Cafe resides proudly on the East Side Boulevard, in the midst of the bustling inner city of Stamford, Connecticut, just about an hour north of New York City. It's a location that indicates a beginning for those who have, and recently serves as a barrier to those who have not. Growing up, it was simply known as The Boulevard—the main artery running through the city of Stamford. Over the years it has succumbed to the urban struggles, and is now clearly defined as the East Side or the West Side. Although the cafe offers a limited menu, it is well known for its irresistible appetizers and Friday night happy hour that features a parade of White and Black corporate brothers, blue-collar brothers, so-called entrepreneurial brothers and let's not forget the Afrocentric brothers (in garb, of course). My point is there is always someone's brother there. My favorites happen to be the chicken fingers with a light duck sauce, followed by a medium-built, well-cooked Cajun-styled (and flavored) blue-collar brother, with a small side of that Afrocentric mentality. He would be my influence for the culture that I seem so distant from.

The oval-shaped windows are mounted with crimson awnings and "Jasper's" most eloquently inscribed in onyx across each. They often serve as theater curtains displaying each of the night's guests as lifelike as a Broadway stage. Multiple bistros effortlessly boast their night's specials with luring street fragrances escaping. Yes is my thought as I parallel park in the space directly across from the entrance of the cafe—it's seldom vacant. As I close my car door, I use one of the many black and ivory street lanterns to identify the caller displayed on my cell phone, assuming it to be Millie, but instead finding that it's Quinn.

"Hey Quinn," I say as I place the phone to my ear.

"Hey Torie! Are you still coming?"

"Actually, I've just arrived."

"Are you walking from the parking lot?" he asks noticeably concerned.

"No, I've scooped a space right in front."

"Okay cool, because I was going to have you swing around the front and I'd jump in and park for you. I keep telling you and Simone that things are changing around here. You got to watch your back."

"Thanks! I appreciate the offer, but I'm alright. I'll see you inside in a minute!" I think he worries too much.

While securing my car, I notice other women walking to or from the cafe by themselves. I then look at my reflection in the window and continue to negotiate an understanding of why people can't see me the way that I see me. I mean, everyone acts like I'm not Black. I'm a Black, educated, and confident young woman who just happened to have grown up in a prestigious suburb. As I turn away from the car, my naturally Asian-textured hair swiftly moves with ease across my bare espresso shoulders as it always has, prompting questions of my ethnicity.

I can see Quinn looking in my direction as I cross the street. He's illuminated by one of the many pendant lights hanging from the ceiling. Often those lights are used as an asset for a woman on a good day, but like her worst enemy, they expose all of her liabilities on a bad day. There is very little choice when it comes to Quinn Matthews's appearance. He stands 6 feet 4 inches tall carrying 240 lean sculptured pounds that are coated like a smooth caramel candied apple. His eyes are a glistening rare amber color that I've only seen on a lion, outlined in black with thick brows shadowing them. A cleft divides his chin just as a period completes a sentence. Without a doubt, the man is fine!

Quinn and I have been best friends for well over ten years, ever since we met at a West Side party the summer before I left for college. I allowed Simone (a new acquaintance at the time) to convince me to lie to my mother and sneak out from my hometown of New Canaan into the city of Stamford on a train to meet her with my best friend Millie, who just happens to be Jewish. Unfortunately, Simone neglected to tell me two things—the first being that this party was in the middle of the projects and that Millie would be the only White person there (typically it would be the other way around, and certainly there would never be any projects—mini mansions, but not projects), and second, the last train going back to New Canaan left at 10 p.m. After a lot of panicking and not being able to find a taxi willing to drive through the dark woodsy suburb to take us home, Simone shared that she was sorry, but she had to leave and go home because her curfew was at 11:30 and her mother would be waiting. With that, she left! That's when this awkwardly thin, tawny-colored guy whose hair was braided in longer rows reaching well beyond his shoulders asked why I was so upset. I desperately explained that we had no way of getting home, further complicated because of where we live. Others heckled and suggested that we cop a squat on the Pavilion benches for the night, but this guy—referred to as "Q" by the others—relentlessly pondered our situation while circling the bench where Millie and I sat. He had instantly become our gatekeeper! Suddenly, a city patrol car was in sight. Q grabbed my hand and instructed us to hurry and follow him. As we reached the circled entrance of the Pavilion, Q was able to hail the passing patrol car down. I'm sure it was likely the starkness of Millie's unlikely appearance that had really gotten the officers' attention that night. Releasing my hand, Q approached the car while Millie and I stood behind huddled together looking completely out of place. After a rather brief exchange, Q beckoned us to the patrol car as one of the officers had gotten out and opened the rear door while the other spoke into the two-way radio.

"Come along, young ladies. No worries . . . we'll get you back home," the officer standing outside the car shared.

Although I wasn't sure what was said during the exchange, I did know that I was on my way home! I looked graciously at my new friend Q and smiled.

"I told the officers how you all had gotten off at the wrong stop on the train, and how you'd gotten lost and things," Q said looking directly into my eyes encouraging me to stick to that story.

I stared back at him as he stood and spoke under the street light; I was instantly paused by his amazing eyes. Clearly I was in distress to have overlooked them until then!

"Yeah, we're so happy that you found us and stayed with us! Thank you so much for helping us." I am sure it was those eyes that hypnotized me into reaching up and placing a quick peck onto his cheek before walking towards the patrol car, but not before offering, "Oh yeah, please let that girl who walked with us from the TRAIN (referencing Simone as a stranger) know that we really, REALLY owe her and that I'll be sure to pay her back!" With that, he couldn't even contain his laughter at the idea of this sheepish New Canaan girl having some heart!

"Oh yes, we doooooooooooo!" Millie shouted from the window.

Since then, Quinn has always prided himself in assuming the role of the big brother that I never had, and Simone over hard-tested time became my very best friend.

Still deep in thought about that memory, I find myself smiling when I hear someone calling out to me.

"Torie?" A voice calls from a group of women to my right as I prepare to cross the street. "Torie Lynn Harper—is that you girl?" She calls out again as she abandons the group to approach me. "It's me . . . Niecey."

It was then that I remembered becoming a summer acquaintance of hers and a few others who eventually accepted my invading their West Side community years ago when I had begun to sneak out of New Canaan looking to have fun with people who looked more like me.

"Girl, you are wearing the hell out of that pencil skirt! What are you . . . a size 4? You still dressing your ass off always looking like a page torn from *Harpers Bazaar!*" We exchange a sincere hug and kiss. "Ooooh, you got those new Christian Louboutin shoes that just came out . . . now those are fierce!! Oh, you doing the damn thing . . . looking like you running all kind of corporations."

"Thank you! I just got out of work. Niecey, how are you doing? You look well, and I love your dress!"

"Niecey, you better come on . . . I told you I gotta pee, and now I don't think that food is gonna stay with me either," yells her friend from across the crowded sidewalk.

"Oh, my!" I say instinctively.

"You're still funny, Torie! We can get you out of New Canaan, but we can't get that New Canaan out of you!!" Niecey giggles and gives me a peck on the cheek before catching up with her impatient friends.

At that moment, my thoughts are that you should probably worry less about New Canaan and free your friend from those ghetto-type exchanges. I'm still deep in thought as Niecey shouts from across the street, "Torie, find me on Facebook sometime . . . my name hasn't changed."

The cafe walls are wrapped in textured toffee paint with each adjacent wall lending warmth by placing you in the arms of crimson. Select art pieces are secured in black wooden frames with umbrellas of accent light above them like in a museum. A carport resides at the entrance where valet parking was once an option, until two of the employees from the West Side decided that valet was a synonym for hassle-free (don't have to harm nobody) carjacking, which sent Jasper's liability insurance through the roof. So now it serves as an outdoor dining area with black wrought-iron tables garnished with menus and flickering hurricane lamps.

Quinn seems rather somber; I'm sure he's still reeling over the events at the office today. The day was filled with many surprises. Every available seat in the conference room was occupied to capacity with colleagues unanimously filled with curiosity. Micro-clusters of conversations spilled over creating an acoustical arena that was silenced upon the arrival of Joel Matheson, our CEO, and his corporate entourage. Adding to the cryptic behavior of late, corporate memos were distributed to each colleague as a reminder of the policies and practices surrounding disclosure and our Non-Compete Agreement. Additional angst developed when we all received instructions to sign and return them prior to our scheduled meeting.

A very large veiled table conspicuously occupied the center of the room eliminating what typically would have been additional seating. The late arrivers had to settle for standing room only. Simultaneously, the lights were shut off and holograms appeared on every surrounding wall mirroring the schematics of the model unveiled moments earlier. There had been plenty of grumbles of multiple commercial realtors vying for the bids on the West Side properties. It had been rumored that the unidentified industrialist leading the bid was from the West Coast because they saw opportunity in developing the feel of Rodeo Drive in the middle of the wealthiest county in our megalopolis.

Instantly the room filled with increasing sounds of "oohs and ahhs" as each of my peers moved about the room on a virtual tour of the new and improved West Side, soon to be introduced to the public as Harbor View. Admittedly, I too, was immersed in the moment until realizing that there was an omission for me. That omission was— where will all of the residents go? I scanned the surrounding walls, and just like a magic wand had been waved over a dilapidated inner city, they are instantly transformed into a combination of Disney's Magic Kingdom, Rodeo Drive and the business district of midtown Manhattan. I see how they'd see it as a win-win for everyone. There is a Starbucks next door to a tri-level Barnes and Noble, and adjacent to a museum. Directly across the street sits a Jiminy Cricket Arcade and to the right of that is a Mommy and Me interactive club.

I obviously was on the wrong block because when I turned the virtual corner, I mentally skipped down the street with glee while passing Coach, White House Black Market, Kenneth Cole, Tiffany and Ann Taylor. That's when I nearly collided into Millie! In unison, we both zoomed in on Lucky Brand and began jumping up and down, forgetting for a moment that we were in our workplace. Lucky Brand is our weekend gear of choice; currently, we have to schlep all the way into Manhattan to find one of their stores.

Around me, my ringing telephone competes with the outbursts of laughter. I look over to my left to see what the big attraction is while reaching for my phone. I've never seen Jasper's this packed on a Wednesday night. Wednesday is comedy night, Thursday is live jazz, and Friday is the big happy hour night. Just as I pass two topiaries on either side of the entrance, my phone begins to ring again.

"Hey girl, where are you?" Simone asks.

"I'm in the entranceway."

"Oh, Torie, look over here. We have a table on the other side of the bar near the stage. I'm waving! Can you see me?" Simone asks.

"Yes," I mumble as I rise to my toes adding another inch to my stilettos while scanning over the crowd across the bar occupying the center of the cafe. "Oh, I see you now, Sim," I say and immediately put the phone into my purse and begin taking on the crowd in an attempt to very carefully head in her direction.

The wooden ladder-back chairs blend well with the red oak floors. I scan the crowd and see that Jackie Wallace is here. She's wearing an ivory knit skirt set with four-inch stilettos. Her gold jewelry enhances her outfit extremely well and is often mistaken as costume because of its brilliance. Don't misunderstand me; the outfit is very nice and Jackie is an attractive woman, but it's a fact that she is always squeezing her big ass into clothes that are two sizes too small for her.

Jackie is 31 years old, five feet tall and weighs about 190 pounds. Her flawless mocha complexion compliments her chestnut hair which falls just short of her shoulders into a blunt cut. Whenever Jackie passes by, her cologne lingers. I swear that she bathes in that damn Dolce & Gabbana! Lord help us when she works up a sweat on the dance floor! She is inevitably the first one on and the last one off grinding those mammoth hips shamelessly. She's a very proud and respected young woman—for the most part. However, it is also a known fact that too much Planter's Punch leaves Jackie with no pride. Oh yeah, I saw it coming as she sashayed that ass around the bar trying to get attention from the unfamiliar male faces of the night. Jackie must have sashayed up and down the bar at least ten times and three Planter's Punches too many. On the eleventh trip, she cut the corner of the bar too close and staggered in an attempt to stay on her feet, but it was too late. When I turned around, those stilettos were in the air and her panty-less, bare ass was on the floor getting exactly what she wanted . . . everyone's attention.

While we were laughing uncontrollably, Quinn remained very quiet and aloof likely replaying the day's earlier events at the office. I have to admit it was pausing, I mean, to find out that we were the silent corporation taking on the multibillion-dollar renovation of the West Side. My guess is given that it's been home for Quinn his entire life; he's taking the reveal extremely personal.

"Hey, you!" I turn my cheek to receive the inevitable kiss that's become our platonic greeting outside of work. To my surprise, it was replaced with a solemn, "Hey."

"Are you alright?" I ask. He pauses a moment to take a gulp of his Corona before replying.

"I can't stop thinking about today. It's all kind of crazy right?" Quinn briskly takes another gulp.

It was only in that moment that I realized the conflict of interest present for Quinn. He's clearly been the driving force of The West Side Coalition (WSC) from the conception. Under his guidance, the coalition has gained more ground and media support in thwarting the Harbor View project than ever anticipated. Of course, this was all done with complete unawareness of who was behind that project. These are the things that would appear to be questionable at the time he pursues a run for mayor. He now realizes that he's unknowingly become a double agent. Quinn has covered every aspect of Klein-Matheson's proprietary work by day and thrown up road blocks aggressively by night while working pro bono for the WSC creating multiple cease and desist in their favor. Talk about getting in your own way!

"They had to have known that I worked with WSC as their advisor! I've signed off on every cease and desist as counsel. It's a set up . . . they've played me!!"

"Why do you think that?"

"Torie, think about it. Matheson promoted me as co-counsel with Eric shortly after the media blitz indicating there would be viability in WSC's fight."

"But that's a good thing for you," I said not understanding his concerns.

"Nah, it isn't. He was adamant about only me being accountable for all proprietary contracts."

"That's because he saw you were a fit for the job."

"Yeah, he pitched it as me being the best-suited expert relating to proprietorships."

Struggling to hear him over the loud music I say, "What does this all mean? I don't understand."

"It means that there can be a review under the conflict of interest or Non-Compete Agreement in my contract. With that, all of the legal motions that I've participated in on the behalf of WSC will be thrown out of court, forcing them to lose the appeals that I've already filed."

"Quinn, you didn't know that it was Klein-Matheson; none of us did."

"Yeah, but someone did. And given that I'm counsel, it would suggest that I've been given full disclosure. I could be charged with willful misconduct."

The words, "Was it man?" echoes from over my right shoulder before I can grasp what Quinn has just said.

"Was it what?" an insulted Quinn replies.

"Was it willful misconduct?" The voice now has a face to match. It's Tyrell, another brother from the West Side Coalition who is also Simone's cousin.

I'm not really sure, but it appears this is becoming a little more than a disagreement—not for Quinn—but it certainly seems like Tyrell is looking for a fight.

"I'm just saying, you riding both sides, man?"

With that, Simone shouts across the table, "Tyrell, don't come in here with that bullshit!" Ignoring Simone's instructions, he proceeds to walk closer towards me and Quinn.

"Go ahead with that, man," Quinn instructs as Tyrell invades his space.

I don't know why, but between the tension that I was feeling and the negative vibe now present in the cafe, I move closer towards Quinn ready to protect him in a moment's notice. (Like I can really do anything to stop these two big men.)

"Man, fall back!" Quinn demands as he rises to his feet, turning his face towards the big screen television to remove himself.

"Tyrell! . . . Tyrell!" Simone shouts as she tries to come from around the table to grab her cousin who is now standing toe-to-toe with Quinn. Their nostrils are flared and their eyes are locked.

"What!! You gully like that?" Tyrell repositions to face Quinn directly and now deliberately obstructs the view of the television screen. He continues, "You gonna just let the man line your pockets and take care of you leaving everybody else to fend for themselves?"

At this point, I thought I'd take over from Simone's failing attempts to diffuse the tension and correct Tyrell's misunderstanding of Quinn's knowledge of any of this. I say, "Ty, it isn't like that. We only found out about all of this today ourselves."

"Oh, what do you have to say about this, Miss White Girl?"

I'm probably the darkest person in the cafe tonight, and I'm still called a White girl! We all know it has nothing to do with my color.

"You both driving them fat-ass whips." He's referring to my Audi Q7 and Quinn's Range Rover. "Taking that dirty money right to the bank," he continues.

"Oh, so that's what you think man?" Quinn asks.

Okay, so now he's completely baiting Quinn and I'm thinking . . . Nigel or someone—anyone—get over here and help me out. I know I'm not the only one who sees where this is going, particularly because they've seen these kinds of confrontations on more than one occasion. I on the other hand, have seen a confrontation like this maybe once—if ever.

"Shit, that's what I know. Alright so you tell me, Klein-Matheson, ain't that the place that you and brown sugar over there (looking in my direction) wear them suits to every day?"

Okay, so now I'm really confused. I've gone from "White girl" to "brown sugar" in just minutes. Which is it and who gets to say? I'm sure a stolen glance of my becoming uneasy is prompting Quinn to compose himself, now realizing on his own that he is allowing himself to be swayed into becoming someone he's not.

"You're wrong man . . . you got it all wrong," he says while walking away trying to avoid a physical altercation.

Quinn tilts his chin up to Nigel gesturing that his following words are intended for him only. "Let me holla at you later, man," he follows with giving him some dap.

Quinn uses the expansion between his thumb and forefinger to rub his creased forehead in hopes of releasing the built up tension.

As I stole a glance at Tyrell, I saw anger, disappointment or an indication of his feeling betrayed, given the look in his eyes that are fixed on Quinn as he's walking away. I try to tell Quinn what I'm sensing when Tyrell suddenly pushes between the two of us.

"Oh, so you just gonna walk away?"

I'm sure with Quinn leaving he feels as if he's being dismissed. All I know is that within a second Tyrell yoked Quinn by his collar and they became locked like embattled pit bulls.

"Tyrell!" Sim yells as the table flips over and the chairs follow in a domino effect tumbling over them. These grown-ass men were reduced to imitating boys on the playground fighting—never actually throwing blows, but rolling and tumbling over and over again, neither releasing their grip. My screaming becomes louder as I instinctively reach in to break them apart. Instantly, I feel a grip on my right shoulder, followed immediately with me being involuntarily tossed towards the wall.

"Damn girl, are you crazy? I know I taught you better than that," Simone scolds. In that moment it felt like the old days when Sim would always caution me on the impending danger and snatch me out of the way, during my summer ventures sneaking into the West Side of Stamford.

Nigel and Tank pulled them apart within seconds bringing them each back to their feet while reprimanding them. They are relentlessly staring each other down, panting heavily, yet both willing to resume at a moment's notice.

"Come on now, we don't do this! We're one, man!" A pause and then Nigel asks them, "We're one, right?" Nigel waits for a confirmation before setting either of them free.

"West Side pride, ride or die" is a mantra often chanted by brothers from the West Side doing positive things. Quinn once shared that when he was about eight, a group of grandfathers united and had taken as many of the youth under their wing and made them sign contracts to be their brothers' keepers through life.

"Come on now . . . West Side pride, ride or die."

"I don't know about Q, man," Tyrell questioned causing Quinn to lunge at him but was deflected by Nigel's raised arm.

"What do you mean, you don't know about Q?" Nigel asks completely irritated.

"Just what I said—now you figure it out!" Tyrell instructs Tank to "get the hell off of him" as he shakes himself free. "I'm outta here."

We all watched as Tyrell left, and we each tried to move on from the entire event. I personally can't help feeling protective of Quinn in moments like this. This would be the rare occasion that I'm given to reciprocate for the care he's continuously shown to me over the years.

After turning the corner, I am paused by hues of red and blue beams leaping from the hoods of several police cars. Onlookers are rapidly crowding and obstructing the entrance to the parking lot. It would be the same parking lot that Quinn would have walked to after securing me in my car only moments ago. I blindly fumble as my fingers search for the buttons to lower my windows, not willing to shift my eyes from my search for him. The traffic has come to a complete halt under the direction of the lone police officer using a flashlight to override each of the intersection lights. Quinn hasn't answered one of my three attempted calls. My head is beginning to flood with unwelcome thoughts and concern. Just as I begin making a fourth attempt, my cell phone leaps from my hand and tumbles beneath the gas pedal. It's now completely out of my reach, and I can't attempt to get it as I am now instructed to move on by the officer. Just one moment later, we're all moved to a stop following a familiar female's voice releasing a heart-gripping shrill, "Oh my God!!"

WOMEN ALIKE

Pausing to take a sip from her third Martini, Perry declares, "Say whatever you want, but the truth of the matter is that there is a cultural disparity between those brothers raised and educated in the suburbs and those raised and educated in the inner cities. Now, I've said it, but each one of you was already thinking that."

"Oh, that's a broad view," Simone defends.

Perry rises to her feet, commanding everyone's attention as she passionately speaks while walking across the room with her shoes clamoring against my wooden floors. She nibbles on a celery stick and continues, "Okay, I hear you, but please let me clarify that that doesn't make them any better! Ha ha!" Perry pauses while cracking herself up and continues, "It only means that the shit which they bring with them is just some different shit, and at the end of the day, it's still shit!!" She claps her hands encouraging more laughter from all of the ladies in the room.

"Oh, and I know that's right!" Simone agrees and waves her hand in the air as if she were in a church pew about to give a testimony.

Perry interrupts, "Wait, wait a minute," trying to speak through her own laughter before continuing. "How many times has your man charged you with either thinking or acting like you're better than somebody?" Perry shouts through her giggles and over the ladies laughter. She continues, "The problem with that is the only other somebody in the room is his ass!! Now, what you really want to say is, 'No, I'm better than your dumb ass for arguing with me over something as stupid as this.' But you can't say anything remotely like that because all he'd hear is the stupid and dumb part. Even though he can say all kinds of crazy nonsense, but it shouldn't hurt as if you are wearing some kind of emotional armor. If you were to say half of the unkind things that he pops off from his mouth in frustration, it would be so over, and so unforgiving. Lastly, you would be charged with being less than supportive, blah, blah, blah!" By the time she finishes, Perry is using her perfectly manicured hands as puppets. We're all laughing and nodding in agreement at her special way of making the truth colorful.

I love getting together with all of my friends—old or new, Black or White—it's never mattered to me. What matters is having good food, great company and even better bottles of wine, along with a healthy debate. Tonight is my first time having everyone over since moving to Clock Towers East. I finally decided to move on from The Big House and try life outside of the subdued woods of New Canaan. My Aunt Dot came up from Maryland and helped Simone and I close up the house for future use. We completely moved, unpacked, and decorated my new spacious two-bedroom loft over one weekend. With Simone's skills and my vision, we accomplished a contemporary dream of desert tan walls and chocolate-stained floors surrounded by my ivory suede sofa and sage slipper chairs. In keeping with the warm feeling, the accent wall surrounding the fireplace is painted in pumpkin and plays off my giraffe-print area rug and throw pillows. The rest of the room's ambiance comes courtesy of the recessed and accent lighting. My home décor reverie comes to a halt when Perry's voice brings me back to the moment.

"Tell the truth ladies; don't you sometimes just want to rock his world for no other reason than knowing that you can? Especially after he has rudely said that you've put on a few pounds? Or worse, when he walks in and you have the lights lowered sipping your wine with your music playing and your candles lit minding your own business. Then he walks by as you're talking on the phone, shaking his head and mumbling under his breath, but you hear it . . . bourgeois."

"Bourgeois! Damn, I thought that was my middle name as often as Robert has called me that," Perry replies stepping over the ladies sitting on the floor as she goes to replenish her drink. The room fills with uncontrollable laughter and affectionate shouts of "You are so stupid, Perry!!"

"Seriously, he always calls me that. I just ignore his ass."

"Alright—time to cut her off," I say giggling.

Felicia chimes in with, "I can top that! At least once a month, I'm called a little White girl. I mean what's all that?"

"Don't say that like it's a bad thing," Jamie teasingly defends completely aware of the intended context from past discussions.

"No, for us it's like, 'Oh so you a blancita now, huh mami?'" Yoli added in her chosen Puerto Rican accent as she and her cousin Milagros high five each other.

One guest shouts, "I hear all of that!!"

"Hell, I've gotten that from my man, cousins, and even some classmates when growing up."

"What does bourgeois mean anyway?" Felicia asks while looking into her glass of water.

The room is quiet enough for everyone to witness Perry leaning towards me with a drink and in not much of a whisper say, "And you want to cut *me* off?" Now pointing in Felicia's direction she continues, "That, right there, is without the influence of any alcohol. Yup, that's straight up urban public schools for you! That's so wrongggg!" Everyone within earshot starts to either laugh or protest.

Given some of the reactions, Felicia should be offended, but she decides to ask again anyway, "So, what's it mean?"

Perry sips, trying to use her near empty glass as a muzzle while saying, "See what I mean?" We all burst into a roar of laughter, including Felicia. I thinned my eyes at Perry and charge her with being hateful.

"Seriously, ya'll its bigger, much bigger than what we're talking about," Simone says in a challenged tone. "I mean, it's the constant task of validating ourselves to comfort others. For sisters, we've got to pass the am I acting Black enough test, and the White's test of I'm Black but not to worry, I'm not the kind of Black you should fear. In the workplace we must always be aware of the silent rule of when two or more of us congregate or share lunch that it may be an indication of an impending coup."

The room is becoming somber as each us wrap our thoughts around the reality of our lives, as Simone has just eloquently outlined.

I offered, "Even sadder is often the lack of trust from a man who is playing the lead role in our lives. I don't mean trust as in infidelity. I'm talking about the trust in knowing someone in the most authentic way, trusting their judgment and sincerity, having the ability to accurately anticipate their next move and thoughts." Everyone is stuck on that last thought. "I'm talking about that I got your back, what do you want to do? What can I do to make it better for you kind of commitment?"

"Oh, I hear you Torie—that real ride or die shit. Thelma & Louise, we're going off the cliff together!" Leave it to Perry to get the room laughing again.

"Exactly, but how can I be that if he's constantly uncomfortable with me being me?" I ask.

"Because, he's not uncomfortable, he's intimidated," Perry says in her most serious and untreated dialect of the night. "Look, what's not to like about us? Nah, wait a minute; (hushing the giggling) I'm being serious. We are educated, well-read and well-spoken, visually on our A-game," pointing at her own body. "Most of all, we bring our invaluable, suburban, socially apt mannerisms as their companion at their corporate functions. We make them look good!"

"So then why is he intimidated?" Millie asks and instructs, "Perry, do not tell me again that I will not understand because I'm not Black."

"News flash Mil, your ass AIN'T Black!" slipping back into her relaxed dialect. "I know you all think if you sleep with a brother, you are instantly enrolled in the club!!" Perry laughs harder while falling back into the pillows on the sofa.

"Shut up! To me, a man is a man!!" With a grin on her face, Millie continues, "Besides, I haven't even hooked up with a Black man . . . yet! My motto for life is equal opportunity!"

"Do you want to know why he's intimidated?" Simone offers. Because those same attributes that bring him pleasure make him feel inadequate. He's not being welcomed for his own attributes or merit. For whatever reasons, White America doesn't see Black women as a threat."

"Nope, we just get tagged with offensive stereotypes like assertive, aggressive, outspoken and combative to name a few. The difference is with all of that, we're able to get in where those same doors are bolted and padlocked for brothers," Perry inserts.

"That's true. Sad, but true," I agree. "Almost everywhere they go, they're met with the opposition of social hierarchy or even blatant disrespect."

"What do you mean?" Laurie asks.

"I don't know, it's hard to explain," I ponder for a moment. "I know . . . think of it being in the form of a dismissive hiring manager, or the concierge at a fancy hotel."

"Or like when a taxi driver chooses to ignore and bypass him, but stops for others," Simone adds.

"Yeah, why do they do that?" Millie asks.

"For the same reasons that some police have preconceived thoughts—that he must be a drug dealer based on the car driven or the neighborhood in which he lives. I've seen this for myself—it often happened when my dates would drive me home to the 'burbs."

"Wow, that sucks!" Millie concedes.

"No, I'll tell you what the problem is," Perry chimes in. "The problem is that brothers are seen as triple threats!" She uses her fingers to count the ways. "Their physical strength as displayed in their dominance in most core sports, their intellect and educational designations now has the playing field closer to being leveled than ever, and with that, I'd say there's a big game going on!"

"No objections?" I ask as Perry continues with her defense in our friendly debate.

"Lastly, a brother's genetically inherited very large anatomy. (She's biting her bottom lip to contain her joyful thoughts.) Well, that puts them in a league of their own, and there isn't a Non-Compete Agreement that can ever change that!" She leans forward to high five Felicia.

"RIGHT!" We all chant in agreement.

"Hmm, I'd call that game point!" Perry closed her argument.

While Perry is entertaining everyone with her nearly pornographic illustrations, I used this moment to inquire about Tyrell's condition.

"Sim, how is Tyrell doing?" I ask.

"He's doing much better. The doctor said that if the initial blow from the bat was to the front of his skull, rather than from behind, it would likely have been fatal."

"Thank God Quinn walked up when he did."

"I know. I only wish that during the scuffle that he would have gotten a better look at who it was."

Leaning in, I whisper to Sim, "What's crazy is that Quinn said the guy was White."

"Hell yeah, that's crazy," Simone and I looked at each other while shaking our heads in disbelief.

The laughter has finally paused and the room has become reasonably quiet. With the exception of shouting, that's coming from the direction of the bathroom.

"Where's Jamie?" I asked before Millie and I both get up and head toward the bathroom.

"Jamie, are you okay?" I ask as I walk through the slightly opened door. Tears are streaming down her red face as she throws her cell phone onto the floor.

"What happened?" Millie asks while rubbing her back and placing Jamie's long auburn hair behind her shoulder to get a better view of her face.

"He's a freaking douche!! Brody said that he was going to be working late. Kelly just sent a picture of him kissing some girl!" With that, she bursts into tears all over again.

"Jamie, don't cry," I say hoping to console her, along with the rest of the crowd that has found their way into the bathroom.

"You want to go on a field trip?" Perry asks. "We can go on a field trip and find the two of them and beat his ass!" She successfully makes Jamie laugh—leave it to Perry. "I'm serious! Just say the word and we'll line up the caravan."

Jamie and Perry were as close as Millie and I growing up throughout our years in New Canaan. The difference between Perry and me is that she acquired a better cultural blend with having family to visit and hang out with in the city.

"Yup, I want to go and kick his ass—pathetic jerk!"

"Or, do you want me to hook you up with a brother?" Perry teases.

"Yeah, hook me up," Jamie teases catching us all off guard with her unlikely response as she wipes the remaining tears from her face.

"Be careful what you ask for," Felicia cautions prompting laughter.

Millie goes on record, "Black, White, Asian—they all have the propensity of being an ass."

We all go back into the living room and reclaim our original seating and resume eating, drinking and laughing as we take in the awesome night view of the skyline of Stamford from my floor to ceiling windows surrounding the room.

"Wait! Go back to what you were saying earlier. You know about not being considered as supportive partners?" Millie asks showing the attorney in her.

"So they come home with all of that built up hurt and frustration? Imagine their psyche after having society challenge their existence even before their manhood on a daily basis. The media is continuously blackballing their brand, only showing adverse coverage and making it representative of the whole brand," Simone offers.

Perry says, "Come on, we've all had those experiences when we've stood in front of that damn television and heard someone grammatically murdering the English language and we say, 'Please don't let it be someone Black . . . ughh . . . it's someone Black.' And to add insult to injury, I swear they inevitably find the one toothless brother with his hair half-braided separated by an afro comb using words out of context for his witness statement." Perry cups her hand to mimic a microphone saying, "There you have it directly from one of the residents of this community. I'm Muffy McAllister from Live at Five!" Laughter fills the room.

"Muffy and I both know that, that particular Negro resides at the local shelter and is only available because every other Negro is at work, and the doors to the shelter will not reopen until 6:00 p.m. Now see from the outside looking in, you have received a slanted depiction of a very nice neighborhood."

Perry playfully looks over at Jamie, who now has tears streaming down her face and asks, "Are you laughing? I know your ass ain't laughing! Okay, so don't act like you all don't have them too, especially in known trailer park areas." Jamie laughs even harder as she seems to be moving on and choosing to forget about Brody's shenanigans.

"Seriously, back to our men, with these types of distractions, obstacles, challenges . . . it makes it hard for them to confidently love when your self-love has been so fragmented. Society has our men often feeling inadequate in our own homes," Simone finishes.

"Oh yeah, it's a lot of work," I add.

"All of my friends who date Black men don't seem to have those experiences," Jamie shared.

"I agree with Jamie," Laurie says while placing her naturally curled blonde hair behind her ear. "I mean like my friends say, they're in the best relationships that they've ever had, and they're treated like queens."

Giggling and turning red-faced Jamie adds, "Since you said it first, I'll add that they're far from complaining about the bedroom."

Millie—now clearly reaching her limit—raises her glass and shouts, "To equal opportunities!!" Once again the room fills with laughter.

"Girl, I was pumping gas earlier this week and a White chick pulled up in front of me. Within seconds, a very nice looking brother jumped out of the passenger side, and then he went and paid for their gas. When he began to pump the gas, our eyes locked. His whole demeanor changed. The swagger was gone and replaced with this apologetic, guilty, almost embarrassed look," Felicia shared.

"But why? What's so wrong with him being a gentleman? He's filling the tank for his girlfriend!"

"Okay, and there's where it becomes a problem. We are women alike—and often, but not always—we are excluded from being treated like that queen. You all get the luxury of coming out of the gates being daddy's little princess and later handed off in life to be someone's queen," Perry spoke passionately engaging everyone.

Laurie asks, "Is that not the same for Black women?"

"Hell, no!" Felicia answers not giving anyone else a chance to respond, "Because most of our daddies weren't around."

"That's not true, Felicia," I said compassionately.

She replied combatively, "Maybe not in your New Canaan, Torie, but here in the city, oh pleasssssee!"

"Nah, Felicia's right," Simone says trying to diffuse the debate. "We know that we have many Black families intact where the father is very present and committed; usually consistent with Black suburbia or in the South. At the same time, statistically in our urban communities it is rare when compared to other cultures."

"I just think that often when we come together as a Black couple, we're already fragmented and in a work-in-progress status. We love differently. It's not going to be like the Millie, Jamie and Lauries of the world. Loving is learned just like speech, cooking and dancing. If I didn't have a set of parents in my home teaching me how to love my mate . . . then I am making it up as we go along just as he is . . . and just like learning anything new, like riding a bike or ice skating, it hurts often and may result in breaks until you learn it."

"Got it!!" Jamie concedes. "But that's the same no matter what color you are."

"Well said, Torie and Jamie!"

"To your earlier point, Laurie, your friend is with the same Black man, but his status has now changed. More importantly for him, he's in possession of his competitor's trophy . . . one of YOU!! Now at those same venues that we visited as a couple, he is no longer invisible. Oh no, he is very present and thus not feeling inadequate, allowing you our men at their best." I challenged.

"Oh, did you think that it was hard to catch a decent brother before? Well then, it's open season now with those damn Kardashians and Kendras of the world making our brothers just as trendy as Paris carrying a must-have puppy around at all times!" Perry said without laughter this time.

"So then just go out with White men." We all turned in Jamie's direction at the thought of that.

"Oh, no," someone muttered from within the group.

"I have. Don't say it like it's bad, it's just different. I prefer the humor and banter I've had with a brother," I explain.

"I love our Black men. I love their flava, their humor, their strength, tenacity and loving in each of their chocolate, mocha, caramel, almond, espresso, hazelnut, fudge ways. I'm never giving up on them!" Simone says with conviction.

"You don't have to. Love isn't a color, it's a fit," I offer.

"Torie's right! Just go and find what fits each of your needs and go for it!!" Millie concludes.

༅

"Torie, are you listening to me? It sounds like you're about to fall out over there! Did you hear what I said?"

"What? I'm on the treadmill!"

"I SAID ... they're closing Jasper's!"

"Wait! Wait a minute, Sim!" bidding a pause during her usual rant. "What did you say?"

"I said . . . they're closing Jasper's!"

"Who's closing Jasper's?" I reach to lower the volume on the CD player.

"I don't know who, Torie. All I know is that they're closing it!"

"But why? It can't be because of finances; everybody goes there and it's always packed."

"Torie, you see them coming around buying up everything on the boulevard."

"Yeah, but Jasper's? I don't get that, Sim. Jasper's is iconic."

"I guess I'm kind of surprised too. I mean . . . it's not like it's a Black club per se or known for housing undesirables."

"Uh-oh, per se? Now who's picking up whose language?"

"I know, right? Girl, I have to catch myself sometimes."

"Wow, all kinds of people have come through there. Do you know how many secrets are buried behind those walls?"

"Hell, I can't say that I haven't left a little something up in there too."

"Oh, if walls could talk!"

"Please, we'd have to reenact that scene from that old movie, what was it called? *The Women of Brewster Place*! Yeah that's it . . . remember how they'd torn that wall down? That's just what we'd have to do . . . yep, rip that puppy down!"

"You're a mess."

"Gotta go, sweetie, but I wanted to let you know in case you hadn't heard from your boy Quinn yet. Everyone is going over to Jasper's tomorrow night to put our heads together and lend support to Case."

"Yeah, of course—I'll be there. What time is everyone going?"

"Well, you already know I told Nigel that we better be home in time for Boo-Boo Kitty."

"Who?"

"Girl, *Empire*! You know that's my show and NO, I won't DVR it. Everyone will be talking about it by the morning, and then I'll know what happened. No thank you! I like it how I like everything else—first hand! Yes, I sit there and tweet and spill tea with the best of them . . . oh, that means to comment and share tidbits. WHAT?"

"Sim, I haven't said one word. That's you struggling with your own round-the-way antics. And I know what spilling tea means."

"Mmuahhhh! You know I like messing with you. Alright, I'll catch up with you later."

SIMONE

I began staring at myself in the mirror and feeling quite satisfied with the face that's looking back. It's no wonder that men go out of their way to get my attention, my telephone number or simply the time of day. I'd say that my entire packaging is pretty tight. I mean, my brownstone looks like a page from *Home Beautiful* or should I say, the contents of my place. Or maybe it does after a Saturday dedicated to all the cleaning and scrubbing and tidying. Hell yeah, it looks like *Home Beautiful*.

My annual salary is $125,000.00 in addition to commission from each of the stores that I stock as a buyer. I also receive a monthly spending allowance to use at my discretion. I'm given this in addition to traveling expenses for spending two days a week in Manhattan canvassing Avenue of Americas or having lunch with potential and already existing vendors. The truth is, I've been driving into the city and using the allowance as a personal supplement to afford my ivory Acura MDX. The other three days of the week, I either sit in the office or visit our stores which have already been established as trend setters. If I were to purchase 12 leopard-print skirts with a red patch on the center of the ass, you can believe that at least ten would sell simply because they came from Arial's. Now, if we didn't experience a loss-prevention problem, I assure you all 12 would have sold. Our loss prevention isn't the result of thieves—as in shoplifters. You know, the one that looks as though she's gone broke buying clothes when in actuality she's just a T.A.T.A.R. (Tucking all tags and returning them as soon as possible.) Every once in a while, we'll catch someone who is new at the game; they will have messed up by cleaning the shit at a coin-op rather than at a dry cleaner. It becomes obvious to them as well as me when I place it on the rack with the others and that's when I give them a chance to come clean. "I'm sorry, were you looking for something to accessorize this?" If they're smart, they'll catch the hint and they usually do.

Damn it. My bath water is spilling over onto my bath mat as the phone begins to ring. I quickly turn the water off and reach for a towel to wrap around me while answering the phone.

"Hello? Wait a minute—the answering machine is coming on!" I shout over the machine.

"Hey baby, are you just getting in?" Nigel asks

"No, I'm getting ready to take a bubble bath," I reply.

"Does this mean that my baby could possibly be nude on the other end of this phone?"

"Nigel, for you anything is possible," I offer in my most inviting tone.

"Is that right?" he asks.

"Uh-huh," I offer more seductively.

"Sim, I was thinking that we could grab a bite to eat down in City Island. But now, why don't you take care of the entertainment and leave dinner to me."

"Alright baby, I'll see you when you get here!"

I rush back into the bathroom to mop up the water from the floor, then wrap my hair into a French roll, leaving one spiral curl draped over my eye. As usual, I do a quick check throughout the kitchen to make sure that everything is in order. My hopes are that there aren't any broken promises of wiped up spills or any unpleasant odors from forgotten dishes stashed somewhere. Everything is on point, so I light a few of my favorite citrus and sage candles and turn on some Alicia Keys. After taking the first two sips of wine, I close my eyes and sigh with pleasure gently allowing my palate to release a steady stream of warmth along the walls of my throat. It's so soothing. I attempt to slowly allow my body to become acquainted with the temperature of the water as I climb into the steamy-hot tub. Before I know it, the cross-breeze from the open windows has allowed the water to cool and reach a comfortable temperature. I've become relaxed and slightly intoxicated. I close my eyes and drift off into an array of pleasant thoughts. My mother never played when it came to hygiene; early on she gave copious instructions on keeping my kitty, purse and private clean. Over time the names evolved into cookie, cooch, and dare I say the last? She spoke in truth because she believed that the world wasn't gonna sugar coat it. Once I was in college our conversations and her instructions became more age-appropriate. She'd say, "You shave that bush yet? Don't go looking at me like that. I already know that you're having sex, but what can I do? You'll need to be much cleaner now. Keep that belly button and behind your ears clean, and I can tell you no man wants to be wrestling with no damn bush or be kissing around no sour milk!" I can honestly say that my mother has always kept things on the up and up; she'd always said that the world wasn't going to raise her children for her.

I hear Nigel's key opening the front door. The door shuts and I hear him placing packages onto the dining room table.

"Doll, it's just me. I'm about to introduce this kitchen to the finest cuisine on this side of town prepared by none other than yours truly. Can you handle that?" He repeats himself as he walks towards the bathroom, "The man asked if you could handle it?"

At this point, I raise my eyelids to be greeted by my favorite chocolate fix that has not been unwrapped from his corporate work attire. As I reach up, the bubbles slowly expose my hidden desserts. I pucker up my lips and instruct him to lay it on me.

He teasingly asks again, "Can you handle it?"

I wrap my sudsy fingers around the tip of his tie pulling him closer to me before replying flirtatiously, "Oh yeah, I can handle it." Nigel rolls back the sleeves of his shirt and commences to sponge down my back as we talk about all of our day's events. His fingers have relieved every kink in my neck and shoulders and ignited a fire elsewhere that was quickly extinguished by his call to duty in the kitchen.

Dinner was great! Nigel sautéed shrimp and scallops in garlic sauce with basil and served it over linguini with sun-dried tomatoes, a tossed salad, and garlic bread. After sharing a few glasses of wine, we decided to rebuild the fire that we had started earlier. Both of our emotions seem to be in need of our safe place allowing each of us to release our personal stresses in exchange for passion. Our love making became intense. Our hearts began beating together rhythmically along with our bodies and our eyes locked as though they were having a conversation of their own. Nigel places his open hand onto the small of my back pulling me closer into him as if trying to make us become one. I'm holding on tightly as our bodies seem to be leaving calm waters and rapidly becoming crashing waves. As we reach the shore together, a lump has grown in my throat. Without permission, tears began to flood my face. Neither of us wants to break the silence, so we quietly agree to allow our bodies to carry on with their own conversation which has been communicated so well through our caressing and gentle kisses.

"I love you, girl. You know that I'll always take care of you, right?"
"I know, baby."

Shortly after we'd fallen asleep, I was pleasantly awakened by the sound of a saxophone being played from what I'd thought to be afar. I gently separated our bodies and walked over to raise the window; autumn was certainly on its way. The night air wrapped its crisp arms around me as I stood and watched the different couples heading towards the green where well-known musicians often performed. The sound of crickets and leaves rustling began creating a soothing ensemble of their own. As the lights were dimming at the park, the crowd began applauding and whistling as Najee was being introduced to the stage. My nude body instantly became a silhouette on the wall draped in a sheer curtain. For a moment, it was if I were a dancer on a dimly lit Alvin Ailey stage.

"Did I hear them say Najee?" Nigel asks as he sat up in the bed. I nodded my head yes; I wasn't quite ready to break our silence because I was still enjoying what I had just experienced. Sure, I've made love countless times before, but I now realize that this was the first time that I've been made love to.

"It's only 9:00, why don't we go downstairs and check him out?" Nigel asks as he wraps his arms around me gently kissing the back of my neck. "Let's take a shower, throw on some clothes and go down and enjoy the man."

We carried a blanket and a bottle of wine across to the park and found our own patch of grass to lease for the remainder of the night. The show ended at about 11:00 so we decided to walk down the street to Jasper's and see if we could catch up with Quinn and Torie.

My apartment is about eight blocks from Jasper's. The complex and the park are at the end of the cul-de-sac on East Side Boulevard. So needless to say, I live in the heart of the city privileged to witness the entire ambiance of the tall buildings, bright lights and festive billboards.

Strolling down the street, I'm taken by how beautiful the rows of brownstones are; each has their own brightly lit entrance with tall torch lamps. Perfectly manicured hedges form a fortress around the building with wrought-iron gates separating them at every cobble-stoned walkway. We continued walking down the boulevard holding hands while pausing at each store window exchanging our thoughts and decorative ideas. May would certainly be here before we realized it. By the time May arrives, we will have closed on our stunning rustic craftsman home down in the Cove area of Stamford. I will be Mrs. Nigel Brooks, and soon after, we will have a few little Brooks running around our property. Both Nigel and I are disciplined when it comes to saving money, but we have had to save enough for our wedding. What little we may have left must be set aside for a rainy day. All I can say is thank God for good credit because that's something that the both of us do have—coupled with a combined total of $140,000 in our 401K plans. The fact that we are both first-time homeowners will allow us to withdraw from our funds without a penalty and take advantage of the opportunity to bid on this home at the city's auction of foreclosed properties. Most homes by the water are priced to start at a minimum of $700,000, particularly in the Cove section, but there has been a lot of talk of property values going down and city taxes rising as a result of the crime on the West Side. Nigel said, "Shit, those are my people and our bid is strictly to accommodate us!" With that thought, we walked away with a low bid of $309,000 on a house sitting on two acres of land that was clearly worth twice that amount.

"Do you like that?" I ask pointing at a Calphalon pot rack with a variety of skillets hanging from it. "Oh, look at that, Nigel! They have the stone canister set with stainless steel lids. Look over there; they've got the matching trays with a mosaic pattern in the center." I'm so happy we both agree that the kitchen and living room could remain rustic, yet have a contemporary flare. The kitchen has beautiful travertine tiles in earthy colors resting beneath an enormous island in the center of the room. The living room still has the original hardwood floors. We believe that adding just a touch of contemporary will give us that eclectic feel, so we've decided that the contemporary contribution will come from having our appliances in stainless steel along with installing hanging pendants and recessed lighting throughout.

"We should use this store for our bridal registry. Look at those clay bowls and the pattern on the square chargers—do you see them?"

"Yes, I see it all, doll," he replies with his deep voice and warm smile.

"Are you making fun of me?"

"No; I'm just enjoying you, Simone. These are the things that made me fall in love with you." He pulls me closer and says, "I love you, girl."

Nigel and I continued on laughing and holding hands as we walked to Jasper's. When we walked in, we could hear a group of men yelling in front of one of the large flat-screen televisions. It was a pre-season football game between the Dallas Cowboys and the New York Giants. At another table, State Representative Clyde Hicks and a few corporate brothers were loudly debating whose responsibility it was to rehabilitate the forgotten West Side.

"What up, man?" Quinn asks as he gave up some dap to Nigel.

"Oh, it's all good now that I've checked out that score," Nigel replies as we walk towards the bar.

"Come on, I gotcha man!" Quinn yelled as he raised a full pitcher of beer in the air.

Just as Nigel placed money on the bar and requested that Paul set a tab up for the night, Torie arrived.

"Hey Nigel," she says before greeting him with a kiss. "Can we borrow Sim for a while? It seems that we have a wedding to plan."

"You can have her, but please go easy on a brother's pocket with all that planning!"

"I saw this fierce gown in the city yesterday, and I really can't do justice in describing it."

"Then I guess we'll just have to go to the city," I suggest.

Felicia offers, "Only if it's a business trip on Arial's."

"That's the only way to go. We'll get a limousine and have dinner at the B.B. King Blues Club & Grill and our choice of clubs for the night!" Simone replies.

"We'll have to do it really soon because winter will be here before we know it."

"Let's be all of that for the night," Felicia demanded as she flicked her cigarette ashes.

"When am I ever less than that? Let's call it a sophisticated stag and we can invite the whole crew. We'll get another limo on me."

"Ooooh, Torie, I like that! You would do that for me?" Simone asks as she pressed her cheek against mine.

"Yes, but can we please order our drinks now?" I requested while peeling her arms from around my neck as she nearly chokes me as she jumps up and down with excitement.

The voices were growing much louder and transforming from a friendly debate to a gentlemen's disagreement. As I turn to see who and what had fueled the debate, Mr. Hicks's eyes met mine and he immediately beckoned for me to join them.

"Girl, tell him that you're busy. Don't go over there." Simone negotiated.

"I'll be right back." I walked towards the noise and shouted, "Order a Cosmopolitan for me, please."

I was greeted with that infamous baritone voice requesting, "Miss Harper, help me out here please?"

"Hi Mr. Hicks! How are you?" I've always given him the utmost respect with him being a lifelong friend of my grandfather.

"I'm trying to explain to these gentlemen the importance of our being involved in the rehabilitation of the West Side community."

"Oh," I reluctantly replied while thinking, this is what all that noise was about?

"Would you mind sharing your ideas on the project that you and that fellow Quinn have been working on?"

I'm sure that it was obvious that I was feeling a little uncomfortable as I glanced around the table to identify who I was speaking to.

I replied, "Umm, it's still very premature."

"Some of the most successful projects were launched during what was thought to be premature stages," the man to my left offered.

"Torie, please accept my apologies for not introducing you. This is Larry Parks, CEO of Account Net." Larry stood and extended his hand to me. He then offered me his chair.

"Oh, no thank you. My friends are waiting."

"Well, as I said, our proposal really is premature. However, Quinn and I feel that the West Side is saturated with viable commercial property. Structurally, they are in very good condition and the damages are superficial from neglect, vandalism and graffiti. This is the reason that companies like Matheson are aggressively trying to acquire them from the community through tax lien auctions, and the same reason that they are not seeking demolition permits; they too realize that the structures are intact for the most part." Judging by the looks on their faces, they probably hadn't given much thought to this. I continued, "We believe that the only way to have people respect their neighborhood is by having them feel as though it belongs to them, as well as giving them a neighborhood worth having."

"Are you saying that their community doesn't deserve to be respected now?" Larry asked as his face grew tighter.

"With all due respect, if I were to step on fragments of already broken glass, how much more harm have I really caused?" Mr. Hicks winked at me just like Granddaddy would have after I'd stood tall and put forth a valid argument to Nanna.

"And just who did you have in mind to finance this facelift? Even if you were able to convince someone to buy into such a poor investment, what makes you think that it wouldn't be destroyed in a short matter of time?"

"It's okay; I've anticipated these sorts of questions and I'm prepared to answer them." Looking him directly in his eyes I offered him a response. "Well actually, I have a couple of thoughts." I had everyone's attention. "Before any financial considerations, we would need to organize a diverse group of professionals to become our tactical team."

"Diverse?"

Now that I'd gotten their attention, I continued, "Very. We would need an attorney to handle all legal affairs, an accountant for financials, realtors, and a team of electricians, painters and carpenters."

"That's a pretty tall order wouldn't you say?" Larry asks in the most condescending tone while looking around for support.

"Well Larry, just looking around the table I'm able to count two accountants (pointing at Larry and me). There's one attorney—and a damn good one if I may add (speaking of him). We also have one part-time realtor."

As evidenced by the silence that had come over the table, I had definitely sparked an interest in each of these men. They smirk and look amongst them seeking the next challenger. Needless to say, Larry clears his throat before beginning to challenge.

"Money?" he asks as he rubs his thumb and index finger in circular motion. "Where is the money coming from?"

"What would you say if I said that the money has already been accounted for?"

"I would say don't stop now, baby girl!"

"First, I'm not your baby and I haven't been a girl in a very long time. Furthermore, I suggest that if you or anyone else at this table has an interest in girls and boys that you march yourself to that table over there and volunteer as a mentor." I stand upright after bending down looking at him eye-to-eye as I instruct him.

Mr. Hicks said, "I would correct you myself, Larry, if Torie hadn't already."

"For those of you who want to know where the money is, I'd be glad to share," I offer in a no-nonsense tone.

"Don't pay that old goat any mind—he's just being all he knows—urban!" Clyde responds.

"What are the only structures that are proudly residing at every other corner on the West Side?"

"Liquor stores?" another gentleman replied.

"No, churches," I answer impatiently.

"Just as a pillar supports a sound structure, the church is the pillar of this community. The church doesn't ask for any outside help or money. They rather help those who are in need within the church family using benevolent funds than having some elected official who lives on the East Side making broken promises."

"Who are the members?" I ask rhetorically. "Every parent, grandparent, auntie and uncle who living right here within the community. Hell, we're not busing them in to go to church, they live here," I sigh with passion and anguish.

"She's got a point," another agreed.

"Don't you get it?"

"Over many years it's been in place never being overthrown and rarely challenged. It's the inner-city democracy fueled and protected by the first amendment and its members. It's the Black people's stock market and the tithes are the 401K contribution."

"She's right, man! I can remember serving a term as Treasurer over at Emanuel Baptist" rubbing his chin and shaking his head from left to right.

He continued, "Monk, you remember right?"

"Well anyway, all I remember is the first time I had to open and post the Sunday tithe envelopes, oooooh weee!" He laughs with a phlegm-filled rattle and adds, "Let me just say this—Reverend is bringing in damn near a half-million to a million non-taxable dollars a year."

Mr. Hicks introduced the man speaking as Preston Wallace, the second husband of Jackie Wallace and the proprietor of West Side Reality. It had been said that Jackie had married a wealthy older man who had done quite well after selling a few commercial properties that have since become landmarks on the East Side. Now Larry had become somewhat dumbfounded.

"Who has that kind of money and is dropping it in a church basket?" he asks while scratching the side of his temple and pulling off of his cigarette. Preston had given me a look as if to say I got this, I raise my brow suggesting that the floor was all his.

"Larry, the church asks for those who are able to give tithes, which is ten percent of their income on a weekly basis, and for those can't to give what they are able to."

"Not everyone is going to give that," Larry argues.

"But many will for their own reasons. Some give because the good book has directed us to and we are obedient. Others use it as a tax write-off, and then you have those who think that they can buy their way into heaven. The most faithful are the elderly women who have set a little aside along with their deceased husband's pensions. Now take ten percent of all of that!!"

With that I decide to close my argument. "With the right proposal and plan in place, I'd like to think of the church as being our lending institution. Kind of like a credit union." Well, I certainly have the entire table stirred up and entertaining the possibilities.

"Torie!" Simone yells as she approaches the table.

"Gentlemen, I must go and join my friends, but it was great talking to you!" Mr. Hicks stands and thanks me for coming over. He respectfully kisses me on my cheek and whispers, "I'm sure that you and Quinn will be hearing from us very soon."

IN THE MIDNIGHT HOUR

The room is busy and suddenly too crowded. I'm tired and nothing makes sense anymore. I tell myself to breathe and loosen my hair clip releasing my hair to freedom. Shallow whispers of air are becoming failing breaths noticeably closer together. The lump in my throat is creating an obstruction causing my mouth to fill with saliva. Oh no, it's happening again! At once I'm taken over by a barrage of thoughts and emotions accelerating my heartbeat.

My throat feels like it's closing and every heartbeat echoes in my chest causing it to vibrate like the bass of a speaker. The pit of my chest is becoming hollow with every chord causing a delay in my breathing and an immediate pulse in my temples. I unclasp my beige satin bra gliding the strap across my shoulder and down through the sleeve of my royal blue blouse in hopes of instant relief. "Ahhhh," I sigh. While removing my pants, my leg has become tangled after turning them inside out. I'm feeling more anxious as I frantically hop around trying to free myself from these damn pants!

I then begin to cough. I can't swallow fast enough and saliva once again fills my mouth. It now feels like there's a pocket of air stuck in the middle of my throat and chest. I can't breathe, and even my thoughts are becoming winded. I'm afraid that if I can't breathe, I won't be able to swallow, and I will likely strangle on my own spit.

I feel that familiar racing in my heart and the panic rises to such a fever that I fear I am going to die. I begin spitting into the bathroom sink over and over again. I quickly dial Simone, but hang up on the second ring when I realize that it's almost midnight. Of course this would happen on the rare occasion that Hollis is away on business. I don't want to call him because I know that he will hop the next thing moving to turn around and come home.

I realize that I can't call anyone at this hour, and if I were to call, what would I say? Would I say that I can't breathe because my mouth is watery and my clothes are suffocating me? Surely they will think that I'm crazy. So I decide that I should unlock the deadbolt in the event that I did pass out or something . . . at least it would be easier for the rescuers. Oh Jesus, what's wrong with me?

I remember once reading that when you're having feelings of anxiety, you should sit on the toilet and push down as though you were in labor or having a bowel movement. I quickly snatch my panties off and drop them onto the floor. Hell, nothing else is working, so why not give it a shot? I sat there for what felt like forever—when in reality it was probably about ten minutes—just long enough for me to get my breathing under control. I'd raise my ass into the air while leaning forward to spit and then resume my sitting position and grunt to no avail. Now panicking and not wanting to die, a reoccurring and vivid memory appears of my mother gasping for her final breath as I looked on helplessly . . . and then Nanna Bess six months later. I clutch my left breast tightly in an attempt to slow my heart rate down while heading back to the living room. My tear-filled eyes are cloudy, so I follow the path of clothing under the bottoms of my feet. I get to my destination and pour a glass of wine. At that moment, I remember the pack of Newports hidden in the freezer deep inside several bags to preserve their freshness. I saved them for times of extreme stress— Mommy's death, Nanna's death, and certainly moments like this.

Finally seated on the sofa, I use my arms to pull my legs into my chest. I rock slowly waiting for calmness after gulping down that glass of wine. I begin to cry out in agonizing shrills of pain finally acknowledging all of my losses.

Looking up at the blank ceiling I cry out, "I am all alone, Mother!" Perhaps I can will one last face-to-face conversation with her. I think about Nanna and say, "Help me, I can't do this alone!" And then to both of them, "Why did all of you leave me? I'm not as strong as everyone thinks and I'm scared. Who will take care of me? How could you leave me here all by myself?"

I'm now pacing the floor with a lit cigarette, a nose that's both stuffy and runny, and a face that is soaked from my tears. I tell myself that God knows what's in our hearts. Well, if my thoughts and heart aren't private, and the hymn says what a friend we have in Jesus, then like a good friend, we share truths. And then with clenched teeth, a troubled heart, and no fear—no fear of life, without fear of death and not even fear of God in that moment—the outburst comes. From somewhere deep inside I yell, "So since you already know the truth, then I know that you know that I'm PISSED off. Nanna, you said that God wouldn't give me more than I could bear! You said to call out to him and that he would be here." I'm weeping harder than ever now and I am angrier than I've ever allowed myself to be.

I fall to my knees and look up to heaven, pressing my hand against my stomach to yield the physical pain in the pit of my soul. I say, "God . . . I just want to talk to my mother . . . Please, God!!" I sob like a demanding child in the middle of a tantrum. I bury my face into a pillow on the floor sobbing with defeat until falling off to sleep.

A while later, I suddenly awaken with a feeling of disbelief; I can't remember my mother's face. I feel my eyes scanning the walls of the room frantically as though my memories were stolen while I was asleep. I can't remember her voice . . . the details of her face . . . her smell. What's going on? Oh God, help me. I rise to my feet and reach for a family photograph and cradle it in my bosom with relief.

I haven't forgotten their faces at all. I open the closet where my mother's coat has been since winter; it still carries her fragrance. A folded piece of paper falls out of her pocket; it's a poem in my mother's handwriting.

> *Cricket (A name she'd called me as a child for being most talkative during the night)*
>
> *If there are no words to be spoken from me, quietly listen to the breath of the alto sax or the lyrics of the awaking birds in the early morning, and there I will be among the humming . . . my voice, love.*
>
> *If there are no longer steps that I can dance, look into the shadows and see the rustling leaves from the autumn trees, I will be there passionately dancing the night away.*
>
> *If my spirit can no longer speak, I will shout happiness through the hues of gold and amber, bursts of laughter through the many shades of the jungle's green. The rare whispers of discontentment will reveal itself through the trickling water slowly streaming down a fogged window.*
>
> *Don't be afraid, baby, I will eternally be . . .*
>
> *Mommy*

Finally, I believe that everything is going to be alright. I slip into a peaceful sleep using her coat as a soothing blanket and the words—her words—as the answer to my prayers during this midnight hour. Thank you, Lord.

HOME IS WHERE MY HEART IS

I magine that the welcome sign as you enter the affluent woodsy suburb of New Canaan, Connecticut reads The Next Station to Heaven. The funny thing is, there really is an indescribable sense of peace as soon you enter this special place. We call the center of town the village. It consists of four core streets that provide for most of our basic needs—the ice cream shop, the bakery, the theater, the deli, a family-owned pharmacy, a classic toy store and Pic-a-Pants, which was yesterday's Gap.

As I a drive down the curvy bends of Frog Town Road, I immediately realize how much I love this old town. In fact, I probably love it more today than I did while I was growing up. Maybe I've loved it the same all along and now I've grown to appreciate it. The one thing that I am certain of is that no matter where I am, New Canaan will always be the place I call home.

New Canaan is the place where I had all my firsts. It's the one place that allowed me to be me—just me; not Black or White, not rich or poor—simply me. This town provided me with opportunities to be the best—or not, if I was so inclined. Living here, I never felt different. Hell, until I left, I had never been followed around a store in my life! I had never even been called a derogatory name, more specifically, the N-word.

How did my Black family become fourth-generation residents of New Canaan? Our family story was something that my grandfather was very proud of. He was never too busy to sit me down and tell me that story over again. My great-great grandfather worked as a laborer from around the 1850s to the mid-1860s building the railroad. His skills were unmatched, and because of that, he was paid premium wages and allowed to stay in an old farmhouse that once housed some local shoemakers. He'd acquired his skills because of his fair complexion and the assumption that he was something other than Black, which allowed him to work on the rails in the South and use the opportunity to come up North. He then met and married the seamstress to Mrs. Hampton, the farmhouse owner's wife.

The farmhouse sat seven acres in the rear of the main house with a separate driveway from the west. After the passing of my great-great-grandparents, the owners (who had begun to age as well) were unable to care for the property. My great-grandfather assumed the maintenance of the property as a way of showing gratitude for all those years of housing. My great-grandmother began preparing taking in laundry and preparing daily meals for the owners; my granddaddy was the delivery boy who carried everything up to the main house. At the time of their deaths, the Hamptons had willed the farmhouse and the surrounding three acres to my great-grandparents in lieu of past unpaid wages. The property has been passed on ever since. The house now belongs to me and I'm on my way to check on this very special house.

I can't imagine my life if I had never ended up here. My mother met my father during her junior year at Spelman College. At the time, he was a senior at Morehouse who was being recruited as a running back for the NFL. Auntie said that he never stood a chance with my grandmother, NFL or not, because his skin was too dark and that he would spoil her family's advantages. That is the reason my mother and father eloped when she discovered that she was pregnant with me. As he became a popular player in the NFL, being a husband

and a 23-year-old father became less and less appealing. When I was three, he sent me and my mother to live with my grandparents in New Canaan—temporarily, of course! Apparently, my mother had never sent pictures of me, not because she was ashamed of me—because I was a spitting image of my mom—but I'd gotten every ounce of chocolate from my father. That would be quite disturbing to my grandmother who was conditionally "color struck." In fact, she hadn't written or telephoned them until six months before our arrival.

As I go down the driveway of the farmhouse and enjoy the array of colors displayed on the autumn leaves, I can see the new owners of The Hampton House gathering the fallen leaves in their yard. On any other occasion I would go over and introduce myself, but I am pressed for time because I'm meeting Laurie and Millie for lunch this afternoon.

It's funny. For years we would refer to that house as The Big House, but over the years and a few substantial renovations, the farmhouse is now larger than The Big House, so it's no longer fitting to call it that. Now we call their house The Hampton House and ours The Big House.

I can remember seeing the houses for the first time as though it were yesterday. When we arrived that day, my mother embraced a young woman who looked just like her; both of them were very small-framed with naturally waved hair and almond-colored skin. I knew that had to be my Aunt Dot, my mom's sister. She picked me up and showered me with kisses from head to toe while telling me what a beautiful ebony princess I was. There I was as brown as coffee grounds with silky black curly hair and eyes with thick curled lashes that were the size of two jumbo black olives! Mom brushed my hair away from my face with a little baby oil to relax the curls that were held with two pink barrettes. I was dressed in denim overalls, a pink turtleneck and white Keds with pink laces. I got to wear my special gold earrings and bangle that Auntie had sent me on my birthday.

At the sound of the door opening on the porch, we all turned around. Out came a man who looked like Harry Belafonte. He was wearing a pair of khakis, a burgundy sweater with the sleeves pushed up, and suede shoes that matched his pants. To this little girl, he was as big as a giant! When I looked up, I realized that my mom was crying and this man was consoling her; that man was my Granddaddy. I remember he kept hugging her and asking her questions, but didn't really give her a chance to answer them.

"Why didn't you call me, Lydia?"

"I'm so sorry, Daddy. I wanted to, but I just didn't know what to say."

"I've always told you not to pay that woman and her ways no mind! Your mother doesn't mean any harm—that's all she knew growing up. They taught her that being lighter ensured a better way of life."

Granddaddy told her that he loved her and pulled her back into his arms. He spotted me at his knee caps where I stayed for only seconds before he swiped me up into his arms. I'll never forget that day! After kissing me and squeezing me so tightly, we just stared into each other's unfamiliar faces. His nose was long and narrow with a point at the end—just like my mother's—and just like mine! He had huge arms encircled by a network of veins. I broke the silence asking him if he ate a lot of spinach. My mother and Aunt Dot began laughing as Granddaddy looked baffled.

"Popeye, Daddy," Auntie whispered in his ear.

He replied, "Indeed I do! What about you?"

"I eat it all up," I proudly replied.

We laughed as he carried me toward a really big white house with a black front door and shutters. There were hanging flower pots the same color as my pink barrettes all the way around the porch. He told me what a pretty little thing I was and asked where I had gotten those eyes from. I remember him saying that with eyes like mine, he would never be able to tell me no, nor would he ever want to.

"Bessie, come on down! Lydia and the baby is here!"

My Granddaddy told me that Nanna had been fussing over the bedrooms for a month now. Aunt Dot had all of these packages wrapped and waiting for me. When I opened the first package, there was a baby doll that looked just like me and books with only positive things about African-American children and making our dreams come true. Over time, my aunt made sure that I understood any and everything that would lend to my understanding the differences of cultures, skin colors, languages and behaviors without prejudice. She taught me to be self-reliant, well-read, and to speak with conviction about only those things that I'd seen for myself or deemed to be from a reliable documented source. It wasn't until I became an adult that I understood most of her ways, which are now my ways.

As I got out of my car and walked up the porch steps, I smiled at the warm memory of the two black Nantucket rocking chairs that, in later years, Nanna and Granddaddy would always be sitting in waiting for me to arrive for a visit. Once I opened the front door, it was like the first time. It was as if I could see Nanna at the top of the stairs on our arrival day all over again. There she stood on the staircase looking at her baby's baby. For the first time in her life, my Nanna Bess was colorblind. Within moments, she compared me to my mother as a child and spoke of all the places that she would be taking me and all the foods she would make. As she led me off to my new bedroom, Nanna assured me that if I didn't like lavender, we would change the color to my liking. Little did I know that behind that closed door sat the most wonderful bedroom in the world!

It really was the most wonderful room in the world! It had a huge four-poster bed with a white and lavender quilt. There were many pillows at the head of the bed and a stepping stool at its side. The two windows were dressed in sheer lavender curtains with white plantation shutters. Pictures of Black ballerinas decorated every wall. An overstuffed toy box stood waiting for me to come and play. On one of the two night stands, there was a children's prayer book. My mother and I would say our prayers together each night after Nanna Bess had given me my bath. Mom put a calendar on the wall so that we'd mark off the days together until Daddy would arrive.

Let's talk about my so-called Daddy. Theodore Otis Harper was his birth name. In the NFL he was known as Otis "The Big O" Harper; in the company of my Aunt Dot he was known as Flash. That's the name she'd given him years ago because he was so arrogant that he thought it was a compliment for his style of dress and nice cars. In reality, Aunt Dot named him this for other reasons. If there was a crowd around, my father would take out his wallet and unnecessarily adjust his credit cards or shuffle his money around being flashy. After losing his front tooth in a game once, he replaced it with a gold one that was as blinding as a camera's flash. The weeks and months had gone by quickly and Daddy's phone calls had become less frequent. Every so often, Mommy would sit me down and explain why my father's plan of joining us had been changed again. Each time it was harder for her to hide her tears, and even to a child, her explanations lacked creativity. But it didn't matter to me, it just meant that I was able to play with Granddaddy longer and I could continue being Nanna's little baker.

During those days, Nanna Bess had been taking me to church with her. Granddaddy felt that I was much too young to understand and that I should only attend Sunday school. But no, she didn't listen. Nanna kept on taking me. Reverend Johnson talked about the devil all the time and how he is responsible for all of the bad things that we do. At the pulpit he'd say things like, "Oh yeah, it's the devil that we've got to learn how to fight, so that he stays out of our lives and so that we can stay out of trouble! Amen, Amen! Beware of the devil— he hides behind pretty things!" I didn't know much about the devil, but I'm pretty sure that he helped me to make that decision to take Nanna's false teeth and put them on the scarecrow in the garden!

Being a child, I took things literally. One Sunday when we got home from church, Nanna went to cook dinner and Granddaddy was watching a baseball game. I was a little bored because my mother wasn't home, and Aunt Dot was in her room talking on the phone and smoking one of her tiny cigarettes that smelled like Granddaddy burning leaves. Left to my own devices, I went outside to play. I was in Nanna's garden and I started thinking about what Reverend Johnson was saying about the devil hiding behind pretty things. So I started picking the flowers one by one to see if the devil was hiding behind them. When I couldn't find him, I began digging up the dirt. Then I heard Nanna Bess yelling, "Lord Child, what are you doing?"

There were flowers all over the ground with dirt on top of them. I poked out my lips and began to cry. She demanded, "Child, you better answer me!" I began to cry even harder and decided to run while shouting back at her, "I was looking for the devil, because I was gonna kick his ass." Nanna chased me with a broom from the front of the house and around to the back. She kept yelling, "Oh, sweet Jesus, don't let me catch this hussy!" Just as I reached the porch taking two steps at a time, Nanna was catching up to me and the broom was even closer, Granddaddy came.

"What's going on out here? Don't you hit this child, Bessie!" Granddaddy demanded as he raised his chin and thinned his eyes at her.

"Granddaddy, I was trying to kick the devil's ass for getting me in trouble the other day with Nanna's teeth." Before I was able to plead my case, I burst into tears and buried my head in Granddaddy's lap.

"Bessie, I told you that child was too young to understand church."

Later that evening, I'd made a big-girl decision; I wasn't going to eat my dinner because Nanna had cooked it and I wasn't talking to her. I asked Mommy to give me my bath instead of Nanna, and she obliged. My mother kept telling me to come on and get into the water, but I kept forgetting things like my toys, bleaching salts, bubble bath and Ambi skin lightening cream. Mommy looked surprised and she asked, "Torie what are you doing with these things?" I told her that Nanna said that it was our "secret pretty potion." Well, my mother screamed for Nanna to come into the bathroom. When she arrived,

I could tell by the look on my mother's face that Nanna was in big trouble. I stood up in the bathtub with white foamy suds sliding down my glossy brown childlike frame, with my weight shifted to the right giving the appearance of one ponytail sitting higher than the other. I then placed one hand onto my hip like a grown woman and extended the other to point my finger at Nanna and instructed my mother to "kick her ass!" I didn't even get in trouble for saying it either! Oh, my new-found self-expression!

My Granddaddy always said that if you live long enough, you will find the answers or better understand the things that you once were unable to. He told me that there would be other things that we would leave this world not ever understanding—and for me—the value that continues to be placed on skin color is one of them. I knew all along that my Nanna loved me unconditionally, and I later learned that it was her love that frightened her into being concerned about my dark skin. I had no clue about this whole color thing or why my mother was so upset that day. For me I just wanted someone—anyone—to handle Nanna.

I now understand that our race has inherited a profound awareness rather than a consistent appreciation for our uniqueness. Unlike any others, we have been bestowed with a natural color wheel displaying infinite hues of compelling earthy brown, milky crème, golden amber, clay red, sun-kissed copper, indigo, toasted almond, warm fudge, caramel, mocha and it goes on and on. Poor Nanna! She was held hostage by that old "brown paper bag" test. She struggled with the thought that I might not ever be accepted. The idea of value being placed on anyone whose skin color matches the shade of a damn bag or lighter, and believing it to give them preference as a person.

Unfortunately, this gift and array of colors has been lost by placing them in a form of hierarchy ranked from lightest as the purest to the darkest as less valuable. It's created an entire subculture—a division within our culture. Our little dirty secret! The funny thing is that this hierarchy has relatively little value or recognition outside of our race, meaning, to most "Black is Black." Although I can remember growing up and hearing so called exemptions—whatever you want to call them—over the years. "Not like you" or "The *other* kind of Black people" and "Torie, you know what we mean?" At the time, I really didn't know what they meant. Now I can tell you exactly what they meant. They weren't separating us by our skin tones, but rather our behavior and speech patterns (dialect). So, if you are acting like a fool, then you are a fool! Nobody cares if you are a light-skinned fool or a Black-ass fool . . . you're just a fool!!

New Canaan sheltered my awareness of this subculture, but when I hit the grounds outside of here, I was pummeled with it. It was the first time that someone said that they didn't like me and I couldn't figure out why. Then it was followed with names that I didn't understand at the time. These girls called me names like Oreo, Tar baby, Black this and Black-ass that. On the other hand, the young men called me dark and lovely, chocoliscious, Black and sexy and often asked if I had Indian in me. (Where did that come from?) I later learned that was in reference to my "good hair." (Hair that doesn't need to be chemically or heat treated to blow in the wind—another cultural secret!) By the way, I think that's where I learned to use "Black ass" so swiftly and freely in conversations. So, I did what most people would do and that was to migrate towards those who have shown an appreciation for me . . . the guys!!

Okay, so New Canaan doesn't go without its share of my social confusion either. Let's start with the fact that most of my friends lived in mini-mansions with domestic help on staff who resembled me. This never went over well despite my showing stellar respect and empathy. When sleeping over with my friends for the weekend, I would attempt to remove my own plate from the table, turn back the covers for myself at night and rise early to make the bed in the morning. With all of that, I still received rude looks and unkind remarks like "Yankee child" in the midst of Caribbean gibberish or Patois. Another secret division within our subculture within our culture! I learned early that some Caribbean people separate themselves from us Black Americans. Needless to say, after a while I stopped turning back my covers and walked my Yankee ass away from my soiled plate and left them to do their jobs!

As I approach the top of the landing of the second floor, the long hallway is illuminated with sunlight and a mild breeze is blowing from the slightly opened window at the end of the hall. I stop and sit on the bench and look down the staircase as I did as a child, waiting impatiently for Granddaddy to finish tying my sneakers before leaving for our long walks that I affectionately called adventures. I'm sitting here now folded in half, covering my mouth to muffle my uncontrollable laughter as tears are streaming down my face at a memory that is just now making sense.

One night Aunt Mabel and Uncle Walter had a big disagreement after he'd had a few cocktails and a long night of playing Pinochle. I remember Nanna convincing them to stay the night because Uncle Walter was in no condition to drive. Granddaddy had fallen to sleep in his easy chair down in the family room that night. Much later, I'd heard all this commotion at the other end of the hall and remembered Nanna saying, "He did what?" as Auntie Mabel was holding her cheek. Well, the two of them stayed in Nanna's room for a long time. The next thing I remember is loud snoring coming from the guest room and whispering. I got up and watched quietly from my bedroom door. Nanna and Auntie Mabel were walking into that room with Nanna's big sewing basket. It was very quiet for a while except for Uncle Walt's snoring.

"Child, you better stitch faster than that!"

"Bessie, my side is almost done!"

Then the silence was broken! I heard the dull sounds of a broom repeatedly hitting the bed and the snoring replaced with Uncle Walt's shouts.

"What the hell is wrong with ya'll? Ouch!! Damn it! Ya'll better let me out of this bed!!"

I heard my Nanna say, "Walt, I betcha you won't try to put your hands on nobody else!"

Then Granddaddy shouted, "Bessie and Mabel—are ya'll crazy? You could have killed this man."

"Nah, we would have done that if that was on our mind! He'll be alright, ain't nothing hurt but his feelings," Nanna replied.

By this time, my face was so close to the door! I heard Uncle Walt mumbling, "Get me out of this damn bed!" That was followed by the sound of fabric being ripped and Granddaddy laughing.

"Walter, they done sewn you in this bed!" Granddaddy laughed and laughed.

"They better be glad I was tied up in these sheets!" Walt yelled.

"Oh yeah, well I'm gonna let you free to see what you going to do," Granddaddy said, still laughing at him.

"I ain't thinking about them two crazy-ass women. Just get me something for my head."

And while this memory still has me on my back, filled with laughter, it warms my heart knowing the depth of Nanna's strength and convictions.

LONGTIME NO SEE

I could hear the echoes of my footsteps on the street after exiting one of the three black Lincoln Town Cars. Somehow, it feels like a school field trip that I really do not want to attend. My walk is definitely different from that of my stiffly dressed colleagues as we march side by side in our corporate uniforms of either black or charcoal. Each is appropriately accessorized with signature Swiss watches, monogrammed brief cases or leather portfolios close by their sides ready to act as a shield in a moment's notice.

For Yoli and me, it's like going home to our once home away from home. It's been years since life had distanced us from that summer when we had experienced those many firsts in this community. As each member of the project team walks onto a new block, they eagerly update their clipboards while Bryce continues to photograph dilapidated structures that will soon become prime real estate purchased at bargain-basement prices. So consumed at the potential of cashing in and making big profits, they can't see that life still exist in these dilapidated buildings that many call home.

As we continue to walk down each block, Yoli's eyes often met mine. She too recognizes the residents peeking from around the corners of their curtains.

"Yolanda, please be sure to note the building addresses for these that will be leveled," pointing at the same residences we've just passed.

"Yes sir!" she replies.

I swear it's like we have on 3D glasses and they don't—like we can see something they can't. I can't help but feel sad; the place that I was so anxious to see is no longer here. My heart and mind quickly drift back and forth from the present to the past—specifically to that summer. We continue to pass the many memory-filled places that became a real Pandora's Box in my life. The West Side was my first experience of rejection. Oddly enough, it all came from other Black girls, and for that, it was a very hurtful time. I was treated like an imposter because of the way I spoke, the way I dressed and the music I listened to. And my hair—how it baffled them! Somehow my hair texture translated to them that I thought that I was better than them.

I close my eyes and take in the aroma of fresh collards and crispy fried chicken with the distinct smell of Frank's Hot Sauce. The source of all these decadent aromas is just across the street—Miss Mabel's Kitchen. She's the lone remaining business on a block amongst those who no longer exist.

"Bryce, I believe that we have enough supporting visuals for our data to begin our preliminary blue prints," Mr. Matheson instructs.

"Torie, you and Yolanda should expedite discussions that will result in the allocation of a budget for Yolanda to begin negotiating on these properties."

"Why, of course. We actually have plans in place to debrief over lunch today while everything is very fresh in our minds," I respond.

"Great idea! Bryce, please come in my car for the return trip so that we can get started as well."

We head back to Thorne Street right off of West Side Boulevard where our journey on foot began. Patrick and the other drivers were waiting patiently for our return.

"Patrick, I'm leaving two of my prize possessions in your care. Please ensure that they return to the office safely." He then leans in closer and whispers to Patrick, "I'm sure these people don't give you any trouble down here, son."

After watching Fred close the door behind Mr. Matheson, Yoli and I ask Patrick to wait a minute before pulling off.

"Patrick, where ya'll people at," I teasingly mock in the deepest Anglo voice I could offer. "I mean you can handle them right . . . son?" The car filled with uncontrollable laughter.

"Tank, turn this car around and get us to Miss Mabel's before the potato salad and red velvet cake is all gone. (Tank is the only name that he went by when we met him that summer.)

"Word? We wanted some of that fish from The Fry House—that's what the brothers and me were just talking about when you were coming back to the car. We were trying to figure out if you would smell 'em."

"Smell what?"

"The fish sandwiches—if we double bagged them and put them in the trunk."

My man Fred said to me, "You stupid man! How the hell you gonna hide some fish?"

"You were going to put fish in the trunk of this car?" We all began laughing until tears came out of our eyes.

Yoli said, "Tank, I would have wupped your ass if I had gotten out of this car with my freshly cleaned Jones New York suit smelling like fish and Tresor."

"Damn, Yoli! I said I thought about it—I didn't do it!"

Pulling up in front of the store, I got a glimpse of what the past couple of years have done to Aunt Mabel. Instantly I've gone from laughter to guilt. She seems a little slower, but still looks like new money; she's always been a sharp dresser. A tightly kept bun rests at the nape of her neck where it has been positioned for many years. Her arthritic curled fingers seem to make it difficult for her to open the brown paper bag for the customer she's currently serving. That didn't stop her from looking up displaying those perfectly shaped gray eyebrows nearly matching her once brown eyes that have now turned gray. Her almond skin has proven again to be an asset, as you will rarely find a wrinkle on our seasoned women. Our hair may gray and our eyes may begin to weep, but for the most part our skin will endure forever hiding our age.

"My Lord! Child is that you?" It had been many months.

"Is this Bessie's grandbaby and my long-lost niece?"

"Yes, Aunt Mabel—it's me, Torie!"

"Child, you looking like new money!"

"Look, ya'll hurry up and grab your food . . . I'm going around here real quick and play my numbers!" Tank shouts on his way out of the door.

"Hello, Tank!" Aunt Mabel chastises him for his poor manners.

"I'm sorry! Hi Miss Mabel!"

"Tank, wait. I'm going to the bodega with you; I want some of Luz's beans and rice! I hope that she has some pork left."

"Alright, you can come with me, but don't be up in there speaking that mess around me, Yoli. I ain't playing! You know I don't know what the hell ya'll be talking about. Hell, you're probably talking about me!" Tank holds the door for her, always treating us like ladies as he did when we met him years ago. Although he would joke and trash talk with us, he made it clear that no one else was going to be given that privilege. Tank has always made sure that we're straight whenever we pop up in Stamford.

Aunt Mabel has to be at least 84 now because Nanna would have been 80. I remember Nanna saying that she had taken her under her wing when she was a freshman at her new upper school and that the other children were teasing her because she was so shy. Aunt Mabel lied and told them that she was her baby sister just raised by another family to help her mother out, and that if anyone wanted to mess with her, that they would need to go through her. From that day on, that lie vanished and became truth as they became closer than any blood sisters. I'm sure that it was easy to believe given they looked very similar with their toasted-almond complexions and naturally wavy black hair. The only makeup that either ever would wear or needed was a coral matte lipstick and a little brow pencil that Aunt Mae clearly has retired. They were our local Rosa Parks, Coretta Scott King and Dorothy Height—always in attendance at every church meeting, NAACP rally and fundraiser with a missionary need.

Coddling me tightly into her chest, I realize that her bosom— once a man's dream—had now become deflated flesh tightly tucked and hoisted up by a Saxon-Kent brassiere.

"Oh baby, where have you been hiding?" She asks while pulling back and taking a look at me from head to toe. "You are sharp child. You got that from me . . . indeed you did. Of course, I'm the one that taught Bes," she says proudly.

My eyes flood with tears and my heart with shame and guilt as I hug her as I weep. Rubbing my back she continues, "It's alright baby, it's alright! You and I are all that we have left, Torie." Coddling me tightly into her chest while rubbing my back is something she'd done in my youth to comfort me during longer church services. As quiet as it's been kept, she's comforted a few men in that same manner after Uncle Walter's passing.

"I'm so sorry Auntie Mae! I've missed you so much!" I just couldn't bring myself to tell her that the real reason I'd been avoiding her was that with Mommy and Nanna gone, she was likely next and that I just couldn't bear to watch another one slip away from me.

"Hush child before you make these blurry old eyes blurrier." Using her apron to wipe her eyes, she says, "I'm not going anywhere anytime soon. I know that's what you got yourself all worked up about."

How did she know what I was thinking?

"Ah huh. I know what you're thinking, but me and the good Lord have plans of our own. We have plenty more people to feed before my work here is done!" With that, she gently kisses me on my cheek and washes her hands before grabbing a spoon to fill containers with banana pudding and a slice of red velvet cake. She calls out to the kitchen for a hot fried chicken breast with a wing and fixins to go.

How did she know what I wanted?

"Child, you've been eating the same thing in here since you could eat table food!" This bag has a pork chop sandwich and a side of potato salad for that young man driving you around. He's been coming here just as long. Now you better find your friends and hurry up and get back to those fancy offices before too long. I saw you walking around here with them men in those suits coming to take over. They aren't the first. I also saw you circle back in the car and that's when I had Roscoe drop your chicken down in the fryer. Now go on, baby. I love you too."

"I'll call you over the weekend. Maybe I can go to church with you on Sunday?" That's something else important to me that I'd abruptly stopped.

"That would be real nice, baby!" she replies as I walk towards the car. "I put an extra slice of the red velvet in the bag for that Spanish friend of yours."

I was trying to leave before she found the hundred-dollar bill I'd slipped in her apron when hugging her goodbye at the counter.

ONE SOCIAL HYBRID TO ANOTHER

"**T**orie, again I am so sorry for the misunderstanding and I hope that this hasn't compromised the accuracy of your reporting."

"Not at all, but remind me please, who is this prospective investor with late submissions?" I ask.

"Brunswick! They've really been on board for some time. There was a breakdown with the timing of their submissions," he defends.

"Eric, this is the first I'm hearing of them." I was really baffled.

"It must be rather daunting for you to stay on top of such a demanding accountability."

"Why is that?"

"Come on, there's got to be some pressure in knowing that the partners heavily rely on the integrity of your metrics, not to mention the obvious time constraints allowed for the compilations."

So now I know that this Mo-Fo knew that he was putting my ass on the block before walking into my office. Okay, I gotcha, player!

"No worries, I can take care of that." As Chief Counsel, I know he knows better than this. He continued to offer insincere apologies for his oversight of the deadline.

"You know if it would expedite the process, why don't we go ahead and eliminate the Working Capital metric?"

"Why would I ever do something like that?" I was clearly curious as to why Eric would ever suggest such carelessness.

"Certainly the preliminary report has shown substantial operating liquidity," he says using a very matter-of-fact tone.

"Fair enough," I reply now standing to assure him that I am in full cooperation and displaying team support as one of his strategic partners.

"However, that report wasn't generated by Klein-Matheson; in fact, it's an external submission from Brunswick's Finance Team. I would never vouch for something that I haven't reviewed in detail."

He rubs his brow and says, "Right, right. I thought I could save you sometime here."

"Nope, we're good. Thank you."

I tilt my head and make steadfast eye contact to ensure that he knew that unlike my colleagues, I wasn't the least bit intimidated by him. With a warm smile and raised brows I ask, "Eric, given the time allotment for a thorough review of all budgetary related submissions, I'd like to pass these on with confidence to my staff accountants as final submissions. Do I have your support in telling them that this is your final submission?"

"Ah yes, of course."

Eric seems to be extremely flustered. I placed the folder onto my desk as he turned to approach the door. I added, "I appreciate the continued support, Eric." With that, my phone began to vibrate giving me a reminder for our M&A meeting with the partners. I'm certain that this has prompted Eric to rush down here to give me this last investor's submission, probably to prevent me from informing the partners of his being incompliant during our updates. I quickly went down the corridor to use the ladies room because the duration of these meetings are so inconsistent.

My phone was ringing as I returned to gather my things for the meeting. A double ring indicated an incoming external call; a quick glance at the display tells me that it's Simone.

"Hey girl, I'm on my way to that meeting. You get two minutes," I say in a rushed tone.

"Girl, take some flavor up in that joint because Lauren won't! Is she still trying to pass for anything other than a woman of color?" Simone asked while laughing. She added, "It's like I want to come over there and just tap her on her shoulder and whisper, 'Lauren, everyone can see you—this isn't a Skype call. They already know that you're Black. You know, the box that you reluctantly checked when hired.' Torie, you came from New Canaan and proudly embrace your Blackness and education."

Lauren has lived on the West Side her entire life until recently; she barely speaks to me and won't even speak to the brothers in the mailroom. What is that shit she's always doing with her head trying to swing her hair pretending like it's so long and bouncy? She looks like she has a nervous tic.

"Simone, don't be so unkind! Besides, your two minutes are up and ill-spent I might add!"

"I'm just saying ..." she hatefully giggles.

"I gotta go!"

"Wait, we are still going to Jasper's after work, right?"

"Sure, I'll call you when I get outta the meeting."

"Is that hater Eric gonna be in there?"

"Of course he is, but no worries. I'm bringing the brown sugar to sweeten his coffee for him, because sipping is all that he will be doing after I shut his ass down. In fact, he was just here looking as if he was up to something. I'm not sure what his goal was, but it was thwarted."

"Good girl! Go in there and teach him a little something and let them all know that we got the memo a long time ago that a mind is a ter-ri-ble thing to waste!"

I rush off the phone not wanting to be late. That would only support that tired old misconception of our always being on "CP" time (colored-people time . . . always late).

Our offices are strategically positioned to face the south end of the building capturing a picturesque view of the Manhattan skyline from the partners' suites. For those of us deemed to be fast trackers, key employees or simply Matheson's up and coming, we share the privilege of our offices placed as neighbors on the same block. Over the past few years, I've perfected my execution of being a skilled valuable pawn in the corporate game. Although this wasn't always the case, as a newbie in the game I've certainly taken a few broadside hits from vying players like Eric with one incident that promptly landed my ass in the unemployment line. It really wasn't so bad; I like to remember it as my summer off with benefits. I had money, insurance benefits and, oh yeah, Sinclair. I'd say that my total compensation package was rather meaty in every way.

Throughout the meeting, I observed Lauren deliberately avoid me, never once making eye contact. I have the utmost respect for any woman and sister acquiring her education and earning the additional credentials to go with it, and to further pioneer as Klein-Matheson's first female and Black attorney—kudos to you. However, I so want to say to her, "Lauren, as Chief Financial Officer, I assure you that I didn't acquire this title from a Cracker Jack box. I earned it as well! Oh and by the way, take a look at our compensation. Oh that's right, you don't have access! I do and I allocate yours!!"

During a brief break midway through the meeting, we all gather around the refreshment buffet and share in idle conversation. I couldn't avoid overhearing another colleague speaking with Lauren.

"Hey Lauren, I had the best Southern dinner at a local restaurant over the weekend. My husband is from the South and misses the cuisine. We had collards, yams and the most delicious pulled pork."

This phony bitch replies, "Collards? What are those?"

Okay, so now I am completely done with her. She allowed Ruth to go on and explain, all in an attempt to disassociate herself from her ethnicity.

"They are the best! You must try them!!"

The meeting was called to resume just in time.

WHAT'S A BROTHER TO DO?

"What up, man?" Nigel walked up on me in deep thought causing the Corona bottle to slip away from my waiting mouth.

"Damn, man!! How you just gonna walk up on a brother shouting like that?"

"So what's up? I mean you sitting over here in this dark corner looking like you're pondering some serious mess."

"Huh?" slightly humored with Nigel's intuitiveness.

"Who is she?"

"What?"

"Man, don't what me! Quinn, how long have I known you? Who is she?" Nigel asked again before being distracted by an unfamiliar patron that just walked in. It's rare to see someone we don't know; for the most part everyone knows everyone whether by face or on a more personal tip.

The cafe is split into sections. There's a dimly lit sports bar set up on the far right with multiple plasmas and bistro tables behind a glass wall called the fish bowl. The wide double doors are usually closed so that our loud cheers and banter don't disturb the other patrons. On the complete opposite side of the big oval bar that's positioned in the center of the cafe is a stage with a smaller dance floor and surrounding tables for live entertainment and poetry. It becomes mad crowded, standing room only up in there when it's a worthy entertainer occupying the stage. Lastly, there's the living room which is actually the bar area and probably the largest section of Jasper's Cafe—with the exception of the restaurant that occupies the entire upper level. The restaurant entrance is separate on the side of the building through the old carport. Case really did a great job with this place. There's a DJ in a loft overlooking the bar and living room; just think of it as a museum, hotel lobby and bar in one. The entire cafe echoes mature occupancy throughout, the ambiance alone can help the weakest brother kick his game up a notch. The major thing that sets this establishment apart from others is Case's intolerance of any drugs running through his place.

"Case! Let me get a round over here! "

"I got the next round man," finishing the bottle in my hand.

"Seriously man, what you holding hostage up in that big ol' head?" He landed an intended timid punch against my upper arm as I rest on only two of the four legs of the chair.

"Man, I'm just trying to make some steps forward on this Coalition business. You know I had to step down as counsel, right?"

"Nah, man."

"Yeah, it's cool! I've just been advising from behind the scene. You know what I'm saying?"

"It's getting done right?"

"Without a doubt man!" He reaches for one of the four cold Coronas that Case sent over. A round of beer in Jasper's usually indicates a set up of two—one and another in the cue.

"What about the job? Were there any ramifications with all of that?"

"Uh huh," shaking my head from left to right taking another swig from the bottle. "Nah, no one has mentioned the West Side Coalition or my affiliation. That's why I took the initiative in stepping down as soon as I knew. I'll tell you this; I'll rest on that if any future arguments arise concerning conflict."

"Oh I hear you. What? And that right there, that's exactly why you would be my counsel. Shoot, my money is always on the brother that's thinking ahead."

"Are you all alright over here?" Case asked as he was making his rounds. He has stayed true to ensuring that Jasper's is received as the upscale venue intended. The cafe is frequented by Whites, Blacks, women and men for different reasons. Some are looking to unwind after a crazy work day or week, others for a good meal and company or just a nice night out. Case had the right idea in weeding out the riffraff by having club music only on Friday and Saturday nights after nine o'clock and with a $20 cover charge or two-drink minimum.

"Yeah, we're good! Case, how've you been man?" Nigel responded before turning his bottle up to his head and tugging on his tie loosening it even more.

"Maintaining, you know what I'm saying? Business has dropped off a little with some of the concerns over the West Side activity lately."

"Yeah, oh yeah," Nigel agreed.

"Of course, the media doesn't help much with their depiction— they make it seem like it's the Wild Wild West over there and are fearful that it will find its way up here to the lower East Side."

"Close enough!!" I chimed in before we all surrendered to insincere laughter over the comparison of our diminishing childhood neighborhood.

"I just hope you and that Coalition can save things before we all go under."

"We're on it! We are on it!" Nigel and I fist bumped in agreement.

"Let me know if you two want some wings or something sent over; it's on the house."

"Appreciate that, man," I rubbed the back of my neck feeling his angst over the recent challenges and wondered would we ever be able to save the old hood.

Tank walked up and grabbed a seat at the table. "Damn, ain't nobody in here," he said while looking around checking out the room filled with mostly male patrons.

"Well that depends on who and what you're looking for." I knew that Tank was looking for sisters.

"I'm looking for some ASS."

"Oooooh!!" Nigel and I shook our heads laughing at Tank's candor.

"You ignorant man," I charge before tossing my beer cap at him.

"Ignorant? Hell, I'm honest," allowing his eyes to continue his prowl while we looked on with laughter.

"He's serious?"

"Hell yeah, he's serious, Q!"

"Oh okay, it's like that? Nigel, the only reason you're not on the prowl is because you're on lockdown, Simone got you all LoJacked and things."

"Man, you fool . . . lockdown?"

"Go on and lift that pant leg, man, and show us that ankle monitor! You got one of them too, huh?"

"Ah Q, don't be over there laughing."

"Why's that?"

"Everybody knows that you've been on a secret emotional lockdown for a minute now."

"Lock down? For who—Jasmine? Man, you're crazy!!"

"Nah . . . Torie, man! What? I ain't so crazy no more, huh?"

"Get outta here, man!" I laugh as I gulp down my second Corona and catch Nigel's head slowly nodding up and down, silently in agreement with Tank. I wonder if it really was starting to show.

After a few brief relationships and a few "more than brief" relationships, I've decided to casually date and focus on my career and the community needs. Jasmine set the tone for that after trading up for a pro player while I was preparing for the bar exam. I admit that her betrayal made me withdraw my trust in most females. Torie is different than most on all levels; she's just real inside and out, no false goods. She appreciates and shares the same desires of making a difference and getting for those in need. She's beautiful and captivating. There I said it; I'd be a liar if I didn't speak of her distinct look.

"Who is that?" Tank asked after capturing a glimpse of a new arrival.

"Go in easy, man," Nigel teased.

"Uh oh, gotta go this brother's being sought after." Tank placed his empty beer bottle onto the table after making lingering eye contact with the young lady seated across the room on a sofa in the living room.

"Be good, man."

"Always!!" Tank looks completely mischievous at Nigel and me adjusting his swagger as he walks across the bar.

"That Negro knows he's fool! He needs to go ahead and find a lady and stay put for a minute."

"Man, I can't EVER remember Tank chill'n with one lady."

"He's a ho! A man ho!" Nigel cracked himself up with that. The effects of that shot of Patron we had are beginning to become apparent. No harm—the brother's just trying to unwind and detach from a week's worth of that hedge fund bullshit that comes with his job. Look at him sitting there unknowingly touting contentment with a simple grin smeared all over his face.

"Come on man, I think our mission's been accomplished." (Referring to our Friday night ritual of indulging in happy hour and leaving well before the night life begins in here.) "Besides, we've got an early morning over at the Community Center tomorrow; we've got to get them Pastors on board, man!" As I reach for my suit jacket, I scowled at the thought of the challenges lying ahead, but more daunting was the idea of failing and what that would mean.

"Speaking of Torie, what you think about that cat Hollis?"

"What? Now you gonna start?"

"I'm serious, man."

"He's alright. I don't deal with him really, I run into him from time to time down at the center volunteering. Why?"

"Simone was saying that he came off at the mouth a little bit the other day."

"To Sim?" I ask rhetorically, knowing that she would've shut him down fast.

"Man, please!! Nah . . . at Torie," I began rubbing my chin with instant agitation.

"So what he's been pushing up on her?" I ask with an interrogating tone.

"No, he didn't hit her; Sim just said that she sees that he's starting to be controlling."

The idea of a man ever putting his hands on a woman is non-negotiable for me, and a man that disrespects any woman that's in my life, like my mom, sister or friend won't be tolerated!!

"I'm gonna get on out of here, man," yawning while picking up my keys and the order of wings to go.

While I walk to my truck, I'm still working out the idea of anyone treating Torie less than careful. She's a gem—a real class act. Torie is stylish but simple; she's chic like Jackie O, Coretta Scott King, and my moms. She defies the imagery of our quietly spoken criteria for being considered beautiful and Black.

"Alright, man!!" Nigel shouted as he was getting into his Audi A6. He and Torie have a steadfast allegiance to the Germans when it comes to their choice of vehicles.

Even with our living in the same dwelling, we don't see each other that often unless planned. Our work schedules and participation in the coalition eat up a lot of our time. Occasionally I'll run into her on a Saturday coming up from our gym in Clock Tower. Usually her hair is tossed on top of her head with random pieces escaping and other sweat-dampened strands clinging against her forehead accentuating her perfectly shaped brows. Her brows aren't arched like the women who deliberately choose to have them shaped like they're asking,

"Huh?" all day. No makeup, oversized bleach-speckled sweats and a tank describes her workout attire; even with that, she looks good. Damn, she's just beautiful.

My cell phone begins to ring as I'm caught in mid-thought of Torie.

"How have you been? What's up?" I ask as I put the Rover in gear turning it around to head in the direction of my caller's place.

"I can do that, but I've got an early morning so I can't hang out long. Do you need anything? Oh, that comes everywhere with me," flirting in response to her request.

"Alright—see you in a few."

COMBAT

T he unfamiliar force to my cheek caused my mouth to fill with warmth and immediately began beating like a heartbeat, only with acute unrelenting pain. My left hand quickly lost its grip of the door knob leaving it barely opened as the other gripped my face in an attempt to suppress the pain and my state of shock. My body began tumbling backward with my head leading in making contact with the bare wooden floor. Between the flailing of both arms and the unwelcome shove from Hollis, the strap of my messenger bag became airborne slipping from across my shoulder and chest repositioning itself around the front of my neck. The bag now rests across my back, miraculously providing a cushion between the floor and me.

With only seconds passing, I was no longer confused! This man was kicking my ass and there was no time to confirm that this was really happening. Hollis then joined me on the floor and straddled either folded knee around my twisted waist while grabbing my shirt and the same strap that had just saved my life. He is lifting and bringing me closer to his face as he shouts. His nostrils flare as they are in need of incoming air from his clenched teeth. We were in combat—fully engaged—and the man who I was once in the trenches with has become my ENEMY!!

I stared back into the raged-filled eyes of the man I no longer knew as he demanded that I admit to being involved with the brother at the end of the corridor.

"Torie, I know that you're creeping with that brother down the hall! Yeah, you think I'm stupid? I saw the number come across the television screen on the caller ID. Damn, girl! Look at what you got us doing!!"

Tears begin streaming down his face. He abruptly releases his grip of the strap and shirt from his hand which repositions the messenger bag beside me, allowing my head to hit the floor. Random flashes of light, with specs of black and white distort my vision as my eyes roll to the back of my head. His spoken words translate as gibberish as I remain still, completely silent and in disbelief that a man, MY man would ever disrespect me and put his hands on me. Likely delirious from the impact, I hear and see my Nanna's face giving me copious instructions on what to do if a man were ever to put his hands on me. Nanna's voice is becoming louder and much clearer as though she's in my presence saying, "Baby, don't you know that a woman's strength is in her legs? If anyone is trying to hurt you, you must hurt them if it means getting them off of you. I don't care how big they are, you size up the room and the contents in it, and there you will find your weapons of defense. You remember that all is fair in war."

I open my eyes as I feel Hollis's body become limp; he's cupping his face into his hands covering his eyes while weeping in shame. I ever so gently reach into my bag that I have yet to forgive for resting beside me rather than beneath me breaking that second fall. I slide my single ignition key out slowly while gripping the small silver cylinder at the other end of the ring. Oh yeah, and just like Pearl Harbor, I take his ass by surprise! I call his name, and as he responds by leaning forward with shame and remorse, I lean back and spray that Mo-Fo right in his face!! When he unfolds his legs to stand to care to his burning eyes, I treat him like the enemy that he has become, and use my legs to flip his ass. I wrestle him on this floor like we are in full-on combat! I guess he didn't do his due diligence before dating me because if he had, he would have known that I was a tomboy until the age of 13! Just as my closed fist landed on his left eye, Quinn appears in my doorway and leaves everything broken on the foyer floor, including Hollis's ass!!

It's been a few weeks since my altercation with Hollis and I've completely immersed myself into my volunteer work down at the community center to fill the void. When I'm not doing that, I'm at the gym working out. I should probably get up now and squeeze in a work out in before Tishie arrives, but the bed is much too comfortable this morning. The silence is broken by a ringing telephone. Who could this be at this hour? Don't they know that it's Saturday? Let me guess, Simone?

"Hello…"

"Hey girl, I know you are not still in the bed—it's 7:30."

"Sim, what do you wannnt?"

"Do you want to go and get our manicures this morning rather than this afternoon?"

"And this couldn't have waited until at least 8:00? You know that Tishie will be here in less than two hours."

"Think of it this way, if we have little diva's nails done at 9:00, we are guaranteed an afternoon of her not touching anything for fear of them getting smudged."

"You have made a valid point!"

"Then we may want to change our standing appointment for nine every other week."

"We really have made her into a little diva. Do you know that I have her savings account up to $4,000 already?"

"Get out of here! Can you be my big sister?"

"Sim, I'm serious! Tishie is going to college if I have to send her myself"

"How long have you been her big sister? It's been at least four years, huh?"

"No, it's been three years, although it does seem as though it's been forever. Sim you should consider becoming a big sister. These little girls aren't anything like us when we were younger. They are like little women lacking jobs, guidance and knowledge of all the things that they should know and knowing everything that they shouldn't."

"Torie, that's your thing—not mine."

The complexion of the conversation was quickly changing. Although Simone and I are very close, our views are very different. My attitude is very simple, if I can help a brother or a sister, I will. Simone's is, get yours like I've gotten mine. I try very hard to respect our differences of opinion, but knowing that Simone came from the West Side and didn't have a lot growing up makes me less tolerant of her "better than" attitude. Don't ever make the mistake of reminding her of her past because then it's on! So be it…

"You really don't give a damn about what's happening on the West Side, do you? Even though it's where you grew up. Our names are probably still on the pavement on Hebrew Place."

Hebrew Place is where I first met Simone. I was about six; she and some other girl were playing hopscotch outside of Aunt Mabel's restaurant as I watched from the window. She confidently walked into the store and went right over to Nanna and asked what my name was and if I could come outside and play with them. To my surprise, Nanna said yes. Simone and I haven't stopped playing since that day, and that other little girl playing hopscotch was Felicia.

"Look Torie, the street signs may be the same and Miss Mabel's kitchen may still be there, but that isn't the same neighborhood that I grew up in. As far as our names being carved in the concrete, I'd gladly bet you $20 on a broke day that we'd find a crack vile dotting the i in Simone!"

"Yeah well, have you ever thought that maybe the reason we have neighborhoods like the West Side is because brothers and sisters in positions like ours grab ours and never look back?"

As anticipated, our voices grew louder and the desire to sway each other in our opinions was the only outcome the two of us wanted to reach. If anyone witnessed this conversation, they'd find it hard to believe that we are the best of friends.

"Look back? I'll tell you what I saw when I looked back—my damn car with two of your so-called brothers going the opposite way in it! I guess that was their way of thanking me for volunteering at the fundraiser. Better than that, they may have thought that my BMW was a generous contribution. So you see, Torie, my contributions are paid for the next 20 years—make that paid in full."

Simone and I both began to laugh at the memory of her running down West Side Boulevard chasing her car and yelling any swear possible. The best was when she ran out of breath and had to stop for a moment. Those bold creeps actually backed up in reverse to offer her a ride! Sim was drenched with sweat and her hair was draped across her face. She looked up and said, "That's my car!" To that, the driver laughed and said, "It WAS your car . . . ha, ha, ha!"

At this point, tears were streaming down my face and we both were gasping for air as she continued to remind me of the names she had called them as they fled with her car. "You greasy toothless Mo-Fo! I know who you are and my brother is going to f---your fat ass up!" Knowing Sim's brother . . . that was hardly an empty threat.

Sinclair is Simone's twin brother; they have always been very protective of one another. I think that it has more to do with the bond that twins have rather than just being siblings. They both have seriously slanted eyes with perfectly shaped brows; their skin is the color of red clay and they both have dimples and high-set cheek bones that provide just enough room for their full set of teeth. With the exception of

Simone being so petite and prissy and Sinclair so big and manly, they could be identical twins, pardoning gender of course. One summer Sinclair and I had gotten pretty close. In fact, I don't think physically we could have gotten any closer. After all was said and done, we both decided that it was just too risky to continue no matter how good it felt. And it felt real good. We're sort of like family, and he is like a brother is what I tell myself after a few glasses of Zinfandel coupled with vulnerable feelings and in the company of Sinclair.

He has certainly become like chocolate cake—always tempting me. From time to time I think, hell, I only want a sliver! Ha! We all know that no one stops after a sliver! There are some things that you don't even tell your best friend; this would be one of them. Although, I've always suspected that she knows because one early morning Sim dropped by without calling (as usual) and Sinclair was just coming out of my bathroom! Anyway, he isn't *really* family.

HOLLIS MOVES OUT

I've lost count of the sleepless nights I've racked up lately. It's been three weeks since Hollis has moved out and I haven't had one phone call from him. I'm sure that's his pride and embarrassment from the unexpected ass whooping Quinn put on him. Just because it's for the best doesn't mean it hurts any less. To be honest, things really hadn't been the same since January when we thought that I'd had food poising. I vomited off and on for three days, all the while trying to get myself together for a dinner party that I was looking forward to.

The party would have given me a chance to discuss possible donations for the community center. The hostess of the party was none other than Claudia Van Exel, who has been seated as chairperson for the non-profit organization Achieve. Achieve historically has provided aid and financial support for many global organizations. Recently they have been recognized as benefactors on a few domestic inner-city projects for their generous donations. I'd met Claudia one other time at Jasper's during a fundraiser for State Representative Clyde Hicks.

Although I was feeling sicker by the minute, I knew that I needed to use this function to my advantage by networking for support to save the after-school programs. Just as I turned around, Claudia was approaching and immediately began with her formalities.

"Hello Torie! How are you, darling?" Her face was so close to mine that I could feel her breath directly on my face. Claudia had obviously prepared her breath to be on its best behavior for socializing. With each word I was forced to inhale wintergreen mints. Within seconds, my mouth began to water and my stomach became upset all over again. I was very light headed and it must have shown all over my face because the last thing that I recalled was her asking me if I was feeling okay.

I don't know how Hollis made it to my side so quickly placing his hand on the small of my back and whispering into my ear, "What's wrong, baby?" The next thing I remember was waking up in the emergency room at Memorial Hospital. Hollis had an ear-to-ear smile on his face as he told me, "We're gonna have to take better care of this mommy-to-be."

The blood tests had shown that pregnancy and dehydration were the cause of my fainting. As Hollis continued to rub my arm and softly kiss my forehead, I struggled to think of a time that I wouldn't have taken a pill because this sister is faithful and would never, ever miss a damn pill. My body was too weak to make Hollis aware of the internal battle that was going on in my mind. I was too dehydrated to shed any tears. In fact, I just kept licking my lips while thinking that he better hand me that plastic pink boat because I was going to be sick all over again! When the doctor entered the room, I began a weak attempt to interrogate him.

"How can this be? I've taken my pill every day."

The doctor replied, "Apparently one got by you."

"Are you sure the test is accurate? Couldn't there be a false positive?"

The expression on the doctor's face as he stared Hollis's direction instantly made me conscious of the hurt that now resided in his face. Gently he released my arm resting it back onto the bed. He stood in silence slipping his hand into his pocket rotating the loose coins. This behavior is a habit of self-discipline that allows him to be thoughtful before speaking; something that he'd prayed that his father would have done in place of the berating name calling he'd witnessed and experienced as a child.

The doctor explained that it was necessary for me to stay overnight to allow the IV to continue hydrating my body. He offered that the nausea should pass as soon as the pregnancy was about 14 weeks along. He then asked if we had any questions. Before completely closing my eyes, I saw the older man walk towards Hollis and place his hand onto his left shoulder like a father assuring his son that it would all work out. He left with the directive that we "be good to each other." I felt Hollis's hand embrace mine as he whispered into my ear, "I got you, baby."

It wasn't until a few days later when I was looking for something in the medicine cabinet when I saw the bottle of antibiotics looking back at me. Then it hit me—that's how this happened!

I didn't know it at that moment, but it wasn't long before I'd be back in the hospital again. I hadn't really had a chance to process the pregnancy before the miscarriage happened. I hadn't yet shared the news with anyone other than Simone and Millie. The loss was probably for the best—at least for me and my life. With all the unforeseen demons that Hollis was harboring, what kind of father would he have been? What kind of life might that have been for any child—for me? I just pray that Hollis gets counseling to rid himself of those demons. He cannot be in any relationship until he fixes all the things inside him. Until then, he's damaged goods and should be taken off the shelf.

KEEPING IT IN THE COMMUNITY

"**B**anks, dry cleaners, bakeries, grocery stores—not just bodegas! We need to see our names on these walls as proprietors," says the young brother as he shouted each passion-filled word to the congregation.

Why does he look so familiar to me? I leaned over and asked Auntie what her new pastor's name was . . . Witherspoon . . . Jonathan Witherspoon, which meant nothing to me so I sat back in my seat and listened. He continued, "Are we not tired of waiting for them to select and approve us for loans at their mercy? Yet we continue to walk that long block to go around that corner daily and weekly depositing our money into our checking and savings accounts, supporting their bank for years." He went on to ask how many of us realize what happens to our money as it's deposited. Many of them looked away in embarrassment for not knowing, and others shrugged their shoulders and waited for him to explain.

"No sooner than you deposit your cash it's likely given to another patron who comes in that branch requesting cash withdrawals . . . I ain't lying. Deacon Paul and Deacon O'Neil—come on over here and help me out. I'm a visual person. I tend to understand better when I can see something. Now I'm going to be the bank teller, and Deacon Paul you can make a deposit."

That isn't too far from the truth, I think to myself. One of the two middle-aged women in the pew behind me whispered poorly, "Don't we deposit into his account every week via the church basket?" The other replied giggling, "And I know that's right!"

Deacon Paul handed Pastor the multiple bills and stepped down from the altar. Pastor places the money in separate piles on the pulpit and asked for the next guest in line—Deacon O'Neil requesting a withdrawal. Pastor demonstrated by removing the same money just deposited by Deacon Paul to fund the withdrawal.

"Hey wait a minute, that's my money!" shouts Deacon Paul.

The cutest little boy slipped off the pew and onto his feet shouting, "I'm not taking my money to the bank no more!" His words got the attention of everyone within earshot before being hushed by his grandma.

"Amen!!" was shouted from more than one member as the congregation grew louder in agreement.

"Now these are the same people who have the audacity not to approve our loans and mortgages when they have our money. Think about it. How often do you see someone come all the way over here on the West Side from the East Side to make a deposit? Who's really brave enough to pack up all their day's gains and drive it on over here where they gotta fear it being taken from them? Why would anyone? If no one is coming over here to make their deposits, then I ask, whose money is in this branch that we frequent? The same bank that tells us no each time we ask for a loan from our money. When I speak, I like to tell you the whole story, not just the piece that will get your attention—that would be misleading. Some would just say, 'I'm sorry, there must be a miscommunication.' You and I know that when someone says that, it's a polite excuse for getting caught in a lie! Am I lying? So before we leave here today, I want to make it clear for each of you that the THEY we are speaking about have nothing to do with Blacks and Whites. That would be too easy, because we know that THEY come in Black too. You see, THEY work in these corporate offices, THEY work as managers and vice presidents at these lending institutions. The influence of money and authority has a color of its own—green—and that is all THEY care about. It's no longer Black versus White—it's the haves versus the have nots. Yes it's tricky now, more complex. We've already seen what happened to a community while waiting for someone else to come to their rescue during Katrina. We live HERE and we call this our home. While some other people may not deem this to be PRIME real estate and would say it has a lack of . . . ah, ah, ah . . . let me see . . . how do they say it? Location, location, location!"

The congregation is roaring with laughter as he continues. "Please allow me to get proper as I go on. Can I do that? Well then I'll start by saying that I beg to differ because if this isn't PRIME real estate, why are we seeing them people suddenly appearing in their suits and fancy camera equipment taking still photos of our buildings and store fronts?"

"Preach, Pastor."

I was enjoying what I was hearing until now, suddenly I'm feeling like that little boy wanting to slide under the pew and crawl on out of here. I wonder if the Pastor had seen me here a couple of weeks ago with Matheson. Why is he staring at me? Damn! I must have been squirming in my seat because I feel Aunt Mabel's cold hand resting on top of mine offering comfort, but it's only made me feel trapped. Clearly, I'm ready to get out of here and this is why people don't like to come!

"Wolves in sheep's clothing is what the scripture says. Crabs in a pot are what our elders say," Pastor said referencing forms of betrayal and deceit.

I can't help but wonder if he's speaking about me, being a part of Klein-Matheson and all. I look around as I wonder.

"God bless the child that's got its own is what the song says. Some people like to think that if you walk into a car dealership or a lending institution and you see a Black individual on the opposite side of the desk that we'll be shown favor. No, no, no—don't believe that. In fact, you should look like you are just browsing until someone else becomes available. See, what people of other persuasions don't understand is that often we'll go out of our way applying more astringent guidelines or rules with someone from our own race to ensure that there isn't the appearance of bias behavior."

I think to myself, I'm sure that he's talking about me, but I'm not like that!

"Oh yeah, we'll do it in the workplace, we'll do it when we have authority and wearing a blue uniform in our community. We can't catch a break. Amen! Amen, congregation. It's a good thing we got the Lord on our side and we are conquerors! Amen. We all got to be accountable for what we do and our purpose in this here life. Sometimes we are intended to be the caretaker of a blessing, only intended to be the vehicle to drive the blessing to the intended destination."

"You ever receive something and before you can get comfortable with having it, it's gone? Seriously it's just gone, whether it was lost or taken, but it's gone."

"Oh yes," someone agreed.

"What's that thing people say . . . umm . . . easy come easy go. Can't miss what you never had. Did you ever think that it wasn't meant to be yours and perhaps it was a test to see if you would do the right thing? Amen. Have you ever found something of value in a public place and rather than take it to the customer service counter, you looked around and placed it in your pocket? And you justify it by thinking that they are only going to keep it for their self if I turn it in. That might have been your test."

"Or what about a large bonus check that you weren't even expecting? Do you do something for someone that you know to be in need, not knowing that they've been praying to God for a needed blessing? Did you bless them as you were blessed?"

I always bless others, I think to myself. I'm not sure why I'm feeling the need to justify myself. I can barely hear the pastor with all this noise in my head.

"Talk to us, Pastor," shouted out from the pew to the far right by the exit.

In a defeated humble voice he asked, "What are you going to do to make a difference? How much longer will you turn your heads? Is it better to feed one or to feed many? I'm not telling you what to do, I'm just a messenger. Find your instructions through scripture. Amen!"

"Amen!!" agreed the congregation.

The piano begins to play softly now as he continues, "I'm not giving up on us . . . when I close my eyes I don't see the boarded up buildings, I don't see the fragmented remnants of sidewalk. I don't see fear or defeat. Let me tell you what I see. Please brothers and sisters, close your eyes with me. Our sidewalks and walkways are dressed in red stone with cherry blossom trees; there are trash containers beside each black wrought iron bench; all of the store fronts are uniformly restored. Mother Mabel, you have neighbors, I can see them. You have a seamstress to the right of you and a bakery to the left. I see a deli across the way and a dry cleaner."

"Yes Lord!" Aunt Mabel shouted.

"Lord, we know without you we are nothing, and Lord we know that you hear each of our prayers and we thank you!! Father God, when others can only see us as we are today and not beyond nor greater, we know that you can. Oh God, we thank you!"

"Thank you, Lord," a Deacon cried.

"Alleluia," another shouts.

I begin to feel a little weird, warm and sad, but within seconds, I feel happiness.

"We give you continued praise as we ask that you build a hedge around our community allowing us to continue calling this our home. We understand that it takes a community filled with love to raise these children with respect and pride. I weep not for me, Lord, but for the children and their mothers who are enduring sleepless nights, for those who are faced with being homeless. Father, we thank you in advance for giving us the victory and drying my eyes, for there will be no need for me to weep any longer as we look to the hills for whence cometh our help we are able to claim our victory!!"

This happiness has me clapping, smiling and now shouting along with the others. Shouts of joy fill the congregation along with tearful praises.

"Lord, allow each of us to leave here today with JOY in our hearts and PRAISES upon our lips knowing that all the glory belongs to you! How many of you know that without him we are nothing? I don't know about ya'll, but without the Lord, I would have never made it! Don't fret for me for these are tears of JOY!!"

The congregation had risen to their feet and drowned each other's shouts of praises. Pastor began to sing a very near rendition of Marvin Sapp's *Never Would Have Made It*, "*Never could have made it . . . without you . . . I'm stronger . . . I'm wiser . . . I'm better . . . much better . . . when I look back over all you brought me through.*" The choir joined Pastor Witherspoon and the congregation embraced the spirit of the Lord being present. Without my permission I began to stand with my hands raised in the air.

I release everything that I've kept so tightly tucked inside of me for the past years with repetitive chants of "Thank you, oh thank you, Lord! Thank you!!" I leave each bad experience and loss right here, particularly the secrecy of my pregnancy. Visions of mommy in that hospital bed appear again, then Hollis straddling me after pinning me to the floor. "Help me, Lord!" I shout as I gasp for air in between tears. Now visions of Nanna's and Granddaddy's empty rocking chairs send my head spinning and begin to flood my mind. My breaths have become shorter and shorter while my praises grow louder as I hear the repeated chorus, "*Oh, I never would have made it Lord without you.*"

Before long, I was shouting and being comforted by the words of Aunt Mabel saying, "It's okay, baby . . . let it all out. It's about time to let it all go." Two ushers dressed in white continue to fan me on either side and the song ended unbeknownst to me, leaving my shouts and praises and the soft spoken words of the Pastor saying, "Let the Lord have his way, don't fight it! Everyone be still and let the Lord have his way."

When the service was over, I sat on the pew beside Aunt Mabel with a new-found feeling of peace that freed me. I was renewed! From that day forward, I never had another anxiety attack. Amen!!

SATURDAY BRUNCH

C lock Tower condominiums have a very metropolitan architectural design; the best part of all is that no two units are alike. I was particularly attracted to my unit for the single wall of exposed brick surrounding the fireplace, high ceilings and Brazilian cherry flooring. The combination provides serious ambiance and acoustics.

On a day like today as I stand here sipping a mimosas and preparing food, it brings back memories of Hollis. I must have drifted off into my thoughts while listening to an old Brian McKnight classic, *One Last Cry*, because it wasn't until I'd heard Quinn ask, "Are you okay," before I realized that I had joined Brian for that one last cry— or that Quinn had even arrived for that matter. I turned around trying to hide my tears.

"Hey, hey! No tears allowed on Saturdays," he said as he handed me a tissue.

"Thank you."

"Are those tears of regret?" he asked while pulling his stool closer to me.

"I must have wandered down an unexpected trip on memory lane," I replied.

"Remember, you can't move forward to get to a new destination if you keep looking back."

"Believe me, it was just a glance," I said as I wiped my eyes.

"Glances are alright, just beware of that deadly U-turn. Do you hear what I'm saying?"

Quinn got up and wrapped his arms around me as my eyes became undeniably welled up. "Torie, a man that steps to a woman even once doesn't deserve her. And you damn sure don't deserve him. I don't care what the brother has on his plate, if he's full, then he should push his ass back from the table! A man . . . a man doesn't put his hand on a lady."

Wiping my eyes I say, "You're right. I really thought that I finally had it right. I made a promise to myself that I wasn't going to give a man the power to hurt me. Once again my self-confidence butts heads with my Black brother's insecurities."

"No, that's his hang up."

Walking around the island counter I thought aloud, "I just can't pamper it this trip. I've got to be able to do me this trip. It just seems that I attract one brother after the next displaying false senses of security."

"Some cats only feel secure when things are going well across the board. The minute a monkey wrench affecting their dough gets thrown in the mix, they start trip'n."

"Why is it my job to keep validating who he is? I know who I am."

"Okay, and that's what being secure is, knowing who you are," Quinn replies.

There's a mild rigidness in Quinn's tone when speaking on matters that involve a woman allowing her to be disrespected or defeated in any aspects of life. It's only intended as encouragement. Lately, he certainly has become an auditor of compliance for me. Everything about him says that he is self-secure. I stopped taking the pill in an attempt to commit to being celibate. One day my period came on without notice since. Anyway, I needed tampons and it was just Quinn and I in my unit that afternoon. When I asked him if he would mind he said, "Hell, they know they're not for me! Besides, my mother made me get them for her and my sisters when I was growing up. I'm an old pro. So, what size do you want?"

He then went on to tell me about the one day that he was embarrassed. His boys were in the store and he'd tried to sneak them onto the counter while they were in the back of the bodega at the cooler. The owner threw him under the bus when shouting, "Pero no, Papi! You no buy tampons with food stamps, no food stamps." He said that he didn't care about the food stamps everyone had those, but tampons!! He assured me that his boys had worn that story out for years.

Like now, he has rolled up his sleeves and washed his hands, pulled up a stool at the island and has taken over preparing the vegetables for the omelets while I'm mixing the batter for the waffles. He knows what needs to be done and just does it.

"Hey, what time is my girl arriving?"

"Who, Simone?"

"Would I bring flowers for Simone?" he replied jokingly.

"Those aren't for me?" I asked teasingly.

"Sorry! These are for my girl, Tishie."

"She should be here any minute now."

Just at that moment, the intercom sounded. "Yes, Otto?" I replied to the doorman in the lobby who speaks with a very present German accent. It had been rumored that he became the anonymous winner of a lottery a few years ago and refuses to move on.

"Miss Tishie has arrived. Shall I send her on her way or will someone be greeting her?" he asked teasingly as we could hear her giggling in the background.

"Tell her that we are not taking visitors today!"

"Very well then, I shall send her away. Although she has said that she will be on her best behavior. Isn't that so, Miss Tishie?"

With that we accepted! Quinn grabbed the flowers and hid them behind his back as he went to meet her at the elevator. Within minutes he'd returned with her on his shoulders and her bouquet of flowers in her hands tickling her nose as she smelled them.

"Torie, look . . . I've got flowers," she blurts out.

"Wow, those are very nice. Who gave them to you?"

"Quinnnn," she says with a prideful smile.

I love watching Quinn's attentiveness towards Tishie and seeing her confidence being nurtured; it reminds me of me with Granddaddy. How I miss that man! Mentoring is sometimes these children's first healthy relationship and sets a barometer for them. This is exactly why it's so necessary and valued. We ate and played board games for the next few hours until her visit was nearly over. Quinn graciously thanked Tishie for the invitation to brunch and went on his way. Shortly thereafter her mother returned to pick her up.

Finally alone, my thoughts quickly turned to unreliable solutions for contending with Eric and all of the recent workplace drama. How am I supposed to pretend that I am on board with the demolishing of a community that I credit with helping me find my way?

A LITTLE INSIGHT

s usual, Perry arrives promptly driving a pearl-colored BMW X5 that's shiny and blemish-free. The sunroof is open illuminating the golden highlights throughout her freshly flat-ironed hair. Her toasted almond-colored face and body glistens as though she's just left the Caribbean. Perry always keeps her cinnamon brows perfectly arched and colored to precisely match her hair, completing an illustration of nature's definition of autumn. But it's not autumn—clearly not. You can tell by her tangerine low-riders, white crocheted halter and flip flops displaying her French pedicure. We are a complete contrast; my hair is Asian black displaying indigo hues in certain lighting. My skin is the deepest shade of brown with dark red tones similar to that of a red velvet cake.

Where we are similar is that we are both cultural "mutts." Like me, Perry has mastered the ability to speak fluent urban dialogue. The comparison ends here, as I deem myself to be authentic and Perry takes the whole assimilation to another level. I find it to be most interesting to say the least; the house Perry resides in is easily 3,500 square feet in one of the most prestigious gated communities in the county. Her daughter attends an elementary school that was ranked number two in the entire United States; tuition is $38,000 per year. Although it's kept quiet, Perry and Robert don't even pay a tenth of Bailey's tuition. They were blessed with a child gifted with a surplus of intelligence, an equal portion of beauty, and most importantly, ethnicity. McClendon Oaks was petitioned to display diversity in their upcoming fall semester. To manipulate the results, they had a representative from the elite school attend Sunday services at select Hispanic and African-American churches because these congregations would accommodate the necessary criteria. The intent was to hold a lottery and identify children from respectful families in the communities that were academically achieved based on their transcript GPAs. Bailey was selected and collectively we couldn't have been happier. Each child born and each groom snatched up becomes a lifelong member of the family, our family.

In no time, Bailey became the cutest plaid skirt-knee sock wearing-IPod carrying-L.L. Bean backpack toting-on her way young sister. Perry soon became a Range Rover driving-horseback riding-golfing-delinquent 438 credit score-life living fraud. She and Robert have become so caught up in their lies—oh yeah, lies. They would lie about everything and to anyone to secure the wrapping on the packaged lifestyle that they were selling to be their own. At every gathering, both of them find a way to insert, "tuition has us working our asses off!" This moment is used to allude to their financial success in a crowd. Oh, but reality! They were a paycheck away from lights out, getting on the bus, Century 21 stick on their front lawn way to the West Side.

Should their personal situation concern me? Well yes, because she's one of my girls and at the end of the day, we might not like each other's ways, but we have loved each other unconditionally and toughly when warranted. Besides, that isn't who she is, it's who HE has made her become. What pisses me off is that when Perry needs to build herself up publicly she offers fantastic untrue successes that immediately dilute my real accomplishments as a single woman. Thank God I don't need the validation from mere strangers to dictate who I am and what I am capable of becoming. Nonetheless, it's becoming more and more of a challenge not to put her ass out on Front Street and expose her not-so-true tales. I mean, I'm the one who bought my home as a single individual with a conventional 15-year mortgage. I'm also the one who has properly disciplined herself to save a minimum of $12,000 a year in addition to the maximum annual contributions to my 401K plan. (And aside from my federal income tax return; that is designated for my all-about-me splurges.)

Do I look a mess? Not at all! I get my hair done every Friday and my nails done every other Sunday afternoon. I purchase my designer clothing at the end of each season, methodically choosing classic garments and colors that will always be staples in my wardrobe. When I have had enough and can't take anymore of her shit, then I speak to my own accomplishments and the possibilities of anyone else being as savvy. But no, she's all set to shoot that down openly.

"Well, Torie, you don't have the responsibilities of a husband or a child, so of course it's easy to live the way you live," Perry says.

No, she didn't just turn her head and dismiss my ass! I quickly rise to my feet and offer with a warm smile that financially, it is all relative. As she reaches for her cocktail—pausing only to thank the waitress and order a tray of fried calamari with the raspberry vinaigrette sauce—Perry replies, "Not really."

"Did she just say 'not really'?" Sim asks. "Perry . . ." now up on her feet.

"Sim," I yell trying to stop her from pursuing it.

"Perry, I KNOW you hear me!" Simone yells. Now she's walking towards Perry saying, "I'm not Torie, so let's not forget that, but I am going to ask you . . . why you continuously think that you can come at her anyway you wish?"

"Sim, please leave it alone," I plead.

Ignoring my request Simone continues, "Perry everybody knows your shit ain't tight and hasn't been on the up-and-up for a very long time. No one would even care about your shit if you would stop trying to look down on everybody else." Perry turns and snarls at Simone while keeping it moving as Jamie and Millie look on, surely thinking . . . not again.

"Stop Sim, this is silly!" I'm tugging on her arm and pulling her in the other direction.

"No, what's silly is Perry thinking that I won't spank her bourgeois ass. Remember . . . she's your friend from New Canaan, not mine! And maybe you should be thinking about who to call a friend, because where I come from, friends don't treat each other like that."

I can see that Simone is becoming extremely agitated, so I suggest that we get going because she has errands to run. Since I was riding with her and it makes for a perfect exit. The beautiful day became a teaser leaving each of us wanting more. Later, we all decided to meet and go to Jasper's knowing that we would be promised a good time.

Later that night after leaving Jasper's and on the way back to Sim's place, they were still laughing at my just-revealed secret.

"Okay, it's not that damn funny!!"

"Oh no, that shit was funny!!"

"After all of these years, I'm trying to figure out how that has gone unnoticed!"

"Whatever."

"No, really. You should be happy it wasn't that crowded."

"Okay, so now everyone thinks they're a comedian tonight?"

"Torie, come on, you have to admit it's pretty funny that Laurie and I both have more rhythm than you."

On cue, Laurie immediately began winding her hips and bouncing her booty like Kendra Wilkinson, inciting even more laughter from onlookers Millie and Felicia. I pick up the closest pillow within reach and toss it at them.

Barely able to speak, Simone asks, "Why didn't you just say 'no thank you' to his request? You clearly fell short in representing sisters. Ha ha!"

I can no longer tell if it's their lingering buzz, or if am I really that bad? Besides, not every Black person automatically knows how to dance . . . that's just another one of those stupid stereotypes. I snatch a glass from her hand and plop down on the corner of the comfy sage sectional and defend, "We didn't listen to R&B and real dancing music in our town."

"Well what did you listen to?"

"Pink Floyd and Lenny Kravitz."

"Pink as in the girl singer Pink? I didn't even know she was out that long," Felicia asked.

"No not her . . . Pink Floyd."

"What did she sing?"

"It's them and nothing anybody can dance to unless you're into head banging and things," Simone said while placing the tray onto the ottoman.

After a few more jokes and many drinks I turned to my girls and asked them to teach me how to dance.

"Girl, it's almost 2:00 in the morning!" Simone replied.

"I'll show you!!" Felicia offered

Laurie and Millie jump up from the sofa to join; Felicia instructs Simone on which songs to play.

"Oooh, I know! Play *Single Ladies*," shouts Millie.

"No, put on that *Cha-Cha Slide* song," Laurie protests.

"Well come on! Get up, Torie!!"

Laurie swirled her honey blonde hair around imitating a propeller as she resumed her seductive dance. There was a time when a sister had a hands-down monopoly being curvaceous; that's clearly no longer the case as I watch Laurie's tiny waist unlikely paired with that big apple bottom! Using a typical brother's description she is "bootyliscious." Laurie is completely keeping up with the beat of the music. Then there's Millie, tossing her wavy brown hair that appears as though it's just been freed from a bobby pin set. She is someone that Nanna Bess would describe as stacked! She's rocking a timeless size-two hourglass figure with a set of 36 DDs custom-packaged from God's assembly line.

Within moments we are all lined up following the instructions of the CD, "To your left three times and cha-cha!" Then onto the Wobble and Electric Slide . . . well, that wasn't as easy for me.

"C'mon Torie! Move your hips!"

"No! You have to wind them up like . . . I know . . . pretend that you have a hula hoop and you're trying to keep it from falling!!"

So excited and determined to teach me, Millie falls onto her drunken knees and grabs my hips and physically moves me while she instructs me to "wind that ass" and "bend those knees a little." The room erupts in hysteria.

"To the left . . . now to the right . . . okay lean back, Tor!!"

"That's it; you've got it . . . now forward . . . and dip!!"

As though planned, all of their arms extend to the ceiling at once, like gesturing a touchdown as they shout and claim a victory of my success.

"How is it that you and Laurie can dance so well?"

"Oh come on, Torie, you know that we were made to participate in Walter Schalk dance recitals and summer stock from the age of six until high school. You would tease us and laugh. Looks like it paid off, huh? Who's laughing now, sister?" Laurie teased.

"So, contrary to what people say, not all Black people can dance?" a very intoxicated Millie shares.

"Hell no . . . not looking at Torie earlier," Felicia giggled.

For the next hour, I learn every possible dance from the running man to the wop and those that none of us can recall the names of. Everyone has fallen asleep either curled up on the sofa or sprawled under a blanket on the floor with the exception of Simone and me.

"Hey, Tor?"

"Huh?'

"What was that bullshit Perry was on earlier tonight?"

"That was Perry just being Perry."

"Seriously, I was going to eat her little ass up. She's always posturing and that shit gets pretty old fast! Doesn't it bother you?" Simone says as she pins up her hair and wraps it with a scarf to preserve it for the next day.

"She's just insecure and probably not very happy inside. I just ignore her."

"Oh, you're good, because if it were me, knowing what you know about all of her personal things. I'd be like, 'bitch, fix your slip; it's showing,' and that would be the only warning her ass would get. Huh, she wouldn't come for me again! Oh, I'd just put it all out there; all of her dirty laundry would be out there!!"

"Sim, don't you think that sometimes I want to?"

"So then, why don't you?"

"Because then I'm no better than she is. It's hard at times, but when I really look at where it's coming from, it's her discontentment with all of the things that she thinks are so great in my life!!"

"And that works for you?"

"Yeah it does, because when she and others stop trying to tear me down, that will be a sign for me that I'm no longer on my A-game and to step it up! But before that happens, they've got to get into my league!!"

Uh-oh! Raising her brows and scratching her head she says, "Well excuse the hell out of me! I didn't see that coming!"

"I'm only kidding!" I laugh at my own gullyness.

"Oh no, you're not kidding!! Don't even try it."

"It's not just Perry. I mean for me, it seems to happen often; in the office and in stores. Anywhere."

"What do you mean? Just say what's on your mind."

"Take Millie and Laurie for example. I've been around both of them since kindergarten. I have never experienced any level of competition; in fact, they'd rather compliment me than criticize me. It just seems that sometimes as Black women, it's difficult to randomly compliment another sister. It seems to require great effort to say something as simple as 'That's a really nice coat' or something like that."

"I don't think that's true. I will compliment a female when she's wearing something that's fierce."

"I can only speak from my experiences, and yes, I do know that you wouldn't have a problem with complimenting, but how often does a sister afford you the same? That's all I'm saying."

"Well, I never looked at it like that."

"It isn't much different from the Only Syndrome."

"What the hell is that?" Millie rolled over and asked while wiping her eyes.

"What?" Simone asked.

"The only syndrome."

Simone and I respond in tandem, "Only room for one Black here!!"

"Sometimes it's hard working in a setting where there's only one other brother or sister. It usually becomes a tiring, silent competition that's launched by the more insecure of the two. Hence suggesting there's only room for one."

"That's stupid!!"

"It comes from a place of feeling chosen or special by default of being the ONE!!"

"Get out of here, you guys come up with the silliest things," Millie says now sitting up. "What time is it anyway?"

"It's 3:45 a.m."

"Well in that case," Millie says falling back onto the pillow on the floor, "Sim, can a SISTER get a blanket?"

"Shut up! I have neighbors, and I keep telling you you're not a sister," Simone teases as she laughs while jumping up to grab a blanket.

Millie remains on her back tossing her head and kicking her legs like a child having a tantrum. I am too a SISTER!"

"Mil, shut up!!" Laurie demanded.

Simone whispered, "Oh, she's a grumpy drunk," to which we all begin to laugh except Felicia who somehow has managed to sleep through all of the noise.

"Hey, you are not my boss!!"

"Really Mil, you're doing this now? You are such a bitch!!"

"Are they serious?" Simone asks after handing Millie her blanket.

"Yup, but they'll be fine in an hour or by morning."

"It IS morning."

With that, we all had fallen asleep. Clearly not one of us will be rising again before noon. Millie decides that we could probably use a good workout to sweat out some of the alcohol we'd consumed last night. I agree, and with it being a gorgeous day, I suggest that we run along the beach. The two of us say our goodbyes to the others and head home to shower and change. We agree to meet at Calf Pasture Beach at 2:00.

Without any thought, I park in a space across from the concession stand as we always had during Hollis's games. I can't help but notice an adorable toddler playing with his mother. I begin to stretch my legs and move my thoughts along while waiting for Millie. Until lately, my anger toward Hollis hasn't allowed me to mourn the loss of our baby. I know that's crazy given that I resisted the idea of even being pregnant at that time. The sight of Millie pulling in to the parking lot stops this chain of thought about babies. Millie's car windows are down and she's singing along with Justin Timberlake at the top of her lungs.

"Nice entrance Mil, and just a tad bit ghetto," I tease.

"Don't be a hater because my man Justin is serenading me."

"Yeah, yeah, yeah! Hurry up! You're late."

"It's the weekend Torie! I'm working on JST time," cracking herself up.

"What?"

"Jewish Standard Time! We're known to have a penchant for being late."

"No, no, no, no, no! We have that covered; it's called CP Time, as in colored-people time. We too have a penchant for being late. But remember what I've said, we don't like to hear it and we don't like to be referred to as colored."

"See, we're more alike than people know."

After allowing her to stretch, we started down the runners' path at a moderate pace chatting in between stolen glances of eye candy.

"So, how are you doing Torie?"

"I'm fine," responding curiously.

"So, you are telling me, that you're fine? Even with all of the preparations going on for Simone and Nigel's upcoming nuptials?"

"Yes."

"Torie, you haven't mentioned Hollis or that situation at all."

"It's called moving on, Mil."

"Got it, but we move on from boyfriends, we move on from bad dates. Hollis was your fiancé, the father of your . . .," she pauses, as I abruptly stop running and look away from her. "Torie, I don't mean to upset you. It's just that you haven't mentioned it, and I'm a little concerned."

"I promise you, I'm fine. It's been a while now," this time said with no agitation at all. Millie's eyes indicate that she isn't convinced.

"Alright listen Mil, remember when I said that I've started going back to church?"

"Yeah?" I'm sure she's thinking what does that have to do with anything?

"Well, I've found my peace; I've left it all at the altar."

She twitches her mouth in search of a politically correct response. "What exactly is it that you left at the altar? What does that mean?"

"Well usually after the collection plate is passed, we have altar call. In our faith, we profess our Lord to be our savior, and because of this during our Sunday worship, we have a ritual where we go to the altar in prayer, at that time we are to leave all of our concerns through prayer at the altar for the Lord to work them out."

"Huh, really?"

"What's the huh for? Don't you pray at the synagogue?"

"Of course we pray during Shabbat services, but we do not pass the plate. Do you have to pay for that altar prayer?"

"No, Mil!"

"Oh because I'm thinking that if that's all it takes, then I will be going to service with you next week and I'm going to pay whatever it costs, then I'm going to the altar and praying these new ten pounds off of my fat ass."

"Mil," shoving her on the back causing her to stumble, "You're an ass! That's blasphemy!"

She promptly gives me a hug and offers, "I'm glad to hear that you are feeling okay, my friend." With that we resume with our run.

Three miles later we're headed back toward our cars soaked with sweat and exhausted. Millie says, "You know, Quinn's been talking about you an awful lot lately." I continue to walk and take huge gulps from my water bottle offering no response, as if I didn't even hear her.

"I'm just saying," she defends.

I stop and reply, "One minute, you're questioning whether or not I've moved on. In the next, you are suggesting I haven't moved on fast enough! Which is it, Mil?"

"I'm only saying what we've all known for a very long time. We've seen that friendship transform into something else over the years, and to be honest . . ."

"Oh, why stop now?" I interrupt.

She calmly resumes with a softer tone as if I hadn't interrupted her at all, "Over the years, particularly after you'd met Hollis, it did become uncomfortable to watch Quinn long for you. And maybe, some of us are curious as to why you haven't considered him; he's handsome, accomplished, kind. . ."

"A very good friend—that's what he is, Mil! So, now go and tell Simone and your other cronies that you have bravely, and I do mean bravely, relayed their collective message . . . and you can also tell them that I didn't bite!"

"Tor. . ."

"Bye, Mil," I say while closing my car door. Do yourself a big favor and decline being the messenger next time!" I rudely pull off as she shouts, "We love you!" I throw my hand and shout, "Whatever," as I continue out of the parking lot.

URBAN MEETS SUBURBAN

"Excuse me, can I get by?" I repeated over and over as I tried to get through the smoke-filled aisle leading to the stalls.

"Excuse me. Ooops, I'm sorry," I offer as I unintentionally bumped into people or stepped on their toes protruding from stilettos.

There were ladies of various ages sitting on the countertops and occupying stalls in groups of two and three with either a cocktail, cigarette or dollar bill carefully folded in one hand with a small straw quickly being hidden in the other as they watched me approaching. Okay, I know what's going on. Hell, I grew up in White suburbia with the real ballers who wore their candy as decorative jewelry strung around their neck. Besides, I watch *CSI, Law and Order* and reality television.

All I want to do is pee; I could care less about the surrounding activity. Furthermore, I have three Gin & Tonics in me that say that it's non-negotiable, particularly because I usually don't drink like this. The ladies around me are seriously acting like this is a straight-up VIP suite as I zoom in on a lounge chair propped up in the corner. It was those same drinks that led me to believe that I was going to be able to whoop that young woman's behind that appeared from behind the door of the last stall that appeared to have been unoccupied.

She was tucked so quietly in the corner behind the opened door engrossed in a private party (if you know what I mean), that she and her dollar bill were clearly caught off guard when I pushed the door further open to assess the accommodations.

"Ah, wait a minute, cause you about to get your ass kicked knocking my shit over!"

Well, can I tell you that her hands juggled better than someone in a circus act dropping nothing as she slid down the back of the door into a squat position in her four-inch stilettos guiding her product and accompanying paraphernalia to a safe landing onto her lap in an upright position? And that's when her eyes met mine.

"Bitch, you came about this close to getting cut!!"

"Cut the bitch!" I heard an onlooker shout.

"There is bathroom etiquette to be followed up in here," she continued while moving her woven hair from in front of her eyes now back in a standing position.

"Ask the bitch for her VIP pass," the same woman shouted with a slurred low-pitched voice.

"Nobody said she can bring her White-acting ass in here."

See, I knew it; they do think that this is VIP. I laughed as I thought of how serious they are.

"All uppity and shit," she yells as she staggers towards the door to leave, certainly not before launching one last demand, "Yeah go on and kick that uppity ass." It might have been more threatening, but in her state of mind she was barely able to recall that you must first open the door before you walk through it!

I turn back towards who seems to be the real threat here, "Look, I'm very sorry that I didn't see you behind the door. All I want to do is empty my bladder and the joint is all yours again. Okay?" At this point everyone else watched on to see how this was going to play out.

"I really tried to work with you, but you are simply unreasonable, and now you gotta go!" I guided her—okay, I shoved her—to the other side of the stall door and locked it before squatting over the nasty urine-filled toilet.

"Oh, so you're a bad-ass mama," she shouts as she bangs on the door. "Well, you gotta come outta there, that's when I'm a stomp you."

"Okay, and when you are doing all of this stomping, am I going to just stand there taking it? I don't think so!" (That's what Gin said . . . you know, as in Gin & Tonic!) I stare into her eyes as I open the door. "So what do you really want to do?" I learned a long time ago that bravado is much like poker—they don't know what I've got as much as I don't know what they have.

I could now hear the murmurs from the onlookers saying, "Oh, I like her" and another, "I told you she wasn't no punk." But quickly they lost interest and went back to doing what they were doing. In a split second my thoughts went all over the place. Why did I let Quinn bring me to this ghetto hole in the wall and without my girls? I cannot believe that I am really about to fight some chick as though we were teenagers. What would my corporate colleagues think if they were aware? If I hurt her will I be liable and will I lose my property? I WILL hurt her if she puts her hands on me.

Too late! The fingers of one hand are directly in my face while her other hand fumbles around inside of her purse. We stared each other down, neither of us wavering. As she pulled her hand from her purse, I was preparing to leap on her ass. All of a sudden her eyes abruptly soften and she said, "Re?"

"Re" is a nickname that only the kids from the West Side ever called me. In fact, they had given it to me years ago because they said that Torie was too white bread.

"Oh shit, girl! It's me, Doreen!"

"Doreen?"

I stared with relief—and then disbelief. Then I stared in disappointment. This is the same young lady who had befriended me and taught me my way around urban streets and how to never let anyone intimidate me. In exchange, I taught her that it was okay to aspire to be more and how to obtain college scholarships.

Doreen was a Business Major who graduated from the Stamford branch of UConn. She was known for being an impeccable seamstress whipping up prom gowns and dresses for many of the women at church. Going to business school was going to support her opening a chain of boutiques.

"Doreen, what happened? How did this . . .?"

"What? Go ahead … ask me how I got like this," she said rolling her eyes then pulling off of her cigarette.

"Well yes, what happened to your degree and dreams?"

"Oh come on, Torie! You know that shit doesn't happen for people like me."

I couldn't believe that someone that I'd seen work so hard to beat the odds, and won, has given it all up. I'm speechless.

"Besides, I needed to feed my babies. Shoot . . . dreams don't do that, and they damn sure don't buy any diapers."

Oh my, she's someone's mother? Then why is she out here like this? I reached down into my purse and grabbed a business card to write my cell number on the back and handed it to Doreen.

"You call me!! Do you hear me?"

"Yeah, I hear you!!"

I put my pen back into my purse and placed the strap onto my shoulder. I'm so angry that I've forgotten all about the mean crowd and push my way by, daring anyone to try me. I look back at Doreen before exiting the smoky room.

"I'll be waiting for your call, Doreen." I no sooner got the words finished when I heard one of the other girls mimic me repeating exactly what I'd just said.

As I'm coming out of the bathroom, Quinn approaches me.

"Hey, I was just coming in after you. What took you so long?"

"Don't ask. It wasn't anything that I couldn't handle." Quinn shakes his head at seeing yet another side of me.

"Come on (still shaking his head at my bravado) let me get you out of this joint."

"Oh, guess who was in the bathroom not looking so well."

"Who?"

"Doreen."

"Who? Kenny's girl Doreen?"

"Yeah, she looks pretty bad; she was in a stall getting high."

"I thought that she'd moved away after Kenny died."

"Died? Kenny died?"

"Yeah, he didn't make it back from his second tour in Iraq."

"Oh my God, that's terrible! She has children too."

"Yeah, they're Kenny's children and they were planning to marry as soon as he returned."

"That's horrible!!"

"Torie!! Where are you going?" Quinn shouts as I go back into the bathroom.

I entered that bathroom as though I had a badge and a holster strapped onto my hips.

"Doreen!!"

"Damn! Here she comes again! Will you get your long-lost friend's ass out of here?"

"What?"

"Doreen, I need to know that you are going to call me. Why don't you give me your number?"

"I said that I'll call, and I'm gonna call!!"

This time, something in her eyes was believable. With that, I left the bathroom.

THE KEY TO LIFE

We stood in his kitchen preparing a Mexican fiesta for our movie night. Quinn was dancing the salsa to Santana and spinning me around in between shaking his hands as though they were maracas. He demands that I acknowledge him to be the master Mexican chef as he tosses the fajitas on the sizzling griddle. I laugh . . . and I smile . . . and then I laugh some more. I laugh at the happiness that he brings to me and I smile at the freedom; freedom from fear. I smile at his respect for peace, the peace that comes from trust, the trust that he effortlessly offers me. I also laugh because I'm on the brink of finishing my second Mojito and realize that Quinn has on a pair of print lounge pants with flip flops and a Knicks basketball jersey. Seriously, it's reducing that man's package by very little; that is at least while behind closed doors. And then he said, "Oh damn, I forgot sour cream. I'll just run downstairs to Klausen's."

"No you don't! I'll go!" I said as I walked placing the near empty glass onto the counter and scanning his attire from head to toe.

"What? You don't like what I'm wearing?" he says in a teasing yet challenging voice.

"It doesn't match."

"Who says?" Quinn asked.

"Everybody knows that prints and patterns don't go together," I say with no concrete evidence of where that had originated.

"Uh-hum, well you can put that with the unfounded 'they say' and who exactly is 'they' anyway? I mean really, who dictates what matches?" Quinn is laughing and looking at his reflection in the window. "A brother can't allow anyone to define him, and especially for what he's wearing. Is an attorney less of an attorney because he's wearing a hoodie and a pair of Nikes? Now I'm really wearing this and Torie. You're coming with me!"

Quinn laughs, turns the burner off on the stove, and grabs his keys and wallet from the top of the refrigerator. To add insult to injury, he throws on a baseball cap and grabs my hand on his way out of the door. All the way down the corridor, in the elevator and through the lobby, Quinn greeted everyone with his naturally well-mannered deep voice.

"Good evening, sir! You look very lovely, miss! How are you tonight?" His chatting continues as we walk towards Klausen's Market, one of the many conveniences here at Clock Towers East.

"Man, let me have that one right there," pointing at a single white calla lilly with a perfectly crisp ecru bow tied to its stem. He places the container of sour cream onto the counter and asks for one of the better single Cuban cigars and a bottle of coconut oil for his trip.

"Somebody is going on vacation?" Marty asks. Simultaneously Quinn nods yes as I stand in his shadow shaking my head no.

"We're on our way to Tijuana," he continues as I begin to blush with embarrassment as I enjoy my single flower.

Marty finally catches on to Quinn's clowning and wishes us well on our trip on our way out of the store.

"Come on mami, dance with papi!" Quinn asks as we walk back through the door of his unit, and my favorite Brazilian jazz vocalist Tania Maria was belting out *Don't Go*. Quinn is so persuasive that I not only dance to that one song, but the next two that follow.

We danced and drank Mojito after Mojito along with our fajitas until we collapsed onto the large pillows on his living room floor. The warmer Quinn's body becomes, his Egyptian musk escapes every freshly cleansed pore, leaving the surrounding air soothing like aromatherapy.

I begin to feel not-so-appropriate sensations in the southern region of my stomach as Quinn's face and slightly moist mouth slowly brushes across my cheeks, while ever so lightly moving forward and backwards against my lips. His eyes meet mine seeking permission to continue, so I grant him that with minimal resistance. I lower my eyelids and place my open left palm against his bicep, pressing the other softly against his chest before completely surrendering. His face becomes warmer and soothing as he continues to lightly brush his mouth up and down the middle of my neck and down to the center of my breast, nestling briefly around and below my navel. The increasing intimacy has caused my heart to accelerate creating an uncontrollable tremble throughout my body. How could something feel so good, yet at the same time physically painful? My stomach muscles are intensely tightening with my breathing becoming rapidly uncomfortable, quickly sobering and forcing me to abruptly resume an upright position.

I let out a loud embarrassing gasp and abruptly push him away.

"Oh Quinn, what are we doing?"

I turn away adjusting my clothing, looking away from him as though we are complete strangers. My body is stiff now offering resistance as he reaches in to pull me closer. Quinn maneuvers into a kneeling position to face me directly guiding my chin between the tips of his fingers demanding eye contact.

"Hey look at me. Look at me . . . it's us . . . it's me. I'm not going anywhere whether we do this or not."

Quinn waited patiently for signs of my ease and gently kissed me on my forehead with a sigh of relief as he felt no resistance while pulling me back into his arms.

"I can't do this. It's not you. The idea of trading off my best friend for desires . . . it's not worth it. It's crazy what were we thinking about."

"I don't think that it's crazy. Torie, I've been seeing you as more than a friend for a while now. I've been falling from a strong like to an involuntary love for some time. . ."

"I'm afraid."

"Afraid of me?"

"No, afraid of this!!"

"Hey! You do know that I would never hurt you?"

"I believe that you would never intentionally hurt me."

Quinn repositions himself to make direct eye contact again, "Torie, I would never hurt you." We nestle and handle each other in a sweet adoring way, as the music quietly plays. Quinn continues to hold and comfort me with random affectionate kisses. I'm suddenly feeling swayed to rethink his proposal.

"I want to give you something." He reaches above our heads and opens the console drawer.

"What's that?"

"What does it look like?"

"A key?"

"Nah, it's not just a key—this key right here will open that door at any time for you. I don't have anything to hide. More importantly, it comes with the responsibility of being the keeper of this brother's heart. You are now holding the key to my heart and soul . . . can I trust you with that?" He then placed the single key into my hand folding it over to secure it.

"Quinn."

"I'm offering full disclosure. I'm putting it all out here—my heart, my truths and my key."

"And that means so much to me."

"Because . . . I'm not afraid of us." staring into my shifty eyes as he pulls me to my feet.

"Quinn?" I said before quickly being hushed with a gentle kiss.

He continues speaking after tilting my face upward to meet his eyes. "Doll, we do it one day at a time . . . and we let our trust, respect and love built through the years of our friendship drive this. I'm willing and capable of leading but I'm secure enough to follow. I'll be right here standing by your side as I've always been. But I'm not willing . . . I can't pass on trying to take it to the next level. I want you in every way. Tell me you got me on this. Are you with me?" Quinn said in an even raspier voice filled with heartfelt emotion.

He pulled me into his arms and began to love me gently. Quinn gave me the best emotionally and physically that I'd ever been given. A long instrumental version of *Ribbon in The Sky* filled the room as Quinn played in tandem, hitting every chord of my being with each high soprano note held to every fast hard alto note from the saxophone solos.

I moaned with extreme pleasure as he held that very last note, proving that he was indeed the master of his extremely large instrument. I must have fallen fast asleep and was only slightly awakened from the touch of the blanket Quinn placed over me.

Sometime later, I felt something unfamiliar against my cheek and turned to be pleasantly greeted by Quinn. I suddenly realized that last night wasn't a dream but in fact, a sweet reality.

"Hey, sleepyhead! It's 8:30 and we're supposed to be down at the community center by 10:00 to start allocating some of the grants."

I smiled at his immediate level of comfort in being with me. I guess it really isn't much different than either of us popping in and out of each other's units early in the morning or late at night as we had for the past year.

"Oww, my head," I groan as I opened my eyes and tried to sit up.

"You can't hang with the Mojito . . . huh?"

"Owww," I groan louder as I force myself to stand up.

"Here, doll." Quinn brushes my messy hair away from my forehead and places an intended healing kiss there after handing me a couple of Advil with a bottle of water.

"What exactly is in a Mojito? Never mind—I don't want to know."

I was picking up the pillows from the floor and folding the throw when I heard the shower come on. He must have gotten up and cleaned the dinner dishes while I slept because the kitchen was already back in its meticulous state. In place of the mess Quinn had set out granola, yogurt, fresh fruit, croissants and glasses of orange juice.

"Why don't you grab some breakfast to ease that headache? I got you all set up in the kitchen," he yells from the bedroom. As I nibble on the fruit, he calls out for me to come upstairs. I actually had never been up to his suite before; it's very different than I'd expected, looking like a page torn from a West Elm brochure. The room is very spacious and masculine with desert tan suede walls and espresso-colored furniture. There were built-in wardrobes occupying the entire exterior wall and a flat-screen television was mounted above the fireplace. The view from his corner unit was impeccable and overlooked the entire downtown.

"Hey are you up here yet?"

"Quinn, it's gorgeous up here . . . and the view . . . wow!!"

"Come in here. I can't hear you!"

"Wow! Wow!" No wonder he couldn't hear me! The bathroom was the size of my guest room. That made sense given he opted out of having a bathtub and a second walk-in closet. The "wow" was in response to the full view of Quinn's rippled flawlessly sculpted caramel body on display behind the wall of glass enclosing his shower. I began to scan the room to avoid gawking at the obvious focal point. The shower walls and floor are dressed from floor to ceiling in the same travertine tile surrounding the fireplace; recessed lights and wall sconces illuminated the windowless room. There were dual shower heads hanging from above and multiple body sprayers throughout in addition to twin bamboo benches that match the floor mats.

He opened the shower door and threw a towel out to me telling me to wrap my hair and come on in. Noticing my hesitation he lowered the lights.

"Oh, my girl is shy!"

"I'm not shy," I replied as I bashfully began looking at the floor.

Quinn is just so confident—not arrogant—but confident about himself and being with me in this way. He waited as I slipped out of my things and guided me through the door after turning off the knob that controlled the second showerhead from the ceiling.

He turned me around forcing my back to him while ever so gently bathing me from the top of my back down to the heels of my feet. He then turned me around to face him so that he could be equally attentive to the front of my body. By this point, I was nearly speechless from holding my breath!

Quinn asked, "You okay?" Is your headache easing up?"

I answered him with, "Oh yeah, it's going away." Truth is, I really wanted to ask how in the hell was my headache going to go away when he was absolutely blowing my mind.

Quinn followed every area that he bathed with soft kisses after cupping water into his large hands to rinse the area. Before long, this man was on his knees and I was resting on one of the bamboo benches holding onto this man as he kept his promise about leading.

We toweled each other dry and Quinn passed me one of his sweatshirts that draped me like a dress so that I could quickly hustle to my unit to get ready and meet him down in valet.

I pulled into Starbucks and ordered my coffee. As I drove around to pay, I couldn't get over how everything seemed different this morning! My cell phone began ringing before I was out of the parking lot. I see that it's Simone and I'll have to catch up with her later; I'm pushing being on time as it is!

Even before pulling up, I could see that all of the cobblestone sidewalks have been completed and the street lanterns cemented into the ground; it's a whole new world. The first awnings are going up and the local news crew is there capturing it all.

There is a crowd of volunteers surrounding Nigel and Quinn at the entrance of the community center. As I approach, I can see the clipboard that he's holding with what I imagine to be a list of many names already written for various tasks. I raise my sunglasses from over my eyes and rest them on the top of my head, while balancing my coffee and portfolio with one hand. Quinn briefly looks over his sunglasses in my direction to ensure that I notice and avoid the areas not yet roped off with openings remaining in the ground. Before returning to his business at hand, he quickly winks as I successfully manage the course and enter the community center.

The activity room is crowded with prospective proprietors filled with hopes of obtaining a grant to launch their dreams of starting their businesses in the neighborhood.

"Hi, Sister Torie," Pastor Witherspoon offers as he approaches.

"Good morning! I see we have a great turnout. The group of volunteers lined up outside isn't a bad sight either."

"No, not at all."

"Yes, it seems like we have a committed following now. There are those who must see something being done before they can actually buy into it, like the new streets."

"And those streets look beautiful, Pastor!"

"I guess we should get started on seeing some of these proposals; after all, we have a community to rebuild."

It's been over two hours since leaving the community center. This has been one long day following an even longer, yet memorable night! I'm sure Quinn has to be exhausted. I'm wondering if he's okay; he asked me to meet him back here in the lobby of Clock Towers so that we could grab a bite to eat. It isn't like Quinn to be late, and certainly not without calling. I've tried to reach him on his cell phone twice and it's gone directly into voicemail. I decide that I'll try again from my unit once getting upstairs. As I exit the elevator, I bypass my unit and head down the hall to Quinn's—after all, I do have my own key now. As I ponder all that's happened, a flutter of warm sensations run through me as I muse over the entire night. I'm deep in thought when my phone begins to vibrate in my hand. It's Quinn.

"Quinn, is everything alright? I was worried with it getting so late."

"Torie, listen . . . I'm here at the center with an officer."

"What's wrong?"

"Everything's fine. Someone just broke the glass in the Rover; they didn't take anything, they riffled through some paperwork in the back. The officer says they were probably looking for mail to steal someone's identity . . . that's of more value than a stereo these days."

"Do you need me to come and pick you up?"

"No, I'm fine. The insurance company has someone coming out to The Towers first thing in the morning. I'm finishing up with the officer and I'll see you in a few."

"Okay, be careful." I turn to head back in the direction of my place, when an unfamiliar gentlemen and I nearly collide. He appears from the alcove that houses Quinn's lone corner unit.

"Am I on the fourth floor?" he asks with a baffled look.

"No, this is the third."

"Well that explains her not answering. I tell you, these floors are mirrored images, aren't they? Now *I* will be explaining why I am late," he says as he walks by.

I'm now curious and stuck on "Now *I* will be explaining . . .," it's as though he was listening to my conversation.

Just before entering the down elevator he shouts, "Thanks for your help."

WEST SIDE PAVILION

I don't know why Asia has Tishie down there waiting by herself; I keep telling her not to do that. As I pull around the corner, there are broken beer bottles, benches turned upside down and an assortment of trash as far as the eye can see. Although noon, it's still very quiet as it's too early for the participants of last night's questionable activity to rise because they've likely just gotten into their beds.

Quinn's sitting in the passenger side of my car catching a ride with me to the dealership to pick up his vehicle. He's talking on his cell phone confirming his day's itinerary clearly immune to all the things that I'm finding extremely appalling as we drive through the West Side.

"Yeah man, give me about an hour," he says to Nigel on the other end of the phone.

"Cool . . . because I have the paperwork with me anyway."

"Will you look at this girl?" I see a young girl barely holding her baby's hand while having him on the outside curb of the sidewalk, directly in the path of oncoming traffic. She's clearly already mad at the world walking with a single diaper and small milk bottle in her hand. So I roll my window down and say, "Excuse me honey, but can you pick your baby up out of the street? Put him on the other side of you or pick him up. I don't want to see him get hurt."

She rolls her eyes and places her hand on her hip leaving the baby's unsteady legs wobbling on the collapsed concrete as his fingers and tiny wrist helplessly turn left and right trying to hang on. As I slow down she asks, "What you say?"

"I SAID, get your baby out of the street!!" I really believed that she didn't hear me.

Now leaning forward and stealing a peek through the opening of my window and then looking at me Quinn says, "Torie, you better leave that girl alone."

"WHAT?" the young girl challenged.

"Hold on man . . . nah, that's Torie man . . . I keep telling her these young girls gonna spank her."

"Nah, she's shouting out the window . . . I know . . . I know man— that's who keeps encouraging her." Suggesting that my behavior to be similar to Simone. Quinn's now looking at me shaking his head from left to right with frustration, but at the same time, grinning over how bold I've become over the years. That's a complete contrast to when I first ever came to the West Side.

I turn towards Quinn with my brows stitched in response to his comment, "Pleassse and you all are going to STOP acting like I can't defend myself."

The young lady shouted, "BITCH, mind your business! Don't be telling me what to do wit mine."

I looked over at Quinn with my mouth wide opened trying to grasp that I was just cursed out by a barely 16-year-old girl. Physically I can fight, but I'm still in training with Simone on the verbal assaults.

"Man, let me go. . . I'll get with you in a bit."

Ending the call he repositioned himself from a near slouch to an upright seated position. Quinn looked out of the window to the right, the sun briefly reducing his eyes to a squint. After a deep sigh he turned back towards me and solemnly asked, "You done? Can we go now?" as he watches the young lady still staring me down.

"What?" I asked innocently.

"I'm just saying . . . you're supposed to be on this Stop the Violence campaign and you staring that girl down like that is just inciting something. You gave her sound advice, but it's for her to accept it or not . . . and then move on."

"Did I do something wrong?" feeling slightly offended.

"Torie, this is not the forum that's gonna allow us to make the changes."

"Okayyyyyy!!"

"Look, I understand what you're trying to do . . . but we've got to get them into the center and get them on our team before we start coaching." I began staring straight ahead like a child that's just been reprimanded.

"Oh what, so you mad now?" Quinn began tickling me on my side and went on to grabbing the back of my neck between his index finger and thumb forcing me to lower my head and chin into my chest pulling me closer into him making loud kissing sounds and saying in a child-like voice, "I'm shorry . . . don't be mad!"

"Get off of me! Stop! You're going to make me crash!!" I giggle realizing it is impossible to be mad at him.

I turn the corner entering into the heart of the Pavilion where I'd seen Tishie from afar moments ago. Where'd she go that fast? I scan the courtyard and think how excited she's going to be when she sees Quinn with me. I think it's so cute watching her blush when he's giving her positive reinforcement. After all I can't imagine her getting anything positive from Asia's new little around-the-way boyfriend.

"She's over there, Torie. TISHIE!!!!" he shouts out of the window waiting for her face to inevitably light up as she runs towards the car.

"Where's her mother at?" I asked with disgust.

"There she goes over there with that knucklehead Be'Lah. I hear that cat is running things and making a whole lot of enemies."

"Great. That's all Tishie needs to be around."

Tishie approaches the car, completely bypasses me and dives straight into Quinn's arms.

"How's my junior partner doing today?" Quinn is always staying true to encouraging her to become a future lawyer.

"Fine!! Quinn are we going to work a case today?" This is something that the two of them often did.

"No cases today because the firm is closed on Saturdays, but I tell you what, when you get back to Torie's, we can all go and grab some ice cream."

"Yeah! Guess what, Torie?"

"What?"

"We're all going to go and get ice cream later."

"Well then, are you ready to go and get those nails done?"

"Yup!"

All this time, Asia didn't even come to say hello or goodbye other than waving her hand. Quinn was just about to close the hatch when I realized that Tishie didn't have her backpack with her summer reading books.

"Sweetie, where are your books?"

"Oh no! I forgot them upstairs."

"It's okay. We can ask mommy to run upstairs and grab them for us." I look at Quinn and tell him that I'll be right back that I'm just walking Tishie over to Asia to ask her to get the backpack. As I'm walking away, I hear a couple of the elderly women from the church speaking to Quinn about all the good things going on at the center and how the kids needed a safe place to play and do their homework. I'm really not appreciating the fact that fragments of scattered broken glass spread across the courtyard is cutting into the soles of my shoes. Why must Tishie have to yell over this car that's blasting music with inappropriate lyrics in order for her mother to hear her?

"You need what?" Asia shouts back.

"I need my backpack!!" Tishie releases my hand and skips in her mom's direction.

"Wait, Tishie!" I call out while still trying to catch up walking over the unleveled ground and glass fearing any needles.

Asia is visibly annoyed at the interruption asks, "Why you leave it upstairs . . . damn!"

I finally catch up to them and say hello to Asia.

"Hey Torie, how you doing?"

"I'm good, how are you?"

"I'm good!" Asia looks over at her boyfriend Be'Lah and asks him to run upstairs and grab Tishie's bag.

"What bag?" Be'Lah asks taking his last pull from a cigarette before throwing it onto the ground.

"The pink one with the kittens on it," says Tishie.

"Yeah, I got you, Shorty!" he affectionately tugs on one of Tishie's ponytails.

Just as Be'Lah went to take his first steps towards the walkway, two silver cars coming from different directions began speeding towards us with guns firing from every window; one was the same car blaring the music just moments ago. Flying dirt begins swirling around creating a sand blizzard; the air is immediately sulfur-infused like a failing charcoal grill. Random yellow flashes appear not allowing me to reach Tishie. I hear Quinn yelling my name but I can't tell where it's coming from because of the loud screams . . . I soon realize those to be my own. Where did he go? . . . "Quinn!! . . . Quinn!!" I think I'm shouting . . . but my mouth is tightly closed. Why isn't anyone helping us? "Tishie!!" The flashes are much closer and . . . "Ughh," I moan after the last loud pop explodes diminishing my hearing. My ears are ringing now. I can barely hear Tishie's cries before feeling her small hand finally in mine. "I got you . . . I've got you, Tish."

Just as I'm pulling her into my chest, a sudden jolt to my back forces me abruptly onto the concrete with Tishie beneath me. I am immediately besieged with an intense burning and can barely manage to open my eyes before passing out. I wake up with my face to the ground and a heavy pressure on my back that won't allow me to move; I guess this is what they mean when saying dead weight. "Oh

God, have I been shot? Am I paralyzed?" I cry out over and over. The burning . . . and the once warm fluid all over my chest has become cool and sticky. I'm trying to stay awake but there's less pain when I close my eyes.

I hear sirens from afar and lots of crying near but not one familiar voice. An unfamiliar voice instructs with authoritative urgency to "Bring the board over here."

"I've got a pulse on both of them."

"Lieutenant, look there's a child beneath her," said a frantic voice.

"This is crazy! When is this shit ever going to end?"

"Hurry! We need that board!"

In my haze, I can't help but wonder where Quinn is.

"Okay, we're going to need to place a collar on his neck."

Whose neck? Can't they hear me? Whose neck needs a collar?

"No one is to move or unfold his arms from around them until we've secured his head and neck. Is that clear?"

They sound like they're close by and I wonder if they can hear me. I cry out, but nobody answers. Why aren't they answering? I wonder if I was really even speaking.

"On the count lift him off and onto the board. One . . . two . . ."

And on their count of three, I felt that debilitating weight being lifted from my back. The weight was gone, and my body has become riddled with pain as I try to get up. It was then that I heard a voice say, "Miss . . . we are the paramedics and we're here to you help you. Please don't move." They began cutting my clothing off exposing my entire torso to locate where the blood had come from; turns out it was in the region of my breast.

"What is your name, sweetie?" a female medic asked.

"She's going in and out!"

"Miss, can you hear me?"

"Torie . . . my name is Torie."

"Okay Torie, we're almost done; we're going to turn you around and place you onto your other side."

I reach for the hand belonging to the kind voice and will not let go. "I don't want to die," I tell her as I squeeze her hand tightly, feeling as though if I were to let go, then I would go.

She uses her free hand to gently rub the top of my hand and calmly repeats, "You're going to be fine, Torie. I'll stay right here with you."

"Thank you."

Another paramedic calls out, "Lieutenant . . . I've got a single entrance wound exiting on the right side of the chest."

Whose chest . . .shot? . . . I've been shot? I slowly turn my head from left to right with my eyes closed.

"Okay Torie, you're doing great. Stay with us. There are fragments of glass—some small, but a couple of larger pieces are embedded in your back. We'll get you to the hospital and get them out. You're going to be fine."

"Her initial impact with the ground must have been on her back before being turned faced down," one paramedic softly says to the other.

Once turning me and strapping me onto my side, I had a full view and a ghastly understanding of who had been shot and that's when I heard myself scream loud enough to be certain that I really was screaming.

"Quinnnn!! I belt out loudly looking to my left . . ." Tishie!!" I shout even louder as I look to my right. That weight was Quinn shielding both Tishie and me.

"Please let me talk to her. Please!! Just bring me near her! Please!" I sob hysterically.

"We're sorry, but we need to get her to the hospital. We'll do everything we can!"

I look on stretching my eyes widely trying to look beyond the blur as they load Tishie in the ambulance. As they attempt to move me towards another waiting ambulance we pass Quinn, who is lifelessly being lifted from the blood-drenched ground.

"No, no, no! Please let me talk to him," I shout and tug to release the straps securing me to the board. Still holding my hand, the female medic instructed, "Just give her a second," as we passed, allowing me to hear the hopelessness in her voice.

They did so reluctantly. With tears streaming down my face, I take Quinn's lifeless hand and demand, "Quinn, you fight . . . do you hear me gritting my teeth . . . Quinn!! You fight!"

The lieutenant ordered them to quickly remove me despite all of my physical resistance. It was then that I demanded an update on Tishie's condition.

"She's fading and bleeding profusely from a shoulder wound."

"Tishie! Oh no! Please no," I petition.

That was the last I remember before waking up in this hospital bed propped up in a near sitting position. It was explained to me later that I had been sedated to allow them to remove the glass from my body. When it was all over, my wounded body had commanded 76 stitches. I also had a concussion.

Simone and Nigel were waiting by my bedside to inform me of Tishie's condition. They told me she was out of surgery and doing extremely well in the children's pediatrics hospital on the East Side. They'd also said that Asia—who was physically unscathed—hasn't left her bedside. Be'Lah was the least fortunate succumbing to the ambush as the intended casualty.

"Quinn?" I asked unable to wait a second longer.

Simone's face couldn't hide it so Nigel immediately offered, "His body is just having a hard time right now . . . it just needs to rest."

"What are you saying?"

"It's just gonna take a little while before he wakes up."

"But he's going to wake up . . . right?"

"The doctor has said that the bullet wound was clean because it went in and out not affecting anything permanently. He's lost a lot of blood and his body went into shock . . . so they've got him heavily sedated to allow his body to rest and heal. "

"Are his sisters or his mother here?"

"They beat the ambulance here; you know how tight the Matthews are."

"Actually I've never met them. Quinn talks about them a lot, but I was traveling when they had that huge barbecue down in Norwalk, so I didn't go."

"Look girl, you need to get some rest too; we're going to be right here going back and forth between the both of your rooms. Do you need anything right now besides me combing that hair for you?" A soft giggle follows.

"I hope you don't mind, but I asked the girls to wait until tomorrow to come up."

"No, that's fine."

"I called Aunt Dot; you know that there was nothing I could say to stop her from flying in. She should be here early tomorrow morning; Aunt Mabel has been here the whole time and is downstairs getting another cup of tea."

"Thank you." A single tear escaped my eye as I turned toward the window. My only thoughts belonged to Quinn and his recovery.

"Hey, you know I'm staying right here with you. I already informed the nurses' station and Nigel will be staying with Quinn and Mrs. Matthews."

Simone walked Nigel out of the room and allowed Aunt Mabel some alone time with me before being escorted downstairs to her waiting ride. She returned about 20 minutes later with her arms filled with pillows and blankets. "Well I've raided both floors and have gotten Nigel and those set up as well . . . want some Jell-O? I've got cherry and lime, and a few ginger ales for later." Sim was visibly proud of her successful canteen caper.

I smiled and requested the lime knowing that as a child she preferred cherry. I didn't really want either, but I also didn't want Simone to feel like all of her efforts were wasted.

We talked off and on in between medication-induced sleep. I had a chance to share with one of my best friends how frightening this day has been and how even more afraid that I may never get the chance to share it with Quinn.

Just past 9:00 p.m., I heard the room door open even with Simone's snoring. Quietly in came a very short fair-skinned woman with familiar eyes. She walked with a slight wobble. There was something familiar about her face when she turned to me and said, "Torie?"

"Yes?"

"Now I see what all the fuss has been about," she continued as she approached my bedside. "I needed to see for myself this young woman that my son would nearly lay his life down for."

"Mrs. Matthews?" All at once, I felt plagued with guilt.

"Yes baby, and how are you doing?"

"I'm so sorry."

"What are you sorry for? You didn't pull the trigger."

"I can't stop worrying and praying that he'll be alright." I start sobbing all over again.

She looked at me offering ease with those same amber eyes and believing her next words to be true. "Stop worrying—but you can keep praying. I know my child and right now I'm sure he's finding his way back here to see how you made out." She reached across her well-endowed chest to lightly pat my hand above the IV's entrance. "I know it's a scary thing . . . even for us that have seen it time and time again . . . still nothing anyone should get used to."

"I'm fine, just a cut or two," now feeling guilty for comparing a cut to being shot. "Really, I'm fine. Thank you."

"Well it's a little more than that, if they still got you here, baby."

You can see that she was a looker in her day. She's much older than I would have expected, but then I remembered Quinn saying that there is a 15-year gap between him and his oldest sister.

"Promise me that you'll let me know if you need something."

"I promise. Thank you," I humbly said.

"I've heard so much about you from the day you showed up on the West Side. For the first time without being prompted, I'd seen my son initiate his own showers and haircuts." She laughed heartily covering her mouth trying not to disturb Simone. "Anyway, that's about the time a boy starts coming into their good hygiene ways."

"Oh, that boy came running in that house midday to take a shower after seeing the girl from New Canaan . . . hmmm, that's been more than ten years now. Boy, how his sisters teased him! They would tell me, 'Mommy, he don't even say nothing to the girl . . . he just looks at her,' and that would get him so mad!!"

This was all news to me . . . albeit good . . . it's news!! So I smile and listen.

"My son's work isn't done here . . . nope." Visibly choked up and wringing her hands she continued, "You all have to finish making it right around here for the kids coming up . . . and he has to finish his work with you." With a wink and a warm kiss on my cheek she adds, I'm sure I'll be seeing a lot more of you Miss Torie. I'm going to leave you to get some rest. You take care of yourself now."

"Thank you for coming, Mrs. Matthews . . . could you . . . please tell him that I love him?"

"I'm gonna leave that for you to say when he wakes up, but I will tell him that I've been to see you and that you're doing fine . . . and are anxious for him to wake up."

In that moment I saw a compact version of Quinn looking back at me from that door. I have to believe her when she says that he'll be fine. After all a mother must know, right?

"How long you been awake, Sim?"

"Only after I heard someone laughing," she defends.

"I can't believe that she came to see me with everything going on with Quinn."

"Mrs. Matthews has always been a nice woman; it never seemed like they belonged living in the Pavilion, even back in the day when it wasn't so bad. After Mr. Charlie passed, I guess she didn't have much choice. He was a hard-working man, much like Quinn."

Simone and I passed the next couple of hours watching the reality shows on and recalling my first visits to the West Side on the heels of Mrs. Matthews's comments. Simone began laughing so hard at some memory that she couldn't even let me in on the humor. Every time she would attempt to share, she'd falter to laughing harder and unable to speak I then began to laugh at her hysteria with tears now streaming down each of our faces.

"Ohhh gosh. . . Ohhh my gosh. Do you remember when you told your mother that we were going to work on a school project and she later came to the Pavilion wearing a coat over an old-lady nightgown and a belt in her hand looking for you in the middle of the block party? Yes—it was her and Aunt Dot. Do you remember that night?"

"YOU told me that we were going to work on a project!!"

"Oh no, what I SAID was, we're going to the projects . . . your bourgeois ass just didn't know what the projects were!"

We're both now laughing so loudly that a passing nurse opened the door to see if all was well. No matter how many years go by, that story still leaves us doubled over. We've now caused such a commotion that another nurse has come in to check on us. With my head thrown back on the pillow and me cupping my stomach, Simone folded over facing the floor as though she were puking, neither one of us could respond to her query.

"I'm so sorry," the older nurse offered, likely assuming we'd received terrible news and mistaking our laughter as cries. This only caused us to laugh even harder with Simone tapping the floor with her left foot going up and down.

I turned toward the nurse waving my hand, "No, no, no everything is fine . . . we're sorry." She found little humor in my words and offered, "You will need to keep it down . . . others are resting." With that, she sternly slammed the door.

Simone continues to laugh as I talk about that day and my mother and auntie throwing me under the bus in the name of love. That day was my first time seeing anything different than New Canaan!!

I'd never seen projects before. There were brick buildings— some tall, some short—which I later learned were called bungalows. Children were outside having their hair braided while others were playing hopscotch and jumping rope using two ropes at a time. There were tables filled with people playing cards and dominoes as babies ran around clad only in diapers. The only shouts heard came from card players or children screaming for the ice cream truck. Some folks called out "Hot Peas and Butter," an urban game similar to hide and seek. Of course, there was lots of music playing, and lots of laughing, but certainly no gun shots!!

Nigel walked in and cupped his hand like a megaphone and shouted, "Did I hear someone say, 'Hot Peas and Butter, come and get your SUPPER!!'"

We began laughing in unison at the unsolicited outburst of an old urban game that brought us back to memories of a loving community that allowed a village to raise a child . . . literally. In that village, any mother or grandmother residing in the neighborhood and an active church member had the distinct privilege of disciplining you and sending you home. That same mother or grandmother had the same permission to love you unconditionally and spoil you by giving you fresh hot biscuits or slices of their homemade lemon pound cakes.

I began thinking that if I'd never seen it for myself, I too might have believed only what the paper reported. I sighed thinking that Mrs. Matthews is right—we do have to make it better for the children coming up.

Two weeks have already passed and I've only been out of the hospital for four days. Before picking me up from the hospital on Wednesday, my Aunt Dot and Aunt Mabel went by Clock Towers to pack up some of my belongings under Simone's guidance. For the first time in a very long time, I look forward to going to stay in The Big House; it's the place I know that will allow me to feel safe and to clear any fragmented thoughts.

Besides, staying in New Canaan would best accommodate my aunties given that I only have two bedrooms in my unit. Not to mention that my family relies on food and cooking as a means of healing, so they'd appreciate using the kitchen that they alongside Nanna have made many healing meals, time and time again over the years. Equally as important is the fact that it's given me the opportunity to persuade Asia to move into my place with Tishie for a while rather than either of them going back to the Pavilion, particularly with Tishie's impending therapy. Physically, Tishie is doing very well, but not surprisingly her personality has been altered, those once sparkling brown eyes have lost their shimmer. Still the activist she's always been, Aunt Dot has already been in contact with Social Services and local nonprofit agencies to insist on assistance in relocating Asia to a safer neighborhood. She feels that it's best to stay on this during the time that they haven't returned to their apartment to visibly show them displaced gaining more urgent support. Aside from that, it will help Tishie's recovery by having her in a place where she feels safe. And like me, she'll feel much better once Quinn finally wakes up!

The first time I was able to visit Quinn in the hospital was extremely draining; it was nearly a setback for me emotionally. I knew that it was going to be difficult, but I clearly miscalculated my strength. Seeing him just lying there so still with his body temperature cool was unsettling. Every once in a while, he would briefly wince, indicating pain and some awareness. By my fourth and last visit before being discharged, I'd had an epiphany of how much I love this man. I decided that with his recent prognosis being positive and the doctors slowly reversing the sedation that I'd want to thank him and let him know all about my epiphany as soon as he wakes up. I'm just going to tell him that somehow over time, I'd absolutely fallen in love with him, but I want him to be wide awake when I tell him. That's it! I'm going to tell him. I placed his hand back onto the bed softly by his side and leaned forward and whispered into his ear.

"Quinn, I've got something to tell you." It was as if he'd heard me, because his cheeks became flush and his brows repositioned. I took the biggest breath and then I did it. I said it sheepishly, "I've fallen in love with you Quinn . . . and I want you to know that I'll be right here waiting for you." I said it again a second time, though this time with much more ease, leaving me wanting to say it over and over in hopes of loving him back to consciousness.

Quinn's Adam's apple abruptly moved indicating that he was attempting to swallow, but after that he remained motionless for the duration of my visit and my release from the hospital. It was another full week before Quinn actually regained full consciousness and learned all that had transpired on that fateful day. The doctors told Mrs. Matthews that his frustration with his physical weakness, being unstable and depressed was to be expected. Initially Quinn welcomed and insisted on lots of company, but after a while, he became rather aloof and often suggested that he was tired to get people to keep their visits brief. Given that I couldn't drive and was still healing myself, I wasn't able to keep the vigil that it appears Jasmine was able to. I decided to call Quinn to check on him.

"Hello?"

"Hi, is this Charleen?"(Quinn's youngest sister.)

"No it isn't . . . who's calling?"

"Torie. Who am I speaking with?"

"Jasmine," she says with the most territorial tone.

"Hi, Jasmine how are you?"

"Oh hey . . . I'm fine."

"I just wanted to check in on Quinn. May I speak with him?"

"He's had a lot of company . . . and I was just getting him settled . . . you know what I mean?"

"Sure . . . listen, please let him know that I've called."

"Of course I will. Bye-bye."

Over the next month, Jasmine and I danced this dance many times. Quinn had been discharged and was back at Clock Towers for at least two weeks by the time I was given permission to resume driving. By this time; Simone cautioned that she suspected that Jasmine had been making frequent visits to the hospital caring for him as a registered ho. It appeared she was trying to find her way back into Quinn's life by being the dutiful ex in his time of need. The same ex who just happens to have slept with his boy when it was widely assumed that he was being recruited to the pros.

"Hello?"

"Quinn? . . . How are you doing?"

"Hey Torie Harper . . . What's up girl? . . . How are you doing?"

"I'm well. You sound good . . . strong . . . I mean you sound like your old self!!"

"Yeah, it's getting there. So listen, I'm gonna miss Tishie and Asia. I hear that they're getting ready to move into their new place. That was real cool of your Aunt Dot hooking all of that up."

"Yeah, she's good with making things happen." The conversation seemed a little labored and unlike any from our past. I can't help but wonder if he'd heard what I'd said to him at the hospital and was now on the run.

"I've been calling, but it seems that you are resting at those times."

"It's been crazy . . . you know Nigel and the brothers are in and out of this joint."

"I'll be moving back in to Clock Tower next week . . . I've been set free!!" He laughs trying to make light.

"Ah, that's cool . . . it'll be good to have you back here . . . (hearing a door and jingling keys) listen . . . I gotta get going . . . but give me a holla when your back . . . you good?"

"Yeah . . . I'm good!!"

"Alright, girl."

"Bye, Quinn."

What was I thinking? Please let him have been completely unconscious!! I mean, we only slept together that one time. Could it have been wiped from his memory? No, well if so, it will remain gone because I won't be reminding him. I don't know what got into me. But still, I'll be forever grateful for him saving our lives.

It feels so good to finally be back home at The Tower and I'm really glad that Millie, Felicia and Yoli insisted on hanging out and staying with me on my first night home. As much as I enjoyed catching up with the girls, I wasn't dissuading them from leaving when suggested. I guess that I'm not really back 100 percent because I find that my body now requires that I take a lengthy nap around midday.

Wow, I know I was exhausted because when I woke up, it was almost 5:00. It must have been the comfort of being in my own bed because I never sleep in the middle of the day and I've been asleep since noon. I'm starving and I need to find something to eat.

The telephone rang and I saw "Mrs. Charlie Matthews" displayed on the caller ID. I quickly grabbed the cordless from the cradle fearing that something has happened to Quinn.

"Hello?"

"Hi, is this Torie?"

"Yes, this is she."

"Hi baby, this is Mrs. Matthews. How are you doing? Quinn said that you would be back in your place soon, so I took a chance calling."

"I'm fine thank you; I came home yesterday. How are you, Mrs. Matthews?"

"Oh, I'm much better now, knowing that everybody is out of that hospital. That's the reason I'm calling . . . I know that it's last minute, but I decided to cook a dinner and celebrate tonight."

"Tonight?"

"Yes, can you make it? It's nothing big, it'll just be Quinn and his sisters and Nigel. They say that Simone is away for the weekend with her work.

"I'd like that. Thank you."

"Okay, we're at 126 Layton Circle—the tan house with black shutters on the right. See you around 7:30."

"May I bring something?"

"Just yourself, baby!"

After getting out of the shower I slipped on a pair of black leggings, an oversized gray cotton sweater and ballerina slippers. I quickly did up a messy updo, added two sprays of Issey Miyake cologne, a brush of gloss and a few strokes of mascara. Just before leaving I phoned my aunts and shared my plans with each of them so that they wouldn't become concerned with my absence. I sent Simone a text message reading, "OMG!! Mrs. Matthews 4 dinner ETA 7:30."

I made one detour by Angelina's Bakery to purchase a signature chocolate cheesecake to carry with me. I only recognize Nigel's car so I park directly behind it. I am so excited to see Quinn and let him know that I've returned home. Tomorrow I will surprise him with preparing meals and helping him with some of his housekeeping before I am scheduled to return to work in a week.

After ringing the doorbell and waiting, I can smell the aroma of roast beef in brown gravy seeping through the opened windows battling the fragrant collard greens. I hear the distinct sound of loosely worn house slippers being dragged across the floor heading in the direction of the door.

"Hi Torie!" I'm greeted with great warmth by Charlene, who is affectionately called Charlie after Quinn's father.

"Girl, you look good!! Mommy, Torie's here!!"

The house was engulfed with healing aromas of macaroni & cheese and buttery corn bread.

"Bring her on back here, Charlie!" She led me through the hallway of an age-defying Colonial with portraits thoughtfully mounted along the walls. We passed an intact parlor with individual framed pictures resting on the mantel. Leading me directly as instructed, my first destination was the kitchen.

"Hi baby, it's so GOOD seeing you!!" Mrs. Matthews rubbed my back in a circular pattern as if she had healing hands while ordering Charlie to free my hands up from the cake box. I turned my head in the direction of the voices spilling over from the adjacent room. "Go on, everybody is in there."

"Do you need help with anything?

"No, baby. Charlie's gonna help me finish with the table and we'll sit in just a few more minutes. Go on in there!" Mrs. Matthews smiles and appears to be more excited than me making me believe that Quinn is aware of my invitation.

As I turn the corner, Quinn's face offers that he is very pleased to see me. He makes an attempt to leap from the sofa into a standing position to greet me, but his legs beg to differ, causing him to abruptly fall back onto the sofa. I pretend not to see his first failed attempt as he executes the next successfully.

"I hope that you don't mind; your mom phoned and invited me." I give him the warmest embrace my body will allow; I don't want to let go anytime soon. For the first time, his body felt warm again and very much alive. Nigel said hello and vacated the room with Quinn's sister Rhonda giving us a moment.

"Torie . . . Torie . . . Torie." Quinn shook his head as though he was trying to shake out the haunting fears of what could have been on that day.

"Come here." Quinn pulls me into his arms as he deeply sighs and raises his head toward the ceiling trying to suppress his emotions. Hugging me tightly, he sweetly kisses me on my forehead and says, "I need you to stay right here for a minute, girl." He continued, "I know it's been crazy, nobody else really gets it . . . but we're okay Torie . . . we're both okay."

I held on as I sniffled and nodded in agreement, imagining that he too has had many sleepless nights and flashbacks of that day; something neither of us wants to discuss anymore. I'm sure he feels the same as me, just wanting to move on.

Within moments we heard an additional voice coming from the foyer and suddenly the family room became crowded as I see Jasmine standing in the doorway. Quinn and I awkwardly freed each other.

"Hey!!" Jasmine says and walks towards us. "I just told your mother that I was so nervous when I didn't get an answer at your place after calling and knocking on your door. I didn't have her phone number and I was coming to Norwalk anyway, so I stopped by. I wanted to make sure you were okay." Jasmine kisses him on the lips and then looks at me insincerely to ask, "How are you doing, Torie?"

My mouth replies, "I'm good thanks," when I really wanted to say, "I'd be much better if you'd stay the hell out of my way." Instead I gave her a hard blink and left her to translate that.

Mrs. Matthews poked her head into the room as she was removing two oven mitts from her hands. "Okay now . . . ya'll come on and eat." She looks over at Jasmine and says, "I wasn't expecting you, but you're welcome to stay for dinner."

"Mrs. Matthews, you know how I love your cooking! Did you happen to make your famous banana pudding?"

Disappointed that Jasmine accepted her offer to stay, Mrs. Matthews quickly replies, "No, I don't have any banana pudding," refusing to give her any reason to prolong her stay.

Quinn interjects, "Ma, what was that in that bowl in the refrigerator?"

"Baby, that's for the church tomorrow!" said in a tone that suggests he leave it alone.

"That's okay!!" Rubbing his arm before saying, "I like to keep my stuff tight anyway and that banana pudding would have me breaking all the rules." Jasmine smoothes her dress and then looks over at me staring me up and down.

Among other things, I think to myself that there is very little tightly kept on her. I can only hope that she can read my mind right now.

Mrs. Matthews has appeared at my side patting my back again. She takes me by the hand "Come on sweetie, let's go and get you some of that food." I pause to ask her where I can go and wash my hands. "Go right on in there." She reaches into the doorway to the right of us and flips the light switch on.

After I made it to the dining room, I can see Jasmine closely seated beside Quinn, now reaching in to prepare his plate.

"Jasmine?" Mrs. Matthews says while removing the serving spoon and near empty plate from her hand. "Torie is out of the powder room; you can go on in there to wash your hands." Mrs. Matthews carried the serving spoon and plate into the kitchen and returned with a different serving spoon and fresh plate in hand.

The table is prepared like a church dinner for a big crowd. There's a roast, baked ham, macaroni & cheese, fried chicken, string beans with red potato, collards, potato salad, yams and buttery corn bread. I haven't seen a table set like this since Nanna Bess was alive. This dinner was about more than food—it was about family and a whole bunch of love.

Quinn continuously sang his mother's praises for her execution of dinner. "Ma . . . you been cooking for a week?" Quinn shoveled food into his mouth in between compliments. "Slow down, son (speaking to Nigel) . . . That's my mama and my food!!"

"Nigel, you don't pay that son of mine no mind," Mrs. Matthews said obviously giddy that her son was finally home.

"Have I ever? You've known me all my life and I've eaten and slept in your home as if you'd birthed me," Nigel joked.

Mrs. Matthews must have followed my eyes capturing Jasmine eating off of Quinn's plate. "We have plenty of food, Jasmine!!" She's clearly disturbed by her interfering with her baby enjoying his dinner. "Oh, I'm okay," Jasmine giggles still picking pieces of ham off of his plate.

I excused myself by helping Charlie take some of the things back into the kitchen to make room for the desserts; Jasmine never attempted to move from her seat to help at all. I was left alone in the kitchen just long enough to launch a text to Simone, "BTW dinner's great / Jas here & all over Q!!" Simone replied, "I'm sure MM cooked meat, always does, how is it that you have a knife in hand and didn't shank her???" I replied, "LMAO wish u were here!!" Simone replied, "Ok, but I still say shank the ho!!"

Mrs. Matthews walked into the kitchen just as I was putting my phone away. "I want you to wrap up some food and take it on home with you." She certainly won't get an argument out of me. "There's banana pudding on the second shelf for you." I couldn't help but smile remembering that Quinn would always bring some back with him for me.

We all knew that Mrs. Matthews stopped caring for Jasmine after she'd publicly humiliated Quinn by dating his dorm mate on the DL and continued to play head games by denying it when she was caught. We knew it to be true, and soon after, he did too. Quinn nearly failed out of law school that semester over her nonsense.

"I'm guessing that you never gave my son that message?" Mrs. Matthews asked me. She raised her brows waiting on my response.

"It doesn't seem to matter much now."

"You won't know unless you tell him. Oh that . . . child, please. He didn't want her when he had her. Men do that you know . . . keep something around until they get what they really want . . . oh yes, even the good ones! He was just trying to let go of a long dream that hadn't worked itself out yet."

"Yeah, but he was so hurt when they'd broken up."

"Child, nobody wants to be made a fool! Besides he wasn't hurt, he was just embarrassed." She had a valid point so we both giggled at that notion. "Come on now, let's get these desserts out there . . . but don't bring that banana pudding!!" She smiled deviously at me.

THE BIG REVEAL

T hings have changed with me going back to work. The change has been for the better. Things have progressed quickly with the Harbor View Project. Some of the older dwellings have been demolished already, and those only needing facelifts have been completely restored. Construction has even been started on the newer structures. Unfortunately, some families have found themselves displaced earlier than originally thought.

I returned to a voicemail box that had reached its capacity and an e-mail box containing upwards of 300 messages before IT decided to manage my out-of-office notification. There were several well wishes and many internal all-staff updates, while most people followed the instructions of the out-of-office assistant directing them to contact Beth Sheehy, our Controller. However, this one caller was persistent in calling my voicemail periodically. The first five calls were attached to messages that echoed in similarity:

"Hi Torie. My name is Ms. Barrett Johns and I am calling in regard to a finding in your recent mergers and acquisitions audit. I really need to speak with you privately and would ask that you not share this request with anyone until I have had the opportunity to fully disclose the finding with you. I can be reached at area code 203.555. - - - -."

Another call. "Hi Torie, Barrett Johns again. I hoped to have heard back from you by now. Notwithstanding, it is imperative that we speak soon as this matter has become extremely time sensitive. Again, I can be reached at area code 203.555. - - - -."

Final call. "Torie . . . Barrett Johns. I'm so sorry to have heard of your recent experiences, but I'm told that you are doing well and expected back sometime over the next two weeks. I can only imagine that you will be inundated upon returning, but would like to gently caution that we really do need to speak. Again, I'm pleased to hear of your return and I'm sure by now you must have my number. Take care."

How does she know about my personal life? Furthermore, I'm sure that my voicemail never indicated a return date. In addition, there were many recorded hang ups with no spoken messages prior to the final call making it all the more cryptic. I couldn't imagine why this caller wouldn't have just reached out to Eric given that he is the Chief Officer of Legal, and more specifically—the person overseeing all M&A. Suddenly, those suspicious feelings that I was unable to rid prior to being on leave have reappeared.

Returned call. "Hello, Barrett? . . . I'm sorry that I've missed you, but this is Torie Harper returning your calls. I am back in the office and available on both e-mail and voicemail in the event that we continue to miss each other throughout the day. I hope to speak with you soon."

I didn't want to appear anxious but truly the curiosity is starting to gnaw.

The call back comes not long after leaving my message. I saw Barrett's number on the caller ID. Completely out of character and prompted by curiosity, I snatched the phone from the cradle and confirmed, "Barrett?"

"Yes, Torie, I'm sorry that I was unable to grab the call before it leaped into my voicemail."

"Oh, no worries," I offer regaining control over my anxiousness.

"I apologize if my messages have been rather cryptic, but it was necessary for me to keep this under wraps until speaking with you."

"And what exactly are we talking about?" rushing her along.

"I've been obtained by Lytle & Lytle Realty (one of the larger investors of the Harbor View Project) to furtively shadow the entire due diligence and mergers and acquisitions processes done by Klein-Matheson. My clients want to be assured that they are not venturing into any partnerships that are lacking integrity."

"I'm just curious, why you are telling me this?"

"Torie, as the Chief Financial Officer, I think that you should be aware that we can prove there was a deliberate omission during our review of a late entrant."

"I'm listening." No longer seated, I stand and begin pacing the distance that the phone will allow.

"I was to report back to my clients two weeks ago and have pushed them back as long as I can. I haven't shared this with them as of yet, because I don't believe this to represent Klein-Matheson. However, it is evident that it is the work of one of your key staff."

My heart was racing and my head flooded with my own theories of who the perpetrator is; this will definitely clear Quinn's name.

"Torie, is it possible to meet this afternoon so that I may share the supporting documents that will allow you to discern who the culprit is?"

"Yes. What time will you arrive?"

"Oh, I mustn't come there, as my anonymity must remain intact. How about meeting at Barcelona at 1:00?"

"I'll see you then."

Despite the caller's instructions, I've decided to confide in Millie. She is not only a colleague, but also one of my lifelong friends whom I trust unconditionally.

I dial her extension to seek her out.

"And she's back!!" she playfully shouts into the receiver before I can say a word.

"Good morning to you too! Mil, can you meet me downstairs for a minute?"

"Torie, are you feeling okay? . . . Do you think you came back too soon?"

"No, no I'm fine. I need to talk to you . . . can you meet me down in the atrium in about ten minutes?"

"Yeah, of course!! Our usual spot right?" referencing a secluded spot that we typically reserved for topics surrounding men or calls from a doctor's visit.

"Yeah."

"Voy, you're scaring me . . . but you're okay, right?"

"I just need to talk to you."

"I'll be down there in five minutes."

As I approached the hidden alcove tucked behind some of the greens in the atrium, I could see that Millie was already there waiting. She must have walked out after hanging up the phone. Look at her neatly tucked in that stealth gray coatdress accented with a Coach scarf!

"So . . . what's going on?"

"There's someone who has been continuously calling and leaving urgent messages."

"Okay, so who is it . . . Hollis?"

"No!! Where the hell did that come from? It's business related, not personal."

"Then who was calling?"

"That's what I'm trying to tell you . . . I don't know this person."

"Well, what did they want?"

"She . . . her name is Barrett Johns. She said that I should tell no one of this conversation and that it's imperative that she speaks to me in person."

"For WHAT?" Millie inserts with discomfort, "And what are you not supposed to tell?"

"She said that she has proof that someone on the Legal Team is up to no good."

"WHAT?"

"Sshhh, Millie!"

"Why do you believe this person? You don't even know who she is, Torie!!" Millie placed both of her hands onto her tiny waist and looked up to the ceiling in thought. "Barrett Johns? . . . Barrett Johns?"

"I know, but she says that she was hired by one of the investors to shadow the process for integrity. She says that she has evidence, and as CFO she would share it with me to confirm for myself." I can't keep up with Millie as she's managed to pace in these tight hidden quarters.

"Mil!!"

Tugging on her bottom lip in between tapping it she blurts out with conviction, "You gotta tell Liam."

"No!! What am I going to tell him?"

"What you've just told me!!"

"Look, she wants to meet for lunch at Barcelona this afternoon. I'll listen to what she has to say and grab the documents and then see whether there's something to tell or not."

"Okay fine . . . then what time are we going?"

"*We* are not going, *I* am going at 1:00. Millie, it's okay. I've confirmed her credentials and she definitely works for the Roethlisberger Accounting Firm."

"It still sounds rather bizarre . . . yet legitimate . . . but you call me as soon as you get back here."

"Alright, let me get back upstairs; I need to finish up some things before leaving."

"You call me!!" I heard Millie shout out as I headed towards the elevator.

I mouthed the response "I will" as the elevator doors closed.

I arrived at Barcelona 20 minutes earlier than scheduled, but to my surprise, I was told that Ms. Johns had already been seated and was waiting for me. As I approached the booth and the guest that was identified to me as Ms. Johns, she promptly stood and greeted me without an introduction.

"Hi, Torie. Thank you for coming."

"Barrett . . . it's nice to finally meet you." I slid into the booth across from this woman who appears to be a complete contrast of my expectations. Given the brash voice that I've become so familiar with, I'd made up a visual of her being heavier in build with dark minimally attended hair and questionable sexuality. Yup, I made all of that up from her voice.

"I hope you don't mind—I ordered a bottle of Pellegrino and a few tapas," Barrett said as the waiter was approaching the booth with those mentioned in hand.

"No not at all . . . that's fine . . . thank you." I watched her place the linen napkin across the lap of her almond-colored pant suit before running her fingers through her chic auburn pixie that tapered at the peak of her neck. Her voice was completely ill-paired with her thin frame and daintiness; she converses with sincerity through her apple-green eyes.

"Again, I apologize if any of this has landed as cryptic. It really is rather routine excluding the finding of course, and that's why I've reached out to you."

"Yes, I did understand your intentions."

"Great, because given the deliberate appearance of false information, I wanted to give you the opportunity to have someone amend it to accurately reflect Klein-Matheson's reporting."

"I'm a little confused. If you know of an inconsistency, why not just reach out to the Mergers & Acquisitions team?"

Now blotting her lips she says, "Right, well . . . what you are suggesting makes a whole lot of sense. Look, I'm limited as to how much I can spell out legally, but what I can say is that it wouldn't be in my clients nor Klein-Matheson's best interest if we were to place the pistol back into the shooter's hands . . . it could be seen as somewhat negligent."

"Got it!!" So she definitely is saying that it's the work of someone on the Legal Team. It's not Quinn because he was on leave when this had to have transpired.

"I knew that you would . . . as I am also sure with your financial expertise that your eyes are best suited to recognize variables that display inconsistencies."

"One would hope!!"

"Oh please try the empanadas—they are the best!!"

By now, I have found ease in sharing lunch with Barrett and further comforted by the tantalizing whiff of freshly fried fish splashed with citrus that has found its way to our table.

"I have calamari for the ladies!" The server cleared our used dishes making room for the oblong platter cluttered with calamari rings and tentacles flanked with lemon wedges. It was only then that I noticed the conspicuous gentleman seated alone in the booth adjacent to ours. His behavior became consistently noticeable—revolving his head and avoiding all eye contact—never ordering anything beyond his cup of coffee. Really, who comes to Barcelona for coffee?

Regretfully as we finished our lunch, Barrett explained that the documents she'd intended to leave with me were not available. Extremely apologetic, she offered that we schedule to meet again next week as she would have received them at that point. Obviously disappointed, I agreed and asked that she confirm our meeting as soon as possible. With that, we stood to depart our separate ways.

"Thank you for lunch. I will have to come here again."

"I apologize again, but I will get the documents to you." Overhearing that, the menacing man placed his money onto the table and quickly abandoned the restaurant. Maybe he's Barrett's bodyguard or maybe my imagination is getting the best of me.

"No worries, it was nice to finally meet you."

Back at the office, I gathered my things after deciding to leave early. I want to share all of the recent events with Quinn. I know he'd know exactly who the culprit might be and what I should do? In addition this was great news this would clear any lingering suspicions of him. Oh yeah, I've got to call Millie! I decided that I'd call her from my place after speaking with Quinn because I'd likely have more to tell her anyway at that point.

I made it home in record time, completely bypassing my unit and heading directly to Quinn's to tell him all that has transpired.

Knock! Knock! Knock! He isn't answering. Becoming more anxious, I try again. Knock! Knock! Knock! I knocked a little harder this time as I called out, "Quinn!!" after pressing my ear to the door hearing the sudden increase in volume from the upstairs television during a commercial.

"Come on, Quinn!" I think aloud as I knocked one more time before deciding to leave. In that split second my anxiety has been replaced with concern, after all he really hasn't been home from the hospital very long . . . and certainly not on his own, prompting me to wonder where was his aide? I wonder if he might have fallen. Of course this made me recall his near stumble at his mother's home during my visit. As I reach inside my purse to grab my phone, I see the key to his unit that he'd given me and decide to use it as offered.

"Quinn?" I hear the television and running water upstairs and what sounds like an extended yawn.

I headed up the stairs excited to share all of the new findings at work; surely this will offer him relief and allow him to focus only on getting better.

"Quinn!" I shout over the television as I walk through the opened bedroom door. "Quinn, you are NOT going to believe what's happened." The bathroom door began to open, although the water in the shower was still running. There was Jasmine fully dressed but with a towel wrapped around her head.

"He's still in the shower, but he should be out any minute . . . Did you need something?" She smirked while waiting for my response. In that moment, my heart shattered and all of the toxic fumes traveled upward choking and leaving me speechless and absolutely hurt. As though that wasn't enough Quinn shouted out, "Jasmine are you just gonna leave a brother hanging or what?"

"I'll be right there. Umm . . . I've got to go, he's waiting for me. Can I tell him something for you?" I watched her smirk stretch into an all-out smile as she began to turn towards the bathroom door un-buttoning her shirt.

I threw the copies of the information that I'd gathered on my own onto the steps as I ran down the stairs leaving his front door wide open. Once in my car, I subconsciously found myself driving to The Big House. When I arrived, I sat in the driveway clutching the steering wheel before having a complete melt down. This was the first time I'd really cried since the shooting and everything seems to have built up.

I'm done! I'm so done with all of this! Fuck Quinn!! Fuck Hollis and fuck the community!! I am done!!

In that moment, I wept and released and decided that being the not-so-urban girl from New Canaan suited me just fine. I'll sell my unit at Clock Towers and move back into The Big House and live a drama-free life. They can all kiss my ass! It's time they played by my rules. Nobody's gonna tell me what to do, how to do it, when to do it or who to do it with! Fuck them!

IT ALL COMES TOGETHER

There he is again . . . that's the same gentleman from last week at Barcelona. Could it just be a coincidence? I'm not sure about him, but I am sure that I'm feeling a bit uncomfortable. Once again, I confirmed the time on my watch is now 1:20 p.m. making Barrett nearly 45 minutes late. I've decided that I'm going to leave, so I quickly sipped from my glass of Pellegrino and gathered my keys and the empanadas I had wrapped to go.

I was approaching the exit when a waiter beckoned, "Ms. Harper?" How does he know my name?

"Yes?" I'm now curious whether I'd left my charge card behind.

The gentleman has asked that I pass this onto you. He handed me a sealed envelope with my name handwritten in cursive. "What gentleman?"

"Oh, I'm afraid he has already departed . . . just after making his request."

"Thank you." As much as I want to tear this envelope open to see what's enclosed, I think it best for me to get into my car and head back to the office. I walked along the opposite side of the street from where my car is parked and waited for an opportunity to cross busy Main Avenue, carefully looking for anyone who seems to be watching me. The day is rather blustery causing my trench coat to fly open and my hair to impair my vision as it's blown across my eyes.

Once secure in my car, I promptly activate a call by pressing the button on the steering wheel to phone Millie while freeing my hands to merge into oncoming traffic.

"Hey, it's me."

"How did it go?"

"She didn't show today, but remember that man that I said was kind of suspect at Barcelona?"

"Yeah, the one you thought was her bodyguard, driver or something," she interrupts.

"Well HE was there."

"No way!! Did he speak to you?"

"No, no, no . . ."

"Was he dining by himself?"

BEEEEEPPPP!! BEEEEEPP!! A horn suddenly blared.

"What was that? Torie, are you okay?"

"Sorry, sorry!!" I blurted out of the window using my hand to gesture them to pass by.

"Torie, is everything okay?"

"Yes, I just nearly cut off this car. I'm going to hang up before I hurt someone. Meet me at our normal spot in 15 minutes and I'll finish telling you. I have to show you something that was given to me."

"He gave you something? What did he give you?"

"No, it was left for me!!"

BEEEEEPPPP!! Another car sat on their horn as I glided into their lane.

"Voy . . . just hang up!! Hang up because you're scaring me and I don't think that any of this is cool anymore!!"

"I'll be fine . . . besides, I'm almost there."

"Okay, but be careful . . . and if you're not here within 25 minutes I'm going to Liam and telling him everything!!"

"Millie, don't say anything!!"

"Then hurry up and get here!"

"I'm fine and I'll be there. Do not say anything!!"

"Tick tock . . . 25 minutes Torie, or I will tell!!"

Just as I pulled into my assigned parking space, I spotted Millie standing coatless outside of the entrance alongside of the decorative hedges spelling out Klein. She waited for me to exit my car as she continued to generate heat by rubbing her hands up and down against her folded arms while enduring the relentless wind.

"Why are you out here?"

"Liam and Klein are both in the lobby speaking with a client."

"Okay . . . then we'll just have to go to my office." I checked my watch to ensure that my administrative assistant would still be at lunch. Hillary says she likes to take a later lunch because it shortens her afternoon; the others complain that she takes a later lunch to police their comings and goings. Honestly, I'm not that manager who cares about keeping score and I believe that's why my team is so awesome. Besides, most of them are older than I am and I've chosen to trust their discretion.

Before entering the lobby I tell Millie that I would delay my entrance by a few moments and use the time to grab a frappe from the cafe. When I arrived at my office and opened the door, Millie was already seated. Looking at the envelope in my hand she immediately asked, "Is that it?"

"Yes."

"Well, open it!!"

There are copies of multiple invoices paper clipped in stacks spanning an 18-month period displaying a company named Champion Inc. as the corporation invoicing the receivables. Invoices are shown 12 months back and 6 months future.

"I don't know this company . . . what is she trying to tell us?"

Millie sorts through one stack as I look through the others seeking any kind of understanding.

"Champion Inc.—I know that I've seen this name before." I walk around my office staring at the invoice in her hand.

"She's trying to show me something that must be inconsistent with the financials."

"You did say that she mentioned an audit, right?"

"Yes, why?"

"She's showing you the past years Receivables and Sold Ahead . . . which would be considered an includable asset."

"Mil, look at these invoices from a year ago compared to the sold ahead during the same time of the year and to the same clients they've inflated beyond belief."

"Ooops . . . I think we've found our red herring!!"

"But we still don't know whose red herring or who owns Champion Inc . . . and with all of the investors and their subsidiaries, how will we ever find out?" Twirling the back of my earring, I'm thinking that these invoices are less helpful than Barrett probably realized.

"We'd need to see each company's balance sheet submitted to see if we can find the Champion Inc. listed as assets. Trust me when I say it sounds much easier than it is. Those documents are completely secured along with the supporting 941s."

"How are we going to do that?"

"Well, the only other accessible person besides Eric would be Quinn. Torie, he has been calling you over and over again; aren't you curious to hear what he has to say?"

"No, Mil," I say curtly. "Remember I was there; this isn't some kind of hearsay."

"I still believe that there's more to it . . . he's always cared so much about you and I find it hard to believe that he'd throw it all away, particularly after saving your life." She softly smiled to deflect any defense that I might be preparing to toss in her direction.

"Torie, I'm outta here. Don't worry, we'll figure this all out."

"Mil? Are we still on for dinner with Laurie uptown at Gates?"
"For sure!!"

Dinner was great as usual; it's always good catching up with Laurie. Now that I'm back living in New Canaan, I get to see her more often. I'm always so amazed how many of my old classmates really came back here to live after college. We ran into so many friends at dinner and I realize the fortune I've had all of these years in these genuine friendships with really nice people.

"Oh my God, Torie!! You look fab, girl. How are you doing?"

"Madison? . . . Aahhh!! What's up, girl?" I'm on my feet and we are hugging tightly. Maddie has always been a real down-to-earth chick as far back as I can remember; she and I were on the cheerleading squad together.

"Imagine this Tor, I'm someone's mommy."

"No way!!"

"Yuppppp, I am . . . twice. Oh, wait a minute; let me show you." Now she's kneeling on the floor beside the table balancing her purse on her lap while scrolling through her iPhone.

"They're adorable Maddie! The little one looks just like you," passing the phone around the table.

"I knowwww! Can you stand it?" As always, Maddie is moving fast, speaking quickly with jittery eyes with a speech pattern that hasn't changed. Maddie has always placed emphasis on one word in every sentence, dragging it a little longer than the other spoken words, not at all diluting her being a sweetheart.

"The other looks like your sister," Millie shared.

"This is Molly and this ONE is our Sara, aren't they the cutest?" proudly wiping the handprints left over their faces from her iPhone.

"So are you back to stay or whatttt?"

"Yes, I'm back at the house." I had to force a smile with that response because I'm still working through those unsettled emotions. Even though it's been just a brief time, it feels like much longer.

"Okay greatttt, then here take my number and give me yours. Oh, you know whattt? Jeremy Talbot is having a fundraiser down at the stables on the 15th—it starts at 7:00. You should come . . . all of you."

"Come on, at least think about it; everyone will be there and it's a wine tasting event to raise money to support horseback riding lessons for less fortunate children. It's for a great cause and it will be a good time."

"I will definitely think about it," giving her a hug goodbye and ending my night with the girls as well.

Two weeks have gone by and Millie and I are nowhere closer in solving the mystery of Champion Inc. Eric is scheduled to travel to the West Coast this week, finally giving Millie sometime to snoop. In addition to that, I have my own personal dilemma of my Clock Tower unit that still hasn't sold and my contract will expire in another week. The economy has put most sellers in a bad place; I've decided that I'll just rent the unit out until the market changes. Simone and I are still not in agreement about the move or me putting the unit up for sale; she feels that I should give Quinn the benefit of returning one of his many calls and speaking to him. Honestly, I'm so hurt that he would betray my trust. I feel really foolish and played for allowing him to schmooze me like that.

After another quiet weekend in The Big House, I decided to go ahead and meet Madison down at the Talbot Stables. I figured that it would get me out of the house and allow me to become reacquainted with the place I've been calling home for the past couple of months, even if Laurie and Millie both passed on the event. With the autumn weather and the venue, I decided to wear a pair of faded jeans and tan riding boots with a pear-colored turtleneck beneath a Burberry poncho. As I looked in the mirror while strapping my saddle bag across my chest, for the first time, I completely admired who I was seeing. Through all of this, I'd somehow accomplished just being me. Now I am easily adaptable in both urban and suburban lifestyles, toting the best of both worlds. This just "being me" thing can really work.

Down through Weed Street and all the way through Frog Town Road, a left here and a narrow right there, I've made it to the stables. Albeit brief, I did have that "Oh gosh, I'm the only Black person here . . . again" feeling. It's been a long time since I felt like this. In terms of treatment, it means nothing other than I'm the only Black person here. It takes me back to all of the school dances that I had to attend with either a group of girls or an import (a.k.a. one of Nanna's church friend's grandsons). This only became an issue in high school when everyone would begin pairing up midway through the party leaving me solo and sad; that was usually my cue to leave.

Taking a deep breath and recognizing that I am no longer that girl, I get out of the car and make my way towards the barn. From the number of parked cars and laughter escaping the scene, I'd say it's a pretty good turnout.

"Torie!!" Maddie waves while standing outside of the barn doors with a lit cigarette in her hand and a glass of wine in the other. She looks like a forest fire waiting to happen!

"Hey Maddie!" I greeted her with a kiss while trying to avoid her cigarette and my hair becoming the first casualty.

"Glad you came! Come on—let's go and catch up with everyone. You can meet my husband."

"So Maddie, how much tasting have you done already?" I teased.

"Umm huh, let's just say you've got a lotttt of tasting to do if you want to catch up to me!!"

And with that I did! It really is turning out to be a great time. Jeremy Talbot hasn't left my side since my initial arrival. The two of us spent stolen time away from the crowd sitting on stacks of hay catching up for hours; I was taken aback by his willingness to share his sober thoughts about my beauty. I, on the other hand, was a coward not easily giving words to how rapidly attractive he's becoming as the night goes on. I've gotten a chance to see what's inside of him; the outside has always been a given.

"So Torie, after all that you've shared, what's next for you?" Jeremy runs his tan and extremely massive hand through his honey-colored hair. His hands and body are the evidence of someone who once was a star quarterback in both high school and college. Although that would never be a swaying attribute for any of my suitors because it only reminds me of the man I so despise—Otis Harper, my long-lost father.

"I'm not exactly sure; I haven't gotten to that chapter yet." I'm sipping from my glass of wine as I notice that the crowd has thinned out to only a few. Maddie was escorted—or should I say nearly carried—out of here under her husband's supervision about an hour and plenty of wine ago. This prompted Jeremy to realize that he had neglected his other guests through the night.

"I should probably get going myself."

"Don't go."

Jeremy confidently placed his hand into mine creating unsuspecting sensations throughout. Being with him was easy and soothing; he offers an immediate comfort and undisputable trust that I'd never ever experienced before.

"I'd really like to hear more about the chronicles of Torie! Hang out with me for a bit; I just need to go and thank the remaining guest."

"Go. I'll wait." Each of his fingers slowly dragged across the palm of my hand as he released. I watched from afar while he helped the guys load the unsold cases of wine onto the pulley.

I watched every rotation of his flawless body after shedding his sweater leaving him garbed in a white tank, jeans and a pair of Timberland boots.

Ironically, his stature is very similar to Quinn's. Jeremy is 6'6 with definition in areas that reflect a seasoned football player with a face that is often mistaken for Brad Pitt.

"Hey . . . can I ask you for five more minutes?"

"Yeah, I'm fine!!"

Exactly ten minutes later, Jeremy was walking towards me with a bottle of wine and two goblets in a single hand, while waving his sweater in the air gesturing surrender.

"I'm guilty of taking more time than I asked of you . . . but I bear gifts." Raising the bottle of wine and pointing to a table draped with champagne grapes, assorted cheese and crackers.

"Well then, lucky for you I happen to like wine and cheese," flirting right back at him.

"Does this mean I've gotten myself off of the hook?" Jeremy winks at me while taking his sweater to wipe off any hay resting on those exposed biceps before tossing the sweater on the floor and placing a blanket across the stacks of hay.

"Possibly." I was clearly flirting even harder now. Jeremy extended his hand beckoning me to join him on a cushion he'd just prepared using folded blankets to soften the leveled stacks of hay. We picked up our conversation from where we'd left off. I comfortably and candidly shared most of my experiences after leaving New Canaan; he listened intently and did his best to understand the cultural differences. To my surprise, Jeremy had acquired a whole lot of flavor and a little 'sumpin 'sumpin that resembles swagger. He assured me that his time away from New Canaan playing college ball and his two seasons playing in the pros made him culturally aware through some really good friendships that he'd acquired. Good or bad, a couple of glasses of wine often allow me to share exactly what's on my mind.

"So wait a minute. Are you saying that you've spent some time with some brothers? Oh, you have a secret sweet tooth for like what . . . brown sugar?"

He's taking it right on the chin and without entertaining it, "No. Actually, I don't like brown sugar. Never have . . . literally."

Touché! We both just started laughing—and like a seasoned brother—Jeremy moved in on me with his rebuttal.

"What I have is this SICK attraction to a beautiful woman. I've had it ever since we were on a field trip in the second grade and she selflessly gave me half—the biggest half—of her peanut butter and jelly sandwich after I'd forgotten my lunch."

"Oh, my! Ha, ha, ha! You remember that?"

"Yeah!! Who forgets something like that? Come on, it was peanut butter and jelly!! From that day, on I watched you over the years become one of the prettiest, smartest and bravest girls I'd ever seen."

"Brave?"

"Torie, I don't know if I could have gone to a school of 400 where there were less than 15 White students. I don't think that any of us thought about it."

"Oh no, I thought about it, I just didn't talk about it. I thought about it every time there was a dance and you all would pair up, hook up, whatever you want to call it . . . and there I was."

"Do you know that I was going to ask you to the spring dance our senior year?"

"Jeremy, you were not!!"

"Seriously . . . ask Maddie. I set her up with Matt Evans in exchange for your phone number."

I never thought that I needed validation and I probably didn't, but it sure feels good to know that I was liked and by a guy who was able to have anyone that he wanted. Hell, he was the quarterback.

"Why didn't you call?"

"I did call, but see, I wasn't as brave as you. I remember when you finally answered, I pretended that I had a question about a class assignment. We graduated soon after and you were gone for that summer. I never ran into you at parties or anywhere else."

"That was the summer when I ventured into the West Side looking for me." I went on sharing only the highlights and of course, all about my relationship with Quinn; a long friendship traded off for a short-lived relationship. "So now here I am back in New Canaan."

"I don't know of a man who would save your life only to cheat on you. That doesn't make much sense."

"Well he did; I saw it for myself. He and his ex were behind closed doors playing in water."

"Ouch!!

"Yup, ouch!! I left for New Canaan two months ago and haven't looked back."

"What did he have to say about that?"

"Don't know, and I've learned not to care!" Now I'm lying my ass off.

"You haven't spoken to him?"

"He's phoned, but I haven't returned any of his calls. There really isn't anything that he can say." Jeremy is beginning to kill my buzz with all of this Quinn talk. I'd rather find out what he's been up to.

"What about you? I'm kind of surprised that you're not married." I only know this because Maddie told me he was single during the night while she passed me another glass of wine.

"Not married anymore," he displayed a slight wince suggesting that it may not have been that long ago.

"I'm sorry, Jeremy, I didn't mean to. . ."

"You didn't say anything wrong. I wasn't very good at balancing pro ball and marriage and because of that, I am now working through being responsible for turning a very good person bitter. She didn't deserve that."

"Were you married long?"

"Three years, but Brooke and I were emotionally divorced after only six months of being married. After leaving New Canaan, the move into a fast-paced city became a complete distraction for me and I probably should have exhausted all of the novelties before marrying."

"I'm sorry."

"Nah, all of this is just growing pains."

"Growing pains . . . I guess that's a way to look at it." I take a final sip emptying my glass of wine and beginning to feel a little melancholy. The truth is, I'd really like—no, I *need* to finish this night with intimacy. Besides, why not satisfy a curiosity? I didn't come here with that in mind, and to be honest, I thought that I was over that fantasy long ago, especially after being introduced to love by a Black man. First experiences will always be the barometer, right?

I've just made my mind up; I am going to give myself permission to do something that I've never done before if the night permits. I'm going to sleep with this man! Look at him—he's beautiful. Jeremy's translucent blue eyes began dancing a waltz as he looked at me from head to toe.

"Torie, you are so beautiful."

"Thank you."

"Your skin is flawless and chocolate."

"Chocolate, Jeremy?" We both began laughing at that description.

"No really . . . like a pan of brownies before you cut into them or the smooth side of a Hershey Bar. You're just beautiful."

I sat motionless as he fussed over me gently playing in my hair and lightly touching my full lips before confidently placing his thin rouge lips onto mine. With a slightly warm and mildly moist mouth, he circled around my jaw line and nestled beneath my right ear lobe with arousing warm breaths escaping his mouth and nostrils. I placed my fingers through his hair guiding his face back in my direction where he looked into my eyes.

"I'd be lying if I said that I'm sorry for this, and that I should stop." He's biting on his bottom lip and waiting for my response.

"I don't want you to stop."

I've only slept with three men ever—Hollis, Sinclair and Quinn. Each experience was after a long friendship or relationship, and not one of those has panned out by waiting. So if I want to be with Jeremy tonight, I will without guilt or expectations.

Jeremy freed my hair from its clip after removing my poncho and top. He reached up to grab another blanket from the shelf above to cover me. He'd explained that the folded blankets were there for the hay rides on colder nights. This wasn't the case for the barn as it was fully heated.

He sat up beside me releasing the clasp of my bra and softly guided me onto my stomach as he poured warm eucalyptus infused oil from a bottle he had on the shelf. He massaged it into my entire body, sealing each touch with a kiss.

Jeremy slipped under the blanket beside me. All of a sudden it was as if a baton was firmly pressed against the small of my back all the way down my ass. I held my breath in disbelief and have to admit I was damn near afraid!! So that I wouldn't be caught off guard, I braced myself by placing my hand against his thigh to ensure that I would control the timing of any contact from this point on. The funniest thing about stereotypes is that they often pan out to be untrue, at least on this occasion.

"Jeremy," I said as I immediately began to stiffen my body.

"Relax, I'm not going to hurt you."

"Aahhh," I moaned before pushing him away.

"Are you okay? Don't worry, we'll take our time."

I moaned again grabbing onto his upper arms as he made his second attempt. I'm really thinking that I don't want to do this anymore.

"Do you want me to stop? It's okay—we can stop if you want."

"No, I mean I just . . ."

"Sshhh . . . relax. Just relax." Jeremy whispers in my ear while massaging my body into calmness, not rushing to enter me again.

Jeremy spent the next hour introducing me to different ways of being pleasured while enjoying the intimacy that finally allowed my body to welcome him . . . all of him and with much more ease. He often paused to ask if I was okay and whether he was gentle enough, clearly aware of his surplus. I learned a lot from Jeremy that night— the most important lesson being that intimacy has no color.

THE WHIRLWIND

The churches have moved the scheduled date to vote sooner; it will take place tonight rather than at the end of next month. The vote will determine whether or not they will collectively lead in the financial support of the West Coast Coalition's plan to lend and coach prospective minority businesses in the community. They're struggling with whether or not an untried project is plausible and should they risk utilizing the church's money to fund such a perilous project. Harbor View has rapidly shown startling progress that's already given the neighborhood a new look. This has commanded attention from every naysayer.

I can't believe that it's less than an hour away. I'm deep in my thoughts when Mr. Hicks invited himself into them.

"Hello, Miss Harper! Are you about ready to cast that vote?"

"I'd vote this second and the next if they would allow me to."

Always charged by my enthusiasm, he chuckled and assured me that the coming weeks would pass quickly with all that we need to complete. Within minutes, we were all summoned and ushered into the sanctuary. We were all anxiously seated in the sanctuary of the oldest and largest congregation in Stamford—First Baptist Community Church

"Hi baby, do you think you have enough room for an old lady?"

"Aunt Mabel! You came!" I'm always excited to see her now that I've gotten her back in my life. It makes me feel like Nanna Bess is still here with me. After jumping up and greeting her with a hug and kiss, I slid in allowing her to have the first seat in our row.

"Child, this is the stuff that Bessie and I got up in the mornings for," she smiled and placed her hand over mine while using her hand-kerchief to blot the left eye that continuously allowed a single stream to run down along side of her face.

"How've you been feeling, Aunt Mabel?" I've become more con-cerned with the dimming light within her eyes that have been re-placed with a grayish film similar to cataracts. I'm as uneasy with the short shallow breaths that discharge from her nose and the sudden yet long lingering ones from her mouth.

"I'm fine, child. Oh look, here they come!"

During lengthy commentary from each clergyman, my mind drifted to thoughts of seeing Jeremy after the vote, then curiosity about Quinn and back to concerns for Aunt Mabel. The dizzying thought cycle was abruptly stopped with . . .

"We are pleased to share that the vote has been passed!!" The sanctuary erupted into an old-fashioned Baptist jamboree. When I looked over at Aunt Mabel, she was looking up at heaven smiling giv-ing praises and thanks. I rubbed her back and held her hand like Nanna might have.

After an hour sharing in the celebration, I gathered my things and swiped up Aunt Mabel from her lady friends to ensure that she'd gotten home safely. For my own sanity, I made a pit stop by the diner pretending that I was starving so that I could witness her eat some food for myself. I wasn't satisfied until I'd seen her drink most of her soup and half of her grilled cheese sandwich; she insisted on taking the other half on home for lunch the next day.

When we pulled up to her brownstone adjacent to her restaurant, I went in ahead of her and turned on the lights. I placed the sandwich and additional containers of soup that I'd ordered in her refrigerator.

There were quite a few balls of aluminum foil sporadically placed throughout the fridge, with tiny portions of leftovers that couldn't feed one person. There was half of a chicken wing in one, a third of a burger in another, and still others that I couldn't identify. The date on the milk expired over two weeks ago. I poured the sour milk down the kitchen drain and gathered up all of the pieces of foil and their contents and tossed them into the trash and offered a little white lie.

"Auntie Mae, I think the power in the kitchen was out for a while, so I've tossed out the things in the fridge."

"What did you say? The ice box isn't working?" She began slowly walking around and mumbling aloud wondering what happened to her ice box.

"See, it's working now. I'll just run to the store in the morning and replace the things that you need."

"Oh, alright baby."

Thank goodness Roscoe has been there since he was a teen. Actually, he's been running the kitchen at the restaurant for the past few years. Given he's been there from nearly day one, he was taught all of the recipes and executes them flawlessly. Auntie called herself retired from cooking and focuses only on her baking now . . . that's something she can do with her eyes closed and no measuring. Roscoe makes sure that all of her supplies and ingredients are always fresh and available. He ensures that the business is run as it always has been; after all, he's aware that Aunt Mabel has willed the business to him and his son who helps with the cooking.

"Okay, I think you are all set for the night. Would you like me to prepare a cup of tea before I go?"

"Oh no, I couldn't fit another thing in me."

I open the dresser drawer displaying perfectly folded flannel gowns in an array of pastel colors. The air promptly fills with a distinct whiff of old moth flakes and lavender potpourri sachets. I welcome the familiar scent that reminds me of Nanna's linens. I select a pastel blue night gown trimmed with white satin ribbon.

"How about I turn your bed down? Go on and get changed while I'm doing this, Auntie." You can tell that she was enjoying my company despite her complaints.

"Child, quit fussing over me now. I do all of these things on my own."

"I can fuss over you whenever I want too!" Aunt Mabel clearly likes the attention I'm giving her. I'm beginning to feel a little guilty for not doing these things sooner.

"Uh huh, but I'm still your elder!"

I walked around checking each of the windows to ensure that they were secured before going back into the kitchen to pour a glass of water to place on her nightstand for the night.

"Torie?"

"Yes, I'm right here," she seemed a little confused for a minute.

"I couldn't remember if you had gone already."

"Nope, I'm still here. I wouldn't leave without telling you." I've just felt my heart skip a beat with sadness at my first glimpse of her mind slipping some. I watched her reach for the frame of her bedroom door to assist her slowly turning back in that direction.

"Turn on that television please. It keeps me company overnight." She sat on the side of her bed with her tiny ankles being swallowed by the lamb's wool inside of her pink suede slippers.

I stared as Auntie Mabel unintentionally removed me from her presence, and without notice, she is captured within her own memories. Memories that must resonate as being present to her and have prompted her to tightly clench her jaw while she firmly wrings her hands and ponders her thoughts. Aunt Mae's face has softened within seconds. By the smile on her face, I can tell her thoughts have shifted to pleasant ones. She's smiling and mildly rocking and humming hymns and as she continues to look ahead with a blank stare.

I continued to watch as she struggled to be present, not wanting to surrender and slip away.

"Hmmm, hmmm," she hummed, "Hmmm, hmmm. Torie?" She turned looking for me.

"I'm still here, Auntie Mabel."

"Child, I forgot that fast that you hadn't gone yet! This old mind sometimes I tell you! Are you forgetful at times?"

"Of course, everyone is some time or another."

"Oooh, child . . . please don't get like this."

I can't help but think of Nanna Bess saying that she'd want the good Lord to take her on home if her mind were to go. She'd say that it's your mind that allows you to be an individual, to form your beliefs; beliefs and behaviors that become your character. Without the mind, you're already gone.

"Come on and get under the covers."

"You like telling people what to do, huh?"

"Only the ones I love!!"

"Put my bible and glasses over there on that night table please."

"Is right here good?"

"Yes, thank you."

"Torie?"

"Yes, Auntie Mabel?"

"I love you and thank you for everything, baby."

"I love you more and you are welcome." I let her hold my hand just a little bit longer.

"Okay, I'll use my keys to lockup from the outside." Aunt Dot had the good mind of making a copy of Aunt Mabel's keys when she was home and they were caring for me.

"Okay, baby!" She's already started to rest her eyes and drift like a baby that's been fed and changed.

I'll make some calls first thing in the morning to arrange for someone to come in and help with the chores and inventory in the kitchen. Oh, I probably should have them come in and put hand railings and bars around as well. I grabbed a pen from my purse to make a note as the list had gotten longer and I didn't want to forget not one thing that she needs! Particularly, I didn't want to forget about a monitoring system too.

෴

The last few weeks have been amazing; the time that I've spent with Jeremy has been endless. It almost feels like months have passed, when it has only been a few weeks. Honestly, I don't think that we've spent more than five nights apart since our first the night in the barn. We've either elected to crash at his place, which is absolutely incredible, or The Big House with me. Personally, I prefer staying with him at the mill because I feel extremely uncomfortable having a man in my childhood bed, and I dare not use any of the others! There's a very real feeling of my family still being present in the house; that's a good thing, but not when I'm indulging in certain behaviors. We stay up most nights listening to the stream trickling outside of his window; it's very tranquil like a spa, and after one of Jeremy's soothing massages, it's even better than a spa. Sometimes we can feel the water cascade beneath the floors, given that the master bedroom is on the main level. We find ourselves talking about any and everything with so much ease; I've slipped into a real like for this man.

The Talbots purchased the old town mill and renovated it into their home. For the most part, the exterior view from the east would suggest the possibility of it being a working mill; however, the other views paint a very contemporary picture with windows methodically placed from the floors to the ceiling to allow every room to offer a breathtaking view of the hilly grounds and stable.

Jeremy purchased the home from his parents a couple of years ago when they'd decided to move back to his father's hometown of Warwickshire outside of London. He's already invited me to go and visit with him in the spring. I've actually been riding the horses again. I haven't done that in years, but much like riding a bike, you really don't forget. When I was younger and taking riding lessons, I couldn't imagine there being anything better to do as a grown up, then I realized that I had never seen a Black equestrian. That was just one other thing that was a way of life that I knew and later learned to differ from others. We've gone up to Martha's Vineyard, The Hamptons, and I even accepted his challenge of getting on the slopes at Pound Ridge Ski Resort! Okay, so I got on the bunny slopes, but I did it!!

We've even had Tishie come out to visit and ride the horses. Even though she's beginning to like Jeremy, Quinn will always be the one for her. Funny ... I make creative excuses to Tishie about Quinn just as my mother did about my father's absence.

STRENGTH IN NUMBERS

"Touch Down!!" They shout in tandem in front of the largest flat screen television in Jasper's. Its football season and the Philadelphia Eagles are playing the Washington Redskins for the Monday night game. Of course, this game has turned out a large crowd with all of the quarterback hype. In between plays I hear voices escalating from a table to the far right of the crowd. State Representative Clyde Hicks and a few corporate brothers are discussing the collective responsibility it would take to rehabilitate the forgotten West Side.

"I'm ready to go," I say as I hand Clyde the folders I'd prepared for the business proposals.

Always tickled by my enthusiasm, he chuckles and assures me that the next few weeks will pass quickly with all that we needed to complete. With that in mind, Clyde stands up and reminds the others that are still watching the game, and that it is time to join the rest of the WSC team already seated in the private room known as The Wine Cellar. I have to admit that I was extremely relieved when I heard Clyde's response to a member asking about Quinn. Certainly I didn't want his healing to be delayed, but at the same time, I haven't seen nor spoken to him since that day.

"Quinn won't be back for at least another week or two. That hasn't stopped him from working on the things that we need from his home!!"

We welcomed the community in one by one with proposals or business plans waiting to be reviewed or polished to be passed onto the approval phase. While there were a few that simply didn't have merit, there were many that will soon be on their way.

I was thoroughly pleased to see that Doreen had shown up following our call, and came with a more than viable business proposal— probably one of the best.

The passing of the vote allowed the West Side Coalition to approve individual grants up to a maximum amount of $25,000 for each prospective proprietor. We are anticipating the funds will cover the initial costs of launching approximately 15 to 20 businesses, and down payments and closing costs for 25 first-time homebuyers. As a way of paying it forward, each proprietor has agreed that they will each sponsor two college students throughout their four years. Sponsorships will subsidize and provide for the costs of books, general supplies, bedding, clothing and a modest monthly stipend.

This fall has effortlessly proven that we are having an early New England winter. One snow dusting after another determined not to allow the roads to rid themselves of that slippery morning black ice. I've spent most of my time cleaning The Big House and enjoy feeling like Nanna Bess is right here by my side, adding a shake or two of seasoning to make everything just right as she would have in the past. Today I'm carefully using her favorite pots to cook wholesome Southern cuisine, preparing to impress the hell out of Jeremy who is coming to have dinner and meet Nigel and Simone for the first time tonight. It always came as a surprise to most people that I could throw down in the kitchen. Granddaddy would always say, "Bess, that baby girl done put her foot in that pot!" It had taken me awhile to understand that he was giving me one of the highest compliments. I should have known that it was something sweet from the beginning, because Granddaddy would have eaten quietly and tolerated something not so great rather than insult me or my cooking. After putting on a pot of navy beans and rice, washing, seasoning and frying a skillet of chicken, I decided to retire on the sofa and listen to music from Kem while being engulfed in the soothing aroma of buttery cornbread baking in the oven.

The winds forced the porch screen door to abruptly slam making a frightening ruckus. I jumped up from a sound sleep into a seated position waiting for my blurred vision to reset. Let's not forget that I am not yet easy with being back in this big old house all by myself.

"Sorry, it's just me. My arms are full and the wind was quicker than me. Sorry that I couldn't catch the door before startling you." While I recognize the voice to be Jeremy's shouting from the foyer, it didn't bring instant ease—in fact, it set my ass off.

"It smells great in here!!"

Is he really still talking? I'm in here clutching my chest trying to find solace in the fact that I'm not just waking up from another drive by. Like most Black women, I resent the misplaced stereotypes that suggest that we are combative and angry. However, I'm sure that in this moment, the look on my face easily supports them. Has he lost his fucking mind? Perhaps tonight I've left him to wonder if there was some validity to those stereotypes!

"Everything okay?"

Jeremy was sincerely concerned about me, but in that moment, all I could muster was a snarl. Jeremy stood frozen in place, likely not sure what would be an acceptable next step for him. With bottles of wine under his arm and logs for the fireplace cradled in the other, he rephrased his question.

"Are you okay?"

This moment has made me realize that I am not okay; I might have benefitted from going through therapy. I realize that I'm probably not alright and would have benefited greatly by going through therapy

"Yes, yes—I'm okay. It's just this thing that I kind of have about loud unexpected noises lately." My words trigger Jeremy's memory; he's obviously recalling what I shared with him about the Pavilion.

"The shooting!" Jeremy hurries to free his arms from the wine and logs to come and comfort me. "Torie, I'm so sorry! I didn't mean to frighten you and I don't want you to ever be afraid."

"It's okay. You didn't do anything wrong—I must have dozed off. Jeremy, it was just bad timing. Really, I'm fine now!!" He embraces me as long as I needed to be or until I was able to convince him that I was fine.

Once the fire was built and jazz was playing, we decided to take advantage of the romantic setting and use it for a bit of intimacy. This girl has to admit that she had an unexpected passionate quickie right there in front of the fireplace. Fortunately for us, Simone is never on time and even if she was, the extremely long gravel-lined driveway allows no one's arrival to go unnoticed . . . provided, of course that you haven't fallen asleep with music playing loudly.

If I do say so myself, dinner was really good. The fact that both Nigel and Jeremy requested seconds was an indicator as well. Okay, the fact that Simone isn't a cook only leaves takeout as a barometer for my dinner. I have to admit that I was a little concerned with how Nigel would accept Jeremy with Quinn being his boy and all. It was nice to see how well he and Nigel did hit it off, but then again, Jeremy is an extremely authentic kind of guy.

Simone promised me a phone call to inquire about the more intimate details of me being with Jeremy. She said that she would have to live vicariously through me given that she had never experienced being with a White man, nor would she given her upcoming nuptials. But that didn't stop her from confessing that she was curious after seeing the two of us together, given that she'd never date anyone other than a Black man.

"Girl, I want all of the details, ALL of them!"

"Shhh, Sim—he'll hear you," both giggling like in their younger years.

"Oh no, grasshopper, cause you doing something that I have never done and I want to know all about it."

"Sim, you're so crazy!" Now catching up with the guys at the door I give her a peck and say, "talk to you tomorrow." I then lean forward and kiss Nigel goodnight; he in turn lightly pats my back and slightly nods his head to offer his acceptance of Jeremy.

"Jeremy, man, it was nice meeting you."

"Yeah, likewise man, even if you are a Pat's fan." Jeremy grips Nigel's hand while laughing. Under any other circumstances, this would have been the beginning of another cool friendship, much like Brody and Quinn's. It seems that I was nervous for no reason—Nigel and Jeremy really hit it off well.

♘

It's been two weeks and even these bitter winds haven't deterred those who are serious about having the opportunity to own their own businesses from coming back.

"How are you tonight?" I ask as I pass through the hallway.

"Really cold out there tonight!"

Is that Mrs. Walker's lemon pound cake? I was grabbing a cup of tea and now deterring my entrance into the gymnasium to find that cake. Just as I was approaching the table, Mrs. Walker called out proudly raising a brown paper bag in the air. "Hi, baby! I packed you something to take home with you . . . it's your own cake! That's the least any of us can do for you."

"Thank you, Mrs. Walker. I appreciate that."

"We appreciate you, child."

Each table hosts a suitor with a proposal in hand and dream in their heart pitching it to a West Coast Coalition member striving to make it come true. The chatter amongst the many present in the community center's gym is spilling over into the corridors where just as many are waiting for their chance at a new life. They are waiting patiently and respectfully as they indulge in the free baked goods and soft drinks that the church members have organized another indication of our coming all together for a new community.

LE CHÂTEAU

What is it with me and time? Give me two hours and I will always need two and a half; this is for everything except work. If I'm meeting someone for lunch, I'm late. If we're going to the movies, we'll miss the previews. If it's a party, I'm the last to arrive. I am determined not to have those issues tonight. I convince myself that I will be dressed and ready when Jeremy arrives. I'm already off to a bad start as I'm crawling around under my bed looking for the missing mate to my Anne Klein pumps. I'm becoming completely frustrated and perplexed as to how the damn shoe had gotten under there and so out of reach. A flush comes over my face along with a vivid memory of a night with Jeremy that sent the lone stiletto airborne.

I'm not ashamed to admit that I like to talk to my clothes—I always have. I start in the closet and keep going as I make a selection and display it across my bed, fully accessorized of course. The conversation concludes when I am wearing my outfit and giving myself out one final check in the mirror.

I continued making my final choices while the bathtub was filling. Hanging earrings or pearls? I debate the choice standing there in my bra and panties while looking into a huge mirror propped against the wall.

Hair up or down? I placed a clip or two in my hair to see what I was working with when I heard a car headed up the driveway. I look at the time couldn't imagine Jeremy arriving an hour earlier than planned. Who could this be? Whoever it is they have the worst timing. I check my watch again realizing that I have less than an hour to bathe and to dress. I can see the driveway from my mother's old room, so I head in there to grab a look. One thing—and probably the only thing—that I don't care for about the fall is the early darkness, which makes it very difficult to see once the sun sets.

A set of headlights is making their way down the driveway—a set of Range Rover headlights. Shit, shit, shit! I began ripping every clip from my hair and use my fingers to make any improvements. Quinn!! What is he doing here? Within 60 seconds, I became fully engaged in a conversation with myself.

He should have called before coming here. Call . . . let's be honest, that's all this man has done for the past two months, even with me not returning one of them. I look a mess!! I grab whatever's within reach and throw it on.

Quinn's persistent knocks follow the sound of his reluctant footsteps as he walked across the porch. I cowardly hold my breath as I contemplate taking a peek from the window during the long lull between knocks. This is so crazy, how did he and I end up here? Just as I dared to steal a peek, my cell phone begins to flop and vibrate across the sofa table illuminating the entire room with hues of blue. Given the ring tone, it was Simone and her usual poor timing. I instantly gasp aloud while falling forward swiftly brushing the curtain causing Quinn to turn back towards the door that he was walking away from. Left with no other choice, I abruptly open the front door completely agitated.

"Quinn? What are you doing here?"

Angrier than I'd realized, I stood with hurt-filled eyes staring him down like daggers. My mind and heart became flooded with foreign emotions of hate, sadness, and a whole lot of longing.

"Were you standing there just watching me the whole time?" he said in a softly defeated tone with combined looks of frustration and weariness, but certainly not a match for his tenacity.

"Yeah, I was, Quinn!! Why did you come here?" I was immediately chastised by my own conscience.

Quinn leaned against a porch column facing me directly. He was oddly dressed for a Saturday in a charcoal suit with a blue dress shirt unfastened at the neck where his tie hung loosely. He had one hand resting in the pocket of his pants exposing his Movado wristwatch; the other hand massages his jaw as he raises his eyes to the porch ceiling, carefully choosing his next words. Insisting on a face-to-face conversation, he walks toward me. It's then that I notice he is no longer walking with a limp. Damn! He looks and smells so good.

"Torie, even a brother has the right to know what he's being charged with. Just tell me what I've done."

"I was at your place Quinn. I let myself in and Jasmine was coming out of the bathroom and . . . I heard you!! I heard you call out for her to come back!"

I turned to walk back into the house when he grabbed me by the arm. "Wait!" I looked at him and his hand on my arm giving me an instant flashback to Hollis. Quinn intuitively released my arm. "Please talk to me, Torie!!" I folded my arms and listened. "I'm not gonna tell you that that didn't happen," I turned to walk away again. "Wait!! Listen, I can tell you that what you think happened actually didn't."

"Did you sleep with her, Quinn?"

"I wouldn't do that, Torie. Besides, why would I give you a key if I had something to hide?"

I'm beginning to feel confused and foolish all at once.

"I didn't even know that you came by until a day or two later. You and I were still finding our way before the shooting. You put us on pause after that night, a very special night . . . but I was giving you that space because you asked for it."

He's absolutely right. But still if he was really into me, why would he have moved on so quickly? I don't know what to think. Quinn has never been a player or a liar; the only thing anyone can charge him with is being a brother trying to make a way.

"Look, the nurse cancelled a couple of times. Jasmine happened to be there one day and offered to prepare my lunch and help with my shower. I wasn't feeling it, but after she pointed out the obvious—that we were adults, she has already seen me naked, and that I needed help. . . I accepted. She was never in the shower or naked; she threw something on top of her head so that she didn't mess her hair up and then helped me get onto the bench in the shower to sit."

My mind races and I think to myself—oh my God—what if he's telling the truth?

"I know things got really crazy after the Pavilion; I had my own struggles and bout with my manhood. Torie, I would lay my life down for you. I love you."

He just said that he loves me—now he tells me! My head is swarming with all kinds of thoughts.

"Quinn, I don't know what to say . . ."

"Tell me that we're gonna stop all this craziness, right here, right now."

"Quinn . . ." I went to speak but was interrupted by a pair of car lights turning in to the beginning of the driveway. Oh my God, it's Jeremy.

"Torie, do you love me?"

My response was abruptly thwarted by the fast-approaching headlights. Quinn stepped away from me and turned to see Jeremy exiting his BMW looking like he'd just arrived home. Jeremy confidently approached the porch and extended his hand as the two stood side by side looking like the cover of a collector's issue of *GQ*.

"I'm Jeremy. How you doing, buddy?"

"Quinn. Alright, man."

"Look um, I'm a little early, so why don't I give you some time and come back."

"Jeremy, no, it'll only take me a. . ." I said when Quinn interrupted.

"Listen, let me get on out of here and let you two get on with your plans."

"Torie, it was good catching up with you." Quinn softly kissed me on the cheek before extending his hand to Jeremy. "Good to meet you, man." Quinn headed down the steps never making eye contact with me once.

The rear lights diminish as he becomes further and further away. I can feel my heart breaking. My mind is replaying everything Quinn said to me. I somehow manage to suppress my tears as I negotiate a getaway upstairs to shower and dress. Jeremy stays downstairs after becoming occupied with tinkering with one of the door hinges that has come loose.

As the doors to Le Château open, we are immediately swept into the beauty and warmth of this remarkable place. We are greeted by a welcoming melody floating out of the piano and into our waiting ears. The angst that cluttered my mind throughout our ride coming here has quickly surrendered me to the breathtaking ambiance. You can't escape the seductive scent of harvest in the air; the entranceway mesmerizes you with its distinct scent of cloves, cinnamon and apples.

It's been a while since I've been here; there was a time when I came more often for weddings, showers or simply dinner. No matter what the purpose is, each time here is just as captivating as the first. The venue is undeniably known for offering and executing the best French cuisine in the Northeast.

"Thank you," I offered as Jeremy removed my coat and mink scarf to check it.

"You look amazing, Torie."

"Oh, Jeremy!"

All at once I heard a singing. Just as I turn to pass, I realize that the voice belonged to none other than local legend Harry Thompson. It seems that he and his family have come up Route 123 for dinner tonight as well. A lot of us locals frequent Le Château, but clearly this is a random, but greatly appreciated performance. We stopped along with others on our way up the stairs to the Salem Room to take in Harry's emotional rendition of *The Way You Look Tonight*. That song gets me every time.

"Wow!!"

Jeremy turned to me and asked, "You like his music?" He sounded rather surprised.

"Oh yes! I like him."

"He seems like a pretty cool guy."

"Yeah, I think he's great. He's always appeared to be a genuinely humble and sincere person. Yeah, I like him a lot."

"Have you run into him in town yet?"

"No." I'm thinking that I could stand here all night listening to him, but he deserves time with his family and a good meal too.

As I turned to watch the other onlookers, I see Eric entering through the doors of the restaurant. I watched him greet an older gentleman from afar as I stood glaring with curiosity from the stairs of Le Château. He extended his right hand as he used the left to secure the canister containing the schedules I'd just given to him yesterday.

I quickly turn to face Jeremy in hopes of shielding my face from Eric. As we wait to be seated, they passed and entered the Reverend Rainsford Room. Does he really think that I'm THAT girl? Well then, he's lost his mind! He's a liar and a traitor at a minimum, as I recalled our discussion yesterday.

"Torie, it's Eric. Listen, Peterson had to cancel our meeting and it's not looking so good for a future pick up either. We can mark him as a nonviable investor."

"Really, I was so sure that we were closing, I was hanging around in case you needed a new computation."

"Yeah well, no worries; there will be others coming down the pike. Why don't you do something for yourself? It's not often we get an early night . . . run while you can."

"Okay I will, but that's really too bad."

"Torie?" Eric called out before hanging up the phone.

"Yes?"

"I'll just go ahead and shred the documents in the tube rather than run them back over to you."

I accepted his word to be true and went on with my day, and now he's here in Le Château with those same documents.

☙

"Tor," I felt Jeremy lightly nudge me after I'd obviously drifted into deep thought. "What would you like to drink?"

"I'll have whatever Maddie is having."

"French Martini," Maddie offered.

"A French Martini, thank you." I quickly replied trying to ward off the distraction and remember that I'm here with great company for the evening. Anyway, I owe that to Jeremy after his earlier encounter with Quinn. I should probably stop looking around and stay put, because I would imagine that it will be rather difficult for me to blend in this crowd in hopes of being inconspicuous.

Jeremy asked what we each of had decided for our dinner entrees.

"I think I'll have the sautéed striped bass with the apple ginger curry sauce. That sounds delicious."

"I'm going to have the same," Maddie offered.

Jeremy placed his hand onto my lap and periodically rubbed the top of my thigh innocently, like someone would rub a kitty. After dinner and a few drinks later, my curiosity could no longer be contained. So while waiting for dessert, I excused myself to use the ladies room to see if I was able to catch a glimpse of Eric and his guest.

"Wait for me, Torie. I certainly can use a trip there as well," I heard from across the table from the mouth of Sara, who until this point has said very little.

"Sure, come on." I smiled and pretended that I welcomed the company when inside I was thinking . . . can't you kept women even pee on your own?

"Wait, I'm coming too!!" a tipsy Maddie shouted.

"Come on, let's all go to the powder room!" Internally I'm afraid that Maddie will shout my name and draw attention to me as we passed the Reverend Rainsford Room. To my surprise, she's barely said a word.

Maddie begins to refresh her makeup while this Sara was determined to floss. I use this as an opportunity to escape.

"Hey listen, why don't I meet you two back at the table? I believe that I saw an old work colleague."

"Oh yeah, that's fine sweetie!!" Maddie half-heartedly replies as she's having a little trouble lining her lips with the pencil. I raised her hand closer to her mouth and winked. She giggled before leaning in to tell me, "I am SO buzzed." To that I reply, "Nah!" Maddie's little secret is out, she's a lush!! But you gotta love her.

I could see Eric's image captured in the hall mirror, and more importantly, I could hear his entire conversation given that they were seated at the first table entering the room. Eric explained to the gentleman that he had established him as an alias investor using the computations in the canister and that all was well. The gentleman handed Eric an envelope and assured him that there would be more to come.

"Well now that we have that out of the way, let's have some of those desserts you spoke of," Eric requested.

"I would suggest the crème brûlée or the chocolate dulce de leche flan; they are both quite nice."

"Decisions, decisions! It seems that some things are much more obvious than others!" The two laughed at the comparison of the ease in partnering over the simple choice of a dessert.

"I agree," the gentleman offered with an accent that still remained unidentifiable for me.

"Sometimes, we just have to take our chances. I'll have the chocolate flan."

"Great choice," he responds placing an unlit cigar to his mouth.

"Here you are!! Did you find your friend?" Maddie shouts and scares the shit out of me while causing Eric to look back over his shoulder.

"Yes, but we should get back to our guys," whispering as I ducked behind Sara's larger frame.

Dinner was fabulous and we sat around sipping a glass of port in front of the fire. We enjoyed the unidentified pianist who earlier graciously shared his engagement with Harry. We laughed and reminisced about the days before we all had left for college. Honestly, I'm not sure if the stories were actually funny or that it was the intoxication that made us believe them to be. Jeremy is becoming extremely touchy and starting to feel the aphrodisiacal effects of his escargot and brandy; notice that I said *his* escargot because this girl doesn't eat any of that mess. No caviar, no frog legs, no escargot!

"Why don't we get out of here?"

"Why don't we?" It's the response that my mouth is giving him, but my heart isn't in agreement at all after seeing Quinn. Why did he have to come to my house and dismantle me? I was getting over Quinn Matthews!! All of a sudden, Jeremy isn't all that appealing and I hate his laugh—it seems so inauthentic.

Jeremy walks towards me with my coat in his hand opened waiting for me to climb in. He's blushing and gawking at me but not saying a word as though he and I are the only two in this foyer in this very moment.

"Whattt?" I ask bashfully and dragging it out like Maddie would. I feel slightly embarrassed as others walk by—emphasis on the slightly!

"You're beautiful, amazingly beautiful," Jeremy says as he wraps the scarf around me and placing a sweet kiss on the side of my neck.

Okay, so now I'm just crazy!! That's it! I'm crazy—and capable of being a ho! There isn't one inch of this man that is unappealing. And his laugh is the most genuine masculine laugh a man could have. My panties have been moistened twice in less than three hours by two different men. Yup, I'm a quietly kept ho!

I am completely confused and under attack from my thoughts. There was this thing that Nanna Bess would say and I never really understood what she meant, but I'm sure that in this situation it's fitting. So I say, "Oh Satan, you are a liar!!"

"Did you say something, Torie?" Jeremy asked as we walked towards the car.

"Umm, I said that I thought you had a flat tire . . . but it looks fine," he looked down at the tire while holding the door as I climbed in, then handed me the fancy carton with Le Château imprinted across it securing the dessert that I ordered to go. I was stealing a peek of Jeremy as he walked around to get into the driver's seat of the car when I captured a quick glimpse of the gentleman I'd encountered with Barrett retrieving his car from another valet attendant in the rear of us. Jeremy obstructed my view when he stopped for only a second to wipe something from the rear of the car. It was too late—he was gone. Maybe he really wasn't there; maybe I should leave port alone.

Monday morning couldn't have arrived fast enough for me. Unlike most Mondays, today I am up and showered already. There isn't any dragging or negotiating with the alarm clock to shut up. No, not today because I have someone that I must go and see. I reached into the closet and grabbed my Tahari black pant suit, a cream blouse accentuated with a single pearl pendant with a flattering pair of earrings.

"Good morning, Torie!"

"Good morning," I blurt out to each colleague as I catch the elevator to the wing of the Legal Team's department until I reach Eric's happy-go-lucky ass sitting behind the desk in his office.

Knock, knock!

"Come on in, Torie. How are you?"

"I'm great, and you?"

"I couldn't be better."

"Well, that's more than anyone can ask for. Listen Eric, I don't want to take up too much of your time, so I was wondering if I could grab that canister back from you."

I watched Eric's smile diminish acutely.

"Canister?"

"Yes, the schedules were inside of a canister . . . I know that you said that you would shred the documents, but we have so few of those canisters left in our department at the moment, and of course they're on back order at Staples."

"Oh *that* canister. You know I haven't seen it. It was on my desk when I left on Friday; these cleaning people are really getting out of control with taking things."

"No worries, I'm just trying to be a little green."

"So did you do anything special this weekend? I only ask because you were so thoughtful with encouraging me to do something for myself."

"No, as luck would have it my little guy came down with something and I never got to leave the house at all Saturday."

"That's terrible! I hope he's feeling better."

"Oh yeah, just a 24-hour thing."

"What about you? Did you do something special?"

"Who, me? Oh yes! I had the most amazing dinner at this place called Le Château in South Salem. Have you been?"

"Me? No, I haven't gotten there yet."

"Oh, then you've got to try it sometime."

I watched all of the color drain from Eric's face before turning towards the door to leave. "Ooops—I hear Millie! Let me go and snatch her up for our morning coffee." Looking back at Eric's face now, he has the look of relief, replacing the paleness in his cheeks that he had just moments ago. That's exactly when I decided to backtrack and let him know that I'm clearly not that girl to be played with. It's bad enough that he was willing to throw Quinn underneath the bus, but now you want to play with my livelihood! Oh, I don't think so!!

Knock, knock! "Hi, me again," I announced as I stuck my head back into his office completely catching his ass off guard. "Millie is on a call, but I was just thinking," as I reached into my bag and pulled out the elegantly packaged carton from Le Château. You MUST try this dessert; this alone will encourage you to try the restaurant." Eric's eyes nearly popped off of his face leaving him speechless.

"For me, it's always difficult to choose between two of their classics—crème brûlée and what is it called again? Oh yes, the chocolate dulce de leche flan. Anyway, you would think that someone like me could easily make a simple decision!" I stared at Eric as his face displayed multiple shades of red not knowing how to respond.

"Anyway, I've decided that you must have my crème brûlée, this way on the off chance that you don't ever make it to Le Château, you will at least have had their signature desserts. I'm sorry; I meant to say dessert, because saying desserts would suggest that you've had a dessert from there before . . . but it would have had to been a different one like the chocolate to make it plural, right?" I've left him speechless.

"How did you let me get on that tangent?" I placed the package on his desk as he remained speechless knowing that I know. More importantly, he now knows that I'm not that girl!!

Knock!! Knock!!

"Eric, is Torie in? There you are." Millie inquired while pushing the door further open and barreling in.

"Yup, here I am! Are you all set to get our coffee?" I smirked all the way out of his door.

"Yes, sorry for the wait. Oh good morning Eric," she says waving while exiting his office I can't recall him responding to that either.

As soon as we entered the empty elevator, I filled Millie in on everything, even my uncertainty in seeing that mystery gentleman.

"Oh my God, Torie!! You should have told me what was going on."

"What did Eric say?"

"The exact same thing he said when you said 'good morning' . . . nothing! He said nothing."

THE LAST NIGHT AT THE STABLES

The last three months have been incredible. Our weekend getaways have been breathtaking and emotionally cleansing; time that has allowed me to find a way forward. Extremely self-edifying but nowhere as fulfilling as my work and time spent at the community center.

Jeremy noticed that I was becoming more and more distant over the past couple of days. I think that's why he threw this little get-together. Our guests went on laughing about things that no longer seemed as funny to me. The conversations are irrelevant to my life's intent. I thought that I'd slip out quietly to the porch from the very loud room when the last of Jeremy's guests arrive. As I turn to greet them, I'm face-to-face with Brody's obnoxious ass—and he isn't with Jamie.

"Brody, what are you doing here?"

"I was invited. What are you doing here?"

"How do you know Jeremy?" I nervously ask.

"How do *you* know Jeremy?" Brody replies sarcastically. Before I can offer a reply, Jeremy chimes in.

"So . . . you and Torie already know each other? Small world! And you thought that you wouldn't know anyone here tonight."

After being introduced to "whatever her name was," Jeremy takes their coats as I offer them drinks. Brody follows me into the kitchen to help, and I'm sure to give me a hard time.

Once secured in the kitchen I asked again, "How do you know Jeremy?"

"And I'll ask you again, Torie, how do you know Jeremy?"

"Really, Brody?" I whisper through my clenched teeth. "I'm serious."

"Okay . . . Jeremy and I have played softball down at the beach together off and on for years. Now it's your turn."

"Well, who is she?" I ask ignoring his question.

"You don't get to stand here and judge me. Come on Tor, you really want to stand here in judgment of me?" He shakes his head in disgust. "Clean up your own crap before stepping in mine, okay?"

I didn't see that coming and I had no response.

"Quinn didn't deserve that bullshit."

"And Jamie did? Besides, you don't know what you're talking about!"

"I know that you're a bitch."

"And you're a freak'n porch-dick!" Someone should have told Brody that a Black woman does not take kindly to being called a bitch.

Jeremy walks into the room and we abruptly become silent. With a perplexed look he asks, "Everything okay?"

"Yep! Brody was just helping me eliminate some trash."

"Thanks, man!" With that, he turned and went to find his newest flavor of the month.

Jeremy looked at me and asked, "Torie, are you sure you're okay?"

"Yeah, why do you ask?"

Jeremy began rubbing his chin while walking towards me, then resting his elbows onto the railing beside me looking out over the night hills uncomfortably sensing something. With a long conceding sigh, he pulls me into his chest placing his hand beneath my hair, gently massaging the small of my neck. I wrapped my arms around his body and buried my face into his sweater just a little below his neck determined not to show that I was crying, but it was too late. Even with my silent sobs, Jeremy was aware and placed multiple soothing kisses on the top of my head, allowing me the moment that I needed before raising my face from his tear-dampened sweater. He used his thumbs to softly wipe the remaining tears from my face.

"Stay here for a second."

I then heard Jeremy through the partially opened doors asking if our friends wouldn't mind calling it a night. Of course, they obliged without hesitation.

"Is everything okay?" one of our guests asked.

"Yeah, she's just feeling a little under the weather."

"Tell Torie that we hope she feels better," another offered.

"I will do that."

"Goodnight, Jeremy!" I heard as the last couple was leaving.

I'm even more frustrated with myself for not being able to mask this internal battle and compromising Jeremy's night with friends. I was just fine until Quinn's visit the other day.

"You didn't have to do that. I'm so sorry, Jeremy."

"I wanted to," he replies now standing directly behind me, wrapping his arms around my body to shield me from the cold air. We both quietly stared at the indigo night sky accentuating the amazing view.

"I didn't mean to ruin your night. I'm sorry for . . ."

Shaking his head from left to right Jeremy whispers, "Shhhhh . . . don't."

Jeremy leaned down resting his cheek against mine and softly said, "It's okay, Torie. I already know."

How could he know what I've been thinking? Before I can gather the words to respond, he goes on.

"I saw it in your face when he came by the house last week."

"Jeremy, I. . ."

I tried to continue, but the words wouldn't come. Once my body language had shown me surrendering to having this discussion, he softly kissed the back of my head and placed each of his fingers in between mine wrapping our adjoined hands and intertwined arms around us tightly. More importantly I saw it in his face.

"The only reason I know that look is because it's the same look that I had when I first saw Brooke moving on after all of my boyish shenanigans. For me, it was already too late. I don't think that it's too late for you and Quinn."

"What are you saying?"

"That man loves you."

"But I'm falling in love with you," placing my opened hand against his face.

Jeremy closed his eyes and began running both of his hands through his hair before responding. "I believe that you are beginning to really *like* me Torie . . . and maybe you're even on the path to falling in love . . . but you are already in love with him."

"Oh Jeremy, it's so much bigger than that. I *am* falling in love with you . . . but what I have fallen in love with is my new-found life; a life that offers me a purpose and visibly sees me. New Canaan has always been good to me giving me an unshakable foundation—the best head start in life that anyone could hope for. It's treated me like a well-accommodated guest and there's the problem—one should not feel like a guest after a lifetime, but rather a family member. And that is what I've found in this new life—a complete since of purpose and belonging for the first time."

"Did I ever make you feel like a guest?"

"No, no, never!!" I say while kissing him and wrapping my arms around his neck. How do I make him understand that he's perfect and I am afraid to give him up? I don't want to give him up. I don't know if I could come back as who I am now and continue to live this life indefinitely.

"Jeremy, if I'd never left New Canaan, I would have never known there to be a void, but now, knowing this—I can't ignore my spirit's hunger to be culturally fed. I must be absolutely crazy to even consider walking away from this . . . from you . . . from us."

"Nope, you are absolutely amazing for finding yourself and staying true to it. Look, if you don't go, I will always wake up in the middle of the night wondering if you and Lainie have gone off on a night adventure. I can see it now—you riding bare back over the night hills to the next community in need; Lainie tied to a parking meter in front of the nearest brownstone. What kind of life is that for any horse? He turns me around toward the hills wrapping one hand around my waist and the other pointing out at the star-lit hills. There she is at the peak of the hills looking back but unable to stop."

"Aahhh, Jeremy!!" I'm rubbing his hand and nestling my head into his neck as he rests his chin on the top of my head still leaning over me as I giggle in between sniffles.

"You just let Quinn know for me that a Hail Mary pass comes by once, and if he ever drops the ball again, I'm taking it and running straight into the end zone. Tell him that there will be no reviews or instant replays and that score will never come off of that board!!"

"I didn't mean for this to happen."

"For now, Torie, I've got to let you go and be that free agent. I can only hope that one day, you will be back to stay."

We stayed quiet for a while simply enjoying where we are now, at this time and in this moment. We decided that we would take anything beyond this night one day at a time until we've exhausted possibilities for us.

So we did. Jeremy and I stayed true to our future dealing with it one day at a time. Sadly, our availability began to dwindle along with the possibilities of us salvaging us.

Am I crazy? How did I walk away from a man who took an emotional bullet to spare me harm and terminal pain? It's like déjà vu with Quinn taking a physical bullet for me. Emotional or physical, they both have the capability of doing permanent damage.

But then I stop and think . . . there's a man out there who drinks from the same crazy fountain that I do, flooded with the hopes and dreams of making a difference in a community that needs a little help with coordinating resources that they've been unable to see. Someone who has the same spirituality trickling through their being that wakes them as it does me each day. He too celebrates the nuances of a culture that isn't easily duplicated—and yes—he just happens to be Black.

A CONVERSATION WITH THE MAN

My head is all messed up! This whole Torie thing has me trippin'! Come on now, who's ringing my damn phone?

"What up, man? You comin' out? Tank asks.

"Nah man, I just got my head into a lot of things right now." I put that out there in hopes of Tank releasing me from this call instead of tormenting me with how he's found yet another woman who is supposed to be the one.

I'm walking around this joint barely listening to what Tank is saying on the other end of this phone.

"Yeah man, right, right," I'm not even sure what I'm agreeing with. I haven't been working at full capacity since seeing Torie.

"What's up with that Harlem thing? We're still doing the bachelor party thing, right?"

"Yeah, but you do know that I've never been that crazy about Harlem." I drift off again only registering parts of what Tank's saying.

"Man, I feel you on that; nobody knows how things will end up going down." Tank replies.

On the real, I haven't been able to focus on much of anything since that impromptu field trip to New Canaan. I'd never considered the possibility of Torie moving on. Damn, I just didn't see that coming until he came down her driveway. How could I dispute that; it was right in front of me? I have to be honest, seeing Torie with someone was painful; seeing her with a White man was jolting. Other brothers would say that I should have seen that coming with a sister like Torie. I beg to differ. I'm not that brother that believes that as a Black man I have the monopoly over Black women. Regardless of how many women brothers date outside of our race, most of my boys nearly lose their minds when they see a sister with a White man—it's damn near blasphemy! Oh, and I enjoy calling each of them cats out on their hypocrisies!!

"Quinn!! Did you hear what I said, man?"

"I hear you." Tank's clearly waiting for my response—to what I'm unsure—so I throw anything out there.

"You right, look let me get back with you a little later," I petition as I'm becoming agitated.

"Alright man, just let me know what you want to do."

"I'm on it!! Peace, man." I hang up the phone and resume my thoughts of Torie.

I resume pondering my thoughts for my own clarity and I came up with this, the bottom line is that I respect anyone doing his or her thing. Personally, I have an unfaltering love for a sister. She carries an inherent strength that dances with my spirit and fulfills my needs. I find it to be brave, tenacious, unrelenting, and sexy at times.

I decided to do something today that both my mother and father taught me, pray.

"Lord, it's me Q. I know . . . it's been a minute or so since I've called out to you. But I know that you've always been present, it's just that I've been so blessed, I figured there are others that might need your attention more."

I look up at the ceiling, not sure if I'm doing this right, but I'm doing it. My father would often say when I was frustrated, "Son, just ask the Lord to help you," and I would brush him off with, "Yeah, alright Pop. I'll do that." Well here I am.

"So Lord, I need your help! I know that I've found the woman that I want to spend the rest of my life with, but someone else has found her too. I'm asking you to show me how to get my girl back!! Between me and you, if—nah—when I get her back, I'm playing for keeps. I'm gonna ask her to marry me." I found myself standing in the middle of my living room smiling and looking up at the ceiling with both of my cheeks moist with tears.

"I promise that I will cherish and respect her forever. I will love her the way that she deserves to be loved. Lord, I will lay down my life for her if ever necessary, please just get her back to me. Remember now, this is between me and you. Amen." Just while I was sitting there trying to get my thoughts together, I looked up at the clock and realized I promised to meet my boy Brody at Jasper's in an hour. Brody's the coolest White guy I've ever known. That cat has never seen color, even when we were shooting hoops out on the playground.

A SATURDAY OF ESPIONAGE

"**D**on't turn on that light!!" I caution Millie as we open the door to Eric's office.

"How are we supposed to see, Torie? Eric isn't returning until Monday. He's out of town on a business trip until then. That's why I called for you to come and meet me here."

"Mil, what if someone comes by?"

"Relax! It's Saturday and unlike you and your department, we rarely ever come in on the weekends."

Millie flipped the light switch on and began looking through some of Eric's obvious files in the cabinet closest to the door.

We rifled through one file drawer after the next but finding very little to corroborate our suspicions. After a while I'd forgotten that we were doing anything wrong and started instructing Millie.

"Look over there."

"In the closet?" she asked.

"Mil, I don't know—just look. How about beneath his desk blotter, people always hide things there."

"Oh, ewwww!!" Millie cries as she flips over a picture of Eric engaged with two nude women. Another photo shows just his genitals.

"Is that really him? Oh, I knew that he was a pig."

"Sshhh!!"

"I know that you didn't just shush me."

"Seriously, Torie, someone's coming."

"What?" Millie places her finger to her mouth and gestures for me to stand still. Oh my God, my heart is beating so loudly that I can hear the beats echo inside each of my ears, and now my temples are pulsating in unison.

"Someone is coming! The corridor lights just came on!"

"I thought you said that no one was here today—it's a Saturday."

"They're not supposed to be here," she grits her teeth and enlarges her eyes. "Close the drawer and come on, Torie."

"Damn it, Mil!!"

"Just come on!!" She adjusts her clothing and brushes her pant legs straight then places her hair behind both ears followed with a deep sigh.

We quickly go into her office and stand over her desk pretending to be deeply engrossed in what we're looking at, some magazine that she handed to me. We both wait as the footsteps became near.

"Oh hey, Millie! I didn't know you were working this weekend."

Of all people, Lauren is walking in on our espionage tactics. As usual, she didn't acknowledge my presence. Seconds later we both are challenged with our presence after she noticed the door of Eric's office slightly ajar and a stream of light beaming through the opening.

"What were you two doing? Why are you here?"

Millie begins to panic after Lauren demands an explanation and threatens to phone security.

"Wait a minute, Lauren. I'm an attorney in this department as well. I have the right to be here." Millie defends.

"Yes, but not in THAT office," pointing to Eric's open door.

"Lauren, wait!!" I call her back into Millie's office. "Okay, the truth is that we were looking for something. I've received a tip from a very credible source that someone is on the take in your department."

"If that was true, why would someone inform you?"

Millie chimes in, "Like she's only the Chief Financial Officer."

"Well, who is this tipster, and how do you know that she or he is on the up and up?"

"Because I've met her; she's given me evidence."

"Oh, this is ridiculous!!"

"Show her, Torie!!" I'm sure Millie is feeling much like me in this moment, feeling like we haven't anything to lose. So I reach down into the messenger bag that I'd placed on Millie's desk when I'd first arrived.

"What are these?" Lauren asks as she flipped through the pile of invoices I'd handed to her.

"We believe them to be the link to finding the culprit and their intentions." I go on and share our suspicions and my initial meeting with Barrett Johns, as well as sharing the random appearances of the odd gentleman who has shown up on more than one occasion. I also persuaded her to consider that she will likely be linked in the conspiracy being that she is Eric's right-hand girl.

"Oh, hell no! I've worked too long and too hard like a Hebrew to lose my career over someone else's bullshit! Sorry, Millie!!"

"Don't be sorry! My people haven't been Hebrews since being lost. I'm a Jew!"

For the first time, Lauren and I share in laughter at Millie's known desire to shock with her off-color remarks. Shortly after the brief lull, we were back to being serious.

"Just tell me what you are looking for, maybe I can help," Lauren led the way walking in the direction of Eric's office.

After being unsuccessful finding anything, we've come across Eric's locked drawers. Lauren recalled having master keys that she was given after the installation of the department's new cabinetry. With no one else having time or interest, she was the contact person for the project in the office manager's absence.

"Hang on—I'll run down to my office and get the keys."

There are so many keys, each with tiny numbers that coincide with a suitable cabinet. We each grab a pile of keys and began looking for the one with #660 written across it.

"How many keys are there, Lauren?" Millie asked with frustration.

"How many cabinets do you see around the department, Millie?" replying equally frustrated.

"I've got it . . . #660!!" I raise the single key in the air and we all jump to our feet and lean by the sides of Eric's desk.

We all exhaled once that key was inserted and our silence allowing us to hear the lock release from the internal cylinder. The first drawer nothing but more gross photos and chewing gum; the next had his personal expense reports and receipts. The final drawer was filled with multiple invoices paper clipped together in three different piles. Oddly enough, the invoices were duplicated but with phony company logos affixed across the header covering the original logo. There was that single invoice with the odd name of Champion Inc. that I'd returned to Eric from the Brunswick submission. After comparing the invoices we each realized that they were fabricated and used as working capital for the specific investors. Fraud!!

"You were right, Torie!!" Millie blurts out.

Lauren informs us of Eric's scheduled return within minutes despite his anticipated absence as Millie had thought.

Oh, so now she wants to own her ethnicity when she fears being linked to Eric's questionable antics. If I didn't need her in this very moment, I would likely throw her ass right under the bus with him. Now Lauren begins to panic along with Millie once they hear Eric whistling.

"What is he doing here?" Millie asked.

"He called and said that we needed to go over some documents today. His weekend away was cut short by the urgency, that's why I'm here," Lauren replied.

When Eric was seen coming down the long corridor, Lauren locked the drawer and followed my instructions to quickly pass me cups of water from the cooler outside of his office. Being the tallest and somehow the calmest, I stood on his desk and threw water onto the porous ceiling tiles directly above his desk until it appeared wet. "Pour water onto his desktop and blot it with paper towel and leave it gathered in the center of his desk, Millie. We have to make it look as though there was a leak from the floor above." I hopped down from the desk as he entered his office while continuing to pretend to wipe up the spill.

"Oh Eric, you've just missed maintenance."

"When I walked in there was a crowd cleaning up your very wet desk," Lauren chimed in again trying to save herself.

"Millie phoned me after hearing sudden splashes, but she was unsure of where it was coming from so she asked me to come downstairs."

This little conjured-up story might have sold if I was not part of it; he's still pissed about the whole crème brûlée thing. So I decided to taunt him again.

"Eric, I'd probably empty everything from inside those drawers, you know, just in case anything has gotten wet. Need some help?"

Millie and Lauren were not very happy with me in that moment.

"You know, lately you have been like a real freakin' Bond girl!!" She leaned in and whispered, "You are scandalous!!"

KLEIN-MATHESON

"**C**ome on, pick up!!" I shout into an unanswered telephone, "Barrett, pick up the phone!!" I continue to look over my shoulder to ensure that my presence has remained unnoticed as I wait for Millie to arrive.

Ring! Ring! Ring! Finally a female voice answers.

"Barrett, I'm so glad that you've answered, listen . . ." interrupted before I'm able to finish and unable to let her know that I've found Eric to be the culprit.

"No, this isn't Barrett. Who's calling?"

"Is she there please?" I ask abruptly after seeing that Eric and the gentleman from Le Château have followed me here to Barcelona.

"Hello?" She questions as I remain silent and tucked in a niche with my back turned as they pass by.

"Hello? Are you still there?" she asks.

"Yes!! Yes I'm here; I'm sorry my phone must have lost the signal." I feverishly respond as I slip into the ladies room.

"Oh, that's okay, it happens all. . ."

"My name is Torie Harper—is she there please?" interrupting her in the midst of her formalities.

"One moment please," clearly she's offended.

Is it really taking her this long to come to the phone? I want to inform her that I will be sharing everything with Liam and Joel. Millie and I have arranged to meet with them at Napa & Company an hour from now.

Knock! Knock! Someone's knocking on the single-stall bathroom door.

"Yes?"

"Will you be much longer?"

"I'll be out in a minute," I offered to the patron just before the same female voice returned to the phone.

"Hello, Ms. Harper?"

"Yes!!"

"I'm sorry, but it seems that Ms. Johns has left the office."

I placed my finger on the phone display ending the call without extending a thank you or good bye. What am I to do? What if they are outside of the bathroom waiting? Maybe Millie was right, I probably should have told someone sooner. What if they see Millie? Oh my, she doesn't even know that they're here. This thought prompts me to open the door without further concern for myself. As the door opens the patron's hand is raised and clenched preparing to resume knocking.

"So sorry," as I brush her shoulder in passing.

"Oh Millie, where are you?" I wonder as I look down to search for her designated key on my phone panel to call. As I raise my head to approach the exit I place my phone to my ear, swiftly I am silenced by a hand placed over my mouth and pulled through the double doors of the service area for the wait staff.

I squirmed and kicked even more after recognizing my captor to be the reappearing mystery gentleman.

"Who are you?" I shout as he is removing his hand from over my mouth to thwart my bite.

"Sshhh . . . I'm a Federal Marshall," showing me his badge before fully removing his hand from my mouth. "You're okay!! We assured Mr. Klein and Mr. Matheson that you would never be in harm's way."

"What? They're aware of all of this already?" I ask.

"Your friend Millie is back there," pointing to another set of double doors. When the door opened, Barrett Johns was consoling Millie.

"Barrett?" I ask with uncertainty until she turns and faces me.

"Torie!!" Millie shouts running towards me, "Oh my God, I was so afraid."

"Yeah, me too! This is crazy!"

"Did you hear what they're saying Eric's gotten himself involved with?" Her face is still red and eyes glassy.

"No," still looking as Barrett approaches me.

"Torie, are you okay?" she asks while placing her hand onto my back.

"Barrett, they found you too?"

"Torie, I'm sorry that I couldn't tell you, but I am an agent."

"An agent, what's going on?"

"Torie, we are federal agents and we have been investigating a gentleman by the name of Carlo Soto. He is the disreputable investor that Eric has partnered with. He has been in the federal database for some time now throughout the country; he's been investigated for similar money-laundering schemes."

"And Eric's a part of that?" I asked.

"Well, we believe that he didn't knowingly participate in the beginning. But yes, our evidence shows that at some point he chose to willingly participate in exchange for money."

"Wow, what a sleaze!!" Millie charged.

"So I don't understand; when you said that you were hired by an investor for a review, that wasn't true?"

"No, that was true. We were informed by Klein-Matheson's outside counsel of their suspicions after noticing something during a review of their own."

"And the invoices—where did they come from?"

"Apparently those were found overlooked inside the bottom collating tray of the copier in the Legal Department."

Millie chimes in with, "Oh, that bottom tray is difficult to see if you're not familiar with that machine."

"So how did the partners get them?"

"Well, it seems that an attorney by the name of Quinn . . . well he passed them onto the partners and shared his suspicions that went on to be validated."

The other agent informed us that both men and Carlo's entourage have been taking into custody outside of the restaurant without incident and that Liam and Joel are waiting to speak with Millie and me.

"Why don't we give you two a moment to gather yourselves? Let us know when you are ready and we'll escort you over to Napa."

"Thank you," I replied although still in disbelief with all that has taken place. This is like something I'd see on *Criminal Minds*, but thankfully foiled with no casualties.

"I could use a drink right now!" Millie confessed.

"I so understand Maddie when she says, "You gotta bring me something stronger than that!!" We laughed and headed out to be escorted to the partners.

The two stand to greet us upon our arrival; both show signs of relief as well as pride.

"Torie, Millie—please sit and join us," Liam requests.

"What a course of events this day has brought about!" Joel shares.

"I'd say," Millie replies.

"Are you ladies alright?" Liam asks.

"We are, thank you," I reply looking at Millie as I make the choice of speaking for both of us.

"We understand that the agents have explained everything, but do either of you have any questions?"

Again I look at Mil and reply, "Not at this time."

"Well then, I'm sure you are wondering what's on our minds."

"Or maybe not," Joel inserts with a poor attempt at humor.

"Awhile back following the unveiling of Harbor View, Quinn Matthews met with Joel and I to share his findings on the copier and to discuss his position with the Westside Coalition and his allegiance to the community and then offered his resignation."

He never told me that he resigned. He resigned? My mind is unable to absorb what he's said before he goes on speaking.

"Quinn resigned?"

"Yes, but of course we wouldn't accept it," Liam assured the two of us.

"Let us explain; both Liam and I have a profound allegiance to the West Side, hence our investment in the preservation. Our families came here many years ago when Jewish people were not readily accepted other than in communities that bordered predominately Black neighborhoods. The West Side was a place that allowed Jews to have a known community built with merchants, print shops, and bakeries welcoming those to arrive next."

"Yes, it ran all the way down and beyond Canal Street and Water Street," Joel offers.

"I didn't know any of this," Millie offers with great interest.

"Not long after building up a thriving community with increasing businesses, the homes—which had been paltry all along—began to succumb to their ages, collapsed and became eyesores. Businessmen outside of the community saw an opportunity to purchase the land from the Jewish families that wanted to flee the neighborhood for a better place."

"Wow, that is very interesting," I say.

"Over the years, we were determined to slowly buy back the land and rebuild a community that would pay homage to our grandfathers," nodding proudly with glistening eyes.

"We'd call it Harbor View!!" says Joel.

"So we've shared with Quinn that we too have an allegiance. We came up with an arrangement that would allow Quinn to lead in a strategic partnership with the Coalition. We have allocated a substantial allowance to support the revamping of the housing needs for all of the residents impacted by this project."

"That's awesome!!" I shout.

"Oh, more than one might imagine with Quinn driving it," Joel says like a proud father.

"In due time all will see the fruits of our well-intended plans," Liam suggests.

THE WEDDING

"**S**omeone's getting married," I softly sing as I opened the dual ivory doors of the bridal suite. I've just returned from stealing a peek at the eloquently prepared ballroom, awaiting the nuptials of our best friends in less than two hours.

Every detail had been fully executed as meticulously planned and prayerfully hoped for. Upon entering the ballroom, I was drawn to each of the gentlemen in the 12-piece orchestra seated on a double-tier platform adjacent to the entranceway. Their classic attire of ivory jackets and black tuxedo pants sealed with crisp black bows at their neck immediately allowed me to be thrown into my personal images of the infamous Cotton Club. I was privileged to witness the soloists rehearse their renditions of Louis Armstrong's *What a Wonderful World* and Etta James's *At Last*. The music brought goose bumps to my entire body.

Crystal reflections are leaping from a brilliant chandelier above and dancing their way down from the ceiling only to find rest on each raised saxophone and every bowing trumpet.

The room appears to be twice its size as the ivory and ecru paisley embossed linens swathe each table. Each tall illuminated crystal vase displayed freshwater pearls delicately wrapped and intertwined between the golden pepper berries and the long stems of ivory calla lilies. The remaining portions of the strands are ever so gently dangling from the narrowing necks of each vase and resting beneath the accompanying select greens.

"Torie, is everything okay downstairs?" Simone asked nervously. "Is the orchestra set up? Has the DJ arrived yet? Oooh girl, cause I let Tank talk me into using his cousin."

I smiled in awe of how beautiful she looked without a stitch of makeup; she was absolutely glowing like a bronze essence goddess. Veronica transformed Simone's everyday straight blunt into soft curls with random vines of very small sheer white flowers intertwined into select spirals. The copper highlights along the frame of her face, match her new brow color and has instantly softened her otherwise dark features that have always been a contrast to her natural bronze hues.

"Something's wrong isn't it? . . . The flowers didn't get here? . . . Girl, I know that you're not going to tell me they dropped my cake . . . Did they? Torie, say something!!" Simone shouted in panic as she stood to her feet.

"No, no, no Sim . . . everything is just right . . . beyond being just right." I said as I placed both of her hands into mine.

"Really, Torie?"

"Yeah really . . . it looks exactly like the ballroom, Sim."

"Ooooh for real?" Simone says as she holds each of my hands tightly, and begins to lightly jump up and down.

"Yes, really . . . it looks just like the one that we dreamed of as little girls, you know the one where our princess was always beautiful and brown. Well tonight, you are that princess. So IF they had dropped your cake and there were to be no flowers, it would still be just right because you are absolutely breathtaking."

"Stop! You're making me cry."

"No, you're making me cry, and I wish my Nanna and mom could see you today . . . they'd be so proud and happy for you."

"They see me . . . they see both of us . . . every day." We hugged and held each other tightly as we approached yet another chapter in our shared lifelong journey.

"Girl, I'm just so happy! I mean, I feel like I don't have to be afraid ever again. I feel so safe," she said while blotting the corner of her left eye ever so gently with the side of her perfectly French-manicured index finger.

Immediately Tessa came over and blotted Simone's eyes to see if the artificial lashes had dried. She was the MAC artist who had been contracted to apply each of the bridesmaid's makeup today.

"Go on sweetie and let it out—those lashes aren't going anywhere now. But once I apply your makeup . . . you should think only happy thoughts."

"Oh no, I am happy," Simone assured.

"This may sound cliché, but Nigel really is everything I could ever hope for in this world. He is my life mate and what I dreamed and hoped for all of my life and now. . ." she swallows hard and purses her lips to suppress the lump in her throat. "It's like we just co-pilot this whole life thing with the same approach, the same hopes and dreams. So if one of us gets tired, it's okay because we each trust and know that we know exactly how the other would want it done."

"Simone . . ."

"See, that's what I'm trying to say—I'm fine!! Nigel has made everything fine."

"I've been running this race so long that I can barely remember how it started . . . just trying to do anything to help take the pressure off of my mother and make her a little happy. When I was younger, I'd try to have the BEST grades in the class, and then at home I'd try to have all the cleaning done. Just so my mother wouldn't have to come home from her second job and make cleaning her third."

Now my face has just given way to tears and any chance of deflecting them has passed as I listen and remember along with Simone. There were many days that I would even go over and help

Simone with the cleaning and share our poor attempts of cooking so that we could move onto getting her studies out of the way to free her weekend. It never seemed quite fair that Sinclair felt no guilt or commitment about helping at all. That's probably because there hadn't been a father around to guide or direct him. It is kind of funny that in all of these years no one has ever made mention of their father, so I really don't know if he passed away or if he's extinct like Otis Harper.

"I've been tired for a long time but I dare not stop because if I did, I would never have gotten here. If I didn't get here . . . I would have never made it there . . . and THERE is where God placed him. It's as if God was whispering 'you finish that race, child' and I did. And Nigel was right there at the finish line waiting before I ever even knew him."

Tessa completed applying moisturizer to Simone's neck, back and shoulders leaving her draped in a terry robe that fastened just above her breast. After spraying a moisturizing mist, she decided that now would be the perfect time to go back downstairs to collect the rest of her luggage so she could go down the hall to apply Mrs. Jackson's makeup before finishing Simone's. This also allowed Simone and me some private moments.

"Sim, he's definitely been custom-made just for you! Besides, who else other than Nigel would put up with you?" I said trying to lighten the conversation.

"There's someone custom made for you too, Torie."

I looked away knowing that she wasn't going to stop there.

"Why are you fighting it? Quinn is the one. I know that you've been second guessing yourself ever since."

"Sim, another time . . . okay?"

"I'm just saying . . ."

"Look, this is your day and . . ."

"It doesn't have to be just my day. Girl, I'd gladly share this day with you."

I began to feel very uncomfortable with her desires to summon feelings that I've so struggled to suppress, particularly because I knew that he would be in attendance as a groomsmen. I've got a jittery stomach knowing that there will be no way that I can avoid him today. Using my tongue, I brushed across the fronts of my teeth as though I had unwanted lipstick resting upon them; this has become a known indication of me restraining my thoughts from becoming actual words.

"Okay . . . okay . . . Don't get upset."

"I'm sorry. I just wanted to say . . . well . . . I don't want to see you. And I, well, let me just say that Quinn loves you. He's not Hollis. Torie, don't let him be the one that got away. Girl, you know what you have to do."

"How am I supposed to do that? I haven't seen him the night he showed up at my house." Simone means well, and in my heart I know that everything that she has said is exactly what I fear. I invested so much of myself into Hollis that I left myself completely exposed and the price I paid for doing that just isn't worth it. Would Quinn do the same to me? Probably not, but then again I would have thought the same of Hollis. I can't go through that shit again, and yes, I probably should have never slept with him confusing things even more but I've got to focus on me.

I leaned over my best friend and removed the brush from her hand that she was using to softly apply shimmering body bronzer across her neck and chest. I completed it for her as she remained seated looking into the pewter mirror attached to the dressing table.

"I never thought that this could ever happen to me . . . I always thought that it only happened to women like you."

"This is happening for not to you and why would you say something like that?"

"Come on, Torie, you know what I'm saying."

"No, I don't," I replied while trying to remember that it's her wedding day and that we probably shouldn't pursue this conversation because this is one of those that could go either way with the two of us.

"Torie, it really is okay. I mean, it is what it is. I am a girl from the West Side and without you allowing me to shadow you all of these years, showing me proper etiquette, speech and encouraging me to go to college . . . I don't know where I'd be today. I mean, don't get me wrong—Mommy did her best, but she only knows what she knows."

"Sim . . ."

"No, Torie, let me finish," Simone says as she rose back onto her feet. "I'm just trying to say thank you. Thank you for allowing me to see beyond what I've seen all around me my entire life and forcing me to see the things that I couldn't see even within myself. Thank you."

"Well then," I tearfully replied, "I thank you for helping me find my way into my sisterhood in a way that I might not have ever known. Thank you for showing me that Black woman's strength that I'd always seen in Nanna, but couldn't seem to find within me."

We both began to sob and wipe each other's tears away.

"See Sim, you were never walking in my shadow—it was me always hiding within yours."

Shortly after the doors opened to the suite and in came Felicia, Perry, Yoli and Millie squealing with excitement over how beautiful Simone looks. We fussed over her while drinking one or two Mimosas each until we were ridiculously giddy passing the time until Tessa returned.

"Come on, let's make this all about you . . . we need to get going on your makeup so that we can get you in that dress and send you on down to that very handsome impatient man I passed on my way back up."

"Nigel's here?" she asks and smiles with unwarranted relief.

"He's not trying to let nobody else get with you," Perry replies. "Hell, he's trying to get them papers on you fast so that when your ass turns up missing . . . (taking another gulp from her champagne flute) . . . He can get everything, especially that big-ass house!!" We all began laughing as usual at the crazy things that don't cease to come out of her damn mouth.

"You so stupid!!" Simone shouted after throwing a towel at her.

"I'm only kidding, girl. We all know that this day is as important to Nigel as it is for you. That man loves you!!" Perry places a kiss onto her cheek and whispers into her ear that she couldn't be happier for them; she even had the nerve to have a single tear rest in the lining of her eye that released just as she stood upright.

"What made you choose that timeless look of ivory and black tuxedos?" Tessa waited for her response as she continued applying the makeup. "Those brothers look so damn fine—even the ones that aren't normally all that attractive."

Ignoring her last remark Simone replied, "I just wanted it to be elegant with women dressed like women and men as men like in the old days. More than anything, I wanted to keep it classy."

We've been catapulted into the evening with only 20 minutes to go before the ceremony would begin. Simone and I are behind the doors of the adjoining suite in the lavish comfort of quietness again and focusing on the last details of her preparation. Mrs. Jackson has joined us, but she is of very little use at this time given that she is unable to stop staring at her daughter with admiration.

"Just look at my baby girl!" She blots her ageless cinnamon face that nearly matches her bronze dress. The fact that she resembles the famous model Iman and her thin youthful body always made it difficult to pass as anything other than a sister or friend of Simone's, but certainly not her mother.

"Mommy, please don't come in here making me start . . . I've just gotten my makeup done."

"I knew from the first day that I saw those slanted eyes stealing their first peek of me and the world only seconds after arriving that you were finding your way."

"Oh, Mom," Simone sniffled after seeing her mother's eyes well up.

"Oh, no you don't, Simone Renee Jackson. Don't you take this moment away from me; I've been waiting too long! I certainly knew that you didn't have a problem in taking the lead and that you were not going to let any man or anyone else stop you when you had your mind made up."

She giggled with joy of the memory. "It was very telling that you came on out fast and with little notice while Sinclair stayed put for nearly another two hours even with the doctors prompting his little behind."

We laughed at the idea of Sinclair ever being little.

"He's always chosen to approach life the hard way, taking me along with him, always making sure that he's alright. I often remind him that I sport a permanent scar on my belly for a C-section that didn't have to be, messing up this temple!"

Mrs. Jackson walked over to the ottoman and picked up her purse and removed a small manila envelope from inside and walked back over to Simone.

"Now I want you to take this and buy as many pieces of furniture that you can for that big house on the Cove. My baby is moving to the Cove!" She proudly hands the unsealed envelope to Simone.

I couldn't have been happier when Simone and I revealed a bank check in the amount of $25,000.

"Where did you get this from?"

"What do you mean, where did I get this from? Baby, haven't I always had to work more than one job at a time?"

"I know, but why haven't you used it on you?"

"I have everything that I need. As I said, I knew that my baby girl was smart as a whip and that I had to start saving for school early on, but your little smart behind and Torie knowing all about those grants and scholarships paid your way right on through that school."

"Oh. My. God.!!" Simone says in disbelief.

"Oh yes, he sure did have a lot to do with it too," her mother replied and then smiled and winked.

"So anyway, I figured that I would save it for your wedding, but you and that brilliant soon-to-be son of mine had taken care of everything already. So I thought I'd give you a down payment and you all could find a home. I was too late for that too."

"Mommy, stop playing!!"

"Oh, I don't have time to play. I have a wedding to attend and the bride just happens to be my baby."

Simone no longer cared about her hair or make up in that moment as she grabbed her mother from behind squeezing her shoulders so tightly nearly pulling them both to the floor tearfully laughing and kissing her. Mrs. Jackson left quickly and prepares to go and find Tessa so that she could refresh Simone's face with the few remaining minutes.

Now that it was just the two of us, Simone turned to me and said, "I still can't get over the fact that you and Quinn still haven't seen each other."

"Sim, you're the one who had me running around and having me miss the rehearsal. By the time I got to dinner that night, he'd already left."

"Listen, don't say anything about this to your brother; I'm going to hang on to his a little while longer. God only knows what I'll end up letting him use his for," she mumbled while walking out the door.

"Bail." Simone thought she'd whispered it, but to our surprise, her mother obviously heard her and responded, "Don't talk that way about my baby boy; you know I don't play that!!"

When the door closed, Simone whispered, "Aren't you glad you stop creeping with my brother?" I was caught so off guard that I was delayed in responding. "Oh yeah, I knew. We all did. The Sinclairs can't keep secrets! Besides, every time Maxwell's *The Hush* would play, he'd unknowingly ask, 'Hey Sim, where's your girl at?'"

"Whatever," I reply not willing to indulge her. We continued to laugh until Mrs. Jackson returned with Tessa.

As we entered the candlelit ballroom, each calla lily appears subdued and muted in tone providing softness. This was of course a complete contrast to the 200 black-eyed beauty calla lilies gathered in bunches at the end of each row. I remember when Simone first described these flowers. She went on and on about how extraordinary they were! A description I'd never heard her use outside of designer clothing and shoes. Simone told me, "Their stems are the darkest jungle green, and the calla lily itself has this luscious crème yellowish tone with ivory pearl cloaks inside and outside of a classic champagne flute. It opens as a heart shape, but reveals a ruby-black center." Even with that description, it absolutely paled to what I'm seeing today.

The darkening sky has added to the panache by allowing gazing through the translucent ceiling of the tent; the starlit sapphire sky lends priceless ambiance. As we enter the tent for the ceremony, the wooden teak floor is completely infused with an azure glow bouncing off the lighter-colored linens and skipping across the vamps of each of the bridesmaid's black satin sandals. No longer a rehearsal, it's the real thing as the vocalist belts out *At Last*. All the chatter in the majestic tent immediately transforms into "oooohs" as attention is directed onto Simone. She appears at the undisturbed petal-filled aisle escorted by Sinclair, and has finally given us all our first vision of her stunning gown.

Simone is a sight draped in pure white; a strapless ballroom gown with a modified Watteau train cascading from the top of the fastening and beyond the dotted Swiss-fitted bodice. Crystal sequins are glistening and winking down onto the floor shimmering daintily throughout the fabric of her gown's train. Tears began to stream down either side of Nigel's face as he was finally able to see beyond the standing crowd as his stunning bride made her way towards him.

My mind and heart are flooded. How is it that I know that this is so right for them, but I'm unable to know what's right for me? I'm happy for them, yet desirous for myself, but not envious. Giving it more thought I wondered if that is wrong and does my not being envious make it okay?

As I reach down to adjust Simone's train, I witness their eyes meeting. In that moment it's as if we'd all left the tent leaving just the two of them. She hands me her bouquet and joins hands with Nigel as they begin with a prayer and onto their unforgettable vows.

Nigel begins, "Today, tomorrow, and beyond eternity, my spirit exists for you, Simone. It is only for you that I seek to be my best. It is with you by my side each time I've found any success. My queen and mother of our children-to-be, I have found in thee, my friend, my lover and partner to share my future with me. Each day we will stay on his potter's wheel and together we will pray asking God to mold us into one, never to be separated or mildly undone." There isn't a dry eye to be seen following Nigel's heartfelt declaration.

Simone follows, "Nigel, I too have found in thee, my friend, my lover, my partner to share my future with me. It is only for you that I seek to be my best and it is with you by my side that I too have found success. Now from this day forward and all the way through forever, I will be here with you to support you in each and every one of life's endeavors. Each day as we kneel and pray, I will give ear to each word that is said, and with that, I promise that we will continuously be spiritually fed."

Pastor Witherspoon completed the nuptials proudly granting Nigel consent to kiss his bride. And kiss her he did, cradling the frame of Simone's face delicately as if he was handling a porcelain doll, completely oblivious to the presence of anyone else in the room.

The ballroom was suddenly filled with laughter and dancing replacing the sounds of flatware colliding and lightly tapping against glasses throughout dinner. As I lean against a column, I find that I can't stop gazing at Nigel and Simone as they inhabit the center of the dance floor. The horns go on spewing notes that are playing a special song for everyone's spirit. I don't care what anyone thinks, there's something to be said about being dressed up and at a fabulous venue, it just brings out Cinderella in all of us . . . and it feels good!!

Great, now they're playing all of my favorite love songs. The combination of the Ketel One and the total ambiance is beginning to get the best of me emotionally. Who is that brother across the room who keeps staring at me? Okay, so he wants to play cat and mouse, then I'll pretend that I don't notice him looking. Hey wait a minute—he was in the wedding party. He's the guy that Felicia was asking about. Uh oh, here he comes.

"What's a stunning woman like you doing in a corner?"

Damn, how did I not see him earlier, he's gorgeous! I smile and allow him to go on with his game.

"Ooops, be careful," he says as he reaches in for my hand after my shoe slips as I tried to retreat a little. "I'd never let a lady hit the floor as long as I'm around. If she were my lady, I'd just carry her." He smiled, but only after wetting his lips before showing his flawless set of pearly whites.

"Oh, so you'd just carry her—all night?" I indulge him.

"Yeah, if that's what she wanted," he's now flashing my perfect smile right back. He moves closer to me placing him directly in the path of a light from the stage. Will you look at this? He's pure solid chocolate; the kind of bunny that made you happy on Easter. His eyes are slanted resting above chiseled cheekbones and parallel to his deep dimples that appear each time his pouty bottom lip makes the slightest move.

Another slow jam is blaring from the DJ's table while the band has taken a break.

"Come on, let's dance," he says confidently.

"I don't even know you," I respond. Does he think that I'd dance a slow dance? That's a bit intimate.

"I'm sorry, I'm Harlem. And you are?" extending his hand and taking mine.

"I'm Torie. And I still don't know you, and not like that," freeing my hand from his. Just then the guests began clapping as Nigel and Simone reentered the banquet room.

"Wow, they look really good together don't they?" I comment to Harlem.

"Mr. and Mrs. Brooks; I've got to get used to that," a familiar voice chimes in.

Quinn! I wondered how I'd missed him coming up behind us. Harlem turns and greets him as though they're old friends.

"What's up, son?" looking down on Quinn's 6'4 stature by barely an inch.

Quinn raises his head to minimize the slightest disparity in their heights. "When I was a child, I spoke and behaved like a child. There's only men up in here now." The two stood nearly perfectly aligned, yet in stark contrast as Quinn thinned his eyes and tightened his jaw, Harlem widely smiled and nodded his head.

"Alright man, you right," not appearing to be put off. "Man, we gotta get together and catch up."

"That's not gonna happen."

Harlem turns to walk away, but not before saying, "Torie, it was a pleasure meeting you; maybe I'll catch up with you."

To which Quinn replies, "That's not gonna happen either," staring Harlem down wavering not once.

With that, I was left speechless and curious about the obvious bad blood present between the two. When Harlem was no longer within our view, Quinn's demeanor changed immediately as he turned to face me with a much softer spirit.

"You'll let me know, right? If I've breeched any invisible lines drawn, but hopefully not before I get to tell you how good you look." Quinn said as I reposition myself taking in more of that familiar and soothing tang.

"How are you, Quinn?"

"Okay, it's a start . . . you do remember me?" He was staring at me with those endless smiling eyes.

My body has already become flushed with crystals of perspiration resting above my lip and dampness beneath each arm as he briefly places his hand onto my hip while leaning down to kiss me on my cheek. There are no words that I can assemble in this moment that could explain my behavior and avoidance; if there were, they've been lost in Simone's earlier advice.

"Listen (pausing while using his index finger to rub behind his left ear) . . . I really miss you . . . and I umm, well I'm still right here, Torie." Quinn continued with conviction, "You just got to let me know where you are. Baby, I'm right here." Indeed he is, standing here with his arms spread open and his eyes offering an unnecessary truce. And that body, well, let's just say that it's an unfair weapon that's reaping mass destruction on my defenseless heart.

He's not trying to schmooze or kick some scripted game on me. No, tonight he's simply putting it on the line that he's trying to be with me . . . he wants to be with me . . . and I need to be with him.

Without any words, just two easy steps forward, I fall into my heart's secret safe place, right into Quinn's opened arms. I tell him how sorry I am, and with that I feel Quinn's opened arms slowly close around me surely in disbelief that I'd surrendered so easily.

The night went on offering many memories, laughter and sheer bliss as we each took on the challenge of the Soul Train Line, Electric Slide, Booty Call and Cha-Cha-Cha dances in between filling my role as maid of honor and Quinn's as best man.

As the night had drawn to a close, we successfully sent the honeymooners off to their overnight stay at the Ritz Carlton in New York City. Early the next morning they will catch a flight to the Caribbean. I traded up and politely ditched the girls and their after party for the private one that had manifested itself throughout the night with

Quinn. Simultaneously our cell phones begin to ring and we each identify our callers as Nigel and Simone.

"Hey," I shout over Quinn's, "What up, man?" We each tried to discretely muffle our laughter from the muted speakers enduring their obviously plotted teasing on the other end of the phones.

"What do you mean where am I at? Man, listen—you only need to be worrying about what you and that gorgeous bride of yours are doing! On the real, everything was tight man!!" Quinn steals a glance at me and reaches across the console of his Range Rover, then places his hand in mine while making our way back to Clock Towers.

"I just want to holler and say thanks man for having my back," Nigel responds.

"Come on, this is us, man!!"

"You right, alright! Love ya, man!!"

"Yeah, love you too, man. Keep it grown and sexy, but stay safe!!"

I shout to Simone, "Behave, girl!"

She responds, "I'll be as good as you are tonight, how about that?"

"Smooches! Got to go," giggling and mildly embarrassed with her giving voice to my intentions.

As we are now in close proximity to Clock Towers, we are both beginning to display a little angst over our silent curiosities of what's next. Quinn occasionally rests his hand on mine in between making adjustments to the music or air on the dashboard. With all of Sim's recent wedding needs and last-minute outings, I began spending random nights back at the tower. After all, it's still my home.

"You alright?" he asks while lightly tapping his digits across my thigh in tandem with the bass in concert on the CD player while stopped at a red light.

Albeit now completely aroused, I deny it by saying, "Just a little sleepy I guess," as I look at the digits shouting 1:45 a.m. from the green illuminated panel.

"Come here." Quinn leans towards me raising my chin and placing a long warm passionate kiss on me prompts thoughts like I hope that he has his foot firmly on the brake because I'm squirming all over this seat. As he rotates his slightly moist mouth from left to right over and around mine I'm thinking that traffic light better turn green real soon! I am completely rendered weak by Quinn's heated fragrance as his warm body projectiles that tang from every pore.

With an opened palm, I cradled his sculpted jaw shifting his face towards mine. "I really am sorry for being unkind to you." The steering wheel remained secured in between his forearm and inner fold of his left elbow as his shoulders faced me. I gently placed a kiss above his brow before resting my forehead against his as we both look down towards our adjoined hands.

"Green light!!" I wonder why lights always seem to take forever to change over the morning hours. I'm only thinking this now because I would have been at risk of catching an indecent exposure case had there been a longer delay in the light changing.

I reach into my purse to grab my key ring once arriving at valet. Suddenly, rain appears from out of nowhere. We rush in attempt to escape the downpour to no avail and we laugh at our defeat and soaked bodies as we look into the elevator mirrors on our flight up. As we stand at the door of my unit, Quinn reaches for my keys to unlock the door. He smiles when recognizing that the key he'd given to me is present alongside my ignition key.

"You know, sometimes after a real crazy day like today, I find it hard to fall asleep," he looks at the key and then at me again.

"Do you?" I ask smugly trying to see what's on his mind.

"Oh, yeah . . . if that should happen to you tonight, why don't you put this key to good use? I mean, it's probably a good idea to test it anyway."

Oh, so he's forgotten that I've tested the key; he may want to leave that alone! An hour or so later after showering, I contemplate whether it's too late to test that key again. I decide to go for it walking barefoot through the abandoned corridor wearing only his big shirt from our first encounter. When I turn the key and open the door, I find no signs of him, only candles that were recently doused.

I reach the top of the landing and see that he's in bed, bare-chested and fast asleep. I cowardly decide it's best for me to head back to my place. Just as I turn to quietly leave the bedroom, my elbow clips the edge of the door jamb causing a startling thump.

"Hey, where you going? Was that your foot?"

"No . . . my elbow . . . but it's fine," I said as he inspected it for himself.

"You want to put some ice on it?" rubbing his eyes with one hand and innocently adjusting himself inside his boxers with the other.

"It's fine, really," I wasn't going to let on that it was burning.

We end up sitting, talking and catching up on as much as we could before both drifting off to sleep. A very long day became a night filled with occasional spooning, random kissing and a lot of sweet embracing; all of the things a girl hopes for from her man before and after making love. Well, I stand corrected! I now know that is making love, confirming that I'd been made love to all night long. It's nearly noon and we're both fully rested and committed to staying true to each of our daily regime that includes a good intense work out—and so we did!!

JASPER'S CAFE ON THE BOULEVARD TODAY

The sun is relentless and diminishing my view, blinding me with vibrant hues of yellow, orange and of red as I cup my hands over the lids of my eyes seeking relief. Regardless, there's very little that can stop me from proudly taking in the view of a cohesive Boulevard.

"How's it going?" I ask the young waitress greeting me at the entrance.

"I think I'm going to grab a table out back today, for four please," I reply in response to her query of guest count.

I phone Clyde Hicks to inform him that I can be found at one of the outdoor tables around back here at Jasper's. Now there's less noise and we'll be able to enjoy this nice day, given that the outdoor tables which were once located under the old valet carport have been relocated. That's a good thing, another indication of things changing. Case has resumed valet parking here to align his business with all of the others up and down The Boulevard.

Everything has come together. The West Side is a mirror image of the East Side; one continuous cobblestone sidewalk. Tall lanterns align either side of the street resembling soldiers standing at attention. The largest structure down on the far right with a church steeple is the One Faith Credit Union. Yes, the clergy stayed united, and with guidance, became protected members of the FCUA after launching the community credit union. To the left of the credit union is the Community Credit Counseling Agency.

"Hey man, longtime no see," acknowledging this old cat I went to school with, "Are you living back here?"

"Yeah, because of you. You did right by us man. My wife and I bought one of those units over at the old Pavilion. I'll tell you, you the man, Q!!"

"Nah, I'm not the man. We're the people and it's the people making it happen," assuring him that he's part of this too.

"So, what's it like living over there now? You like it?"

"Man, we love it; it's all luxurious and things. It ain't nothing like when we lived there even as kids man." He nods his head with his eyes absent and filled with visions of his happy home. "Yup, man, it's nice! No noise, no violence. It's real nice—it's home."

"That's what I'm talking about; thank you for sharing that," I reach in showing him some love with a quick man embrace.

"I'll tell you what, you got my vote!!" pointing at one of the many mayoral campaign posters displayed around us.

"I appreciate that, man!" I give him dap when a passing car goes by filled with youngsters. They honk their horns as they go by and waving and shouting, "Vote for Mr. Matthews!"

"See what I'm saying? Even the kids know," he shares before walking away.

The Pavilion was leveled one section at a time after weeding out the few families that refused to comply with our new neighborhood guidelines for whatever reasons. We were prepared to make a proud community for the deserving and as many first-time homebuyers as possible. For those who were not yet credit worthy, accounts were established at the Community Credit Union on their behalf; a percentage of their monthly rent is deposited each month to save towards their down payments for the current units they've moved into. Once their credit has improved, they too will be homeowner. Making moves like this ensures that every resident has a vested interest in the community. They began with setting up the first section of prefab townhouses to allow the first families to move in as they leveled the old and replaced with new units. A swift plan was in place to be followed and executed with tightly managed schedules. The contractors leveled and built for months until every family proudly occupied a new home; homes filled with market-dictated amenities, prize-winning landscaping and wrought iron fencing surrounding a welcome sign that reads "Harbor View Pavilion."

Klein-Matheson has proven to be savvier than most, showing this with their choice in partnering with the Coalition as it has served all parties invested and involved. With the Coalition's success in maintaining ownership of more than a third of the real estate on the West Side, it created multiple obstacles throughout the projects intended schematics leaving only two choices—partner or walk away. So whether their decision to fund the restoration of all the commercial dwellings, came from a place of controlling the intended unified appearance along the strip or a more sincere origin, it has landed only winners. This is where Klein-Matheson has shown their brilliance in initiating the Business Sponsor Program that funded the restorations.

Quinn says hello to Joel and Liam as they arrive.

Liam asks, "Are we late, or are you early as usual?"

"Gentlemen, to that I say, you're right on time," humoring the two as they arrive for our meeting.

"What are we drinking . . . seltzer?"

"Seltzer? This is a celebration. Bring us the best bottle you have!!" smiling at the young waitress.

"Look around you; we have collectively done something that could be groundbreaking throughout!!"

"Oh, I second that!!" Clyde Hicks shouts from the aisle as he joins us.

"Well in that case, we must work diligently at getting you that Senate seat, Clyde!" We all nod in agreement.

We ate quickly, celebrated briefly and lingered in details and plans to bring our remaining intentions to reality. Feeling accomplished, we committed to a second gathering in the very near future and Liam and Joel go on their way.

"You know, he's right. What we've done should encourage and take other cities to task."

"One can only hope, sir. Will they ever know what we've done here?"

"Anybody can see if they just look around."

"Got that, but I'm talking about the inner cities across the States."

"I'll tell it from the Senate floor, or you'll do like everyone else, and write a book about it someday!" We both raise our glass and toast.

Mr. Hicks lowered his glass as his face has taken on a more serious look. "Quinn, I wanted to mention that I've seen that brother of Nigel's around a lot lately."

"Who, Harlem?"

"Yes. Every time I leave Tank's new barbershop, I see him over by the International Circle."

The International Circle is a long strip mall of restaurants occupied by a vast variety of ethnic cuisines that has become a landmark for the tourist crowd.

"I can't say that I've seen him doing anything, but you know," as he stood up to leave.

"Alright sir, it's always a pleasure.

Harlem Brooks is a member of the Brooks tribe. He's the eldest of five brothers and was destined to turn a good thing bad early on. He had a full ride all through college acquiring his Bachelors and Masters; a law major, although he never did sit for the Bar because of some trouble he'd gotten himself into.

An educated fool is to be a concern, but an educated thug is to be cautioned. Harlem knows the laws of the land and the way around them, just as well as he knows the alphabet. In the past, he's shown his ability to manipulate corporate deals. It was said that he was seen with Eric one morning at a local coffee shop—bad news! He started off with small local hustles like three-card Monte, pyramid schemes, and always finding some gullible investor for his tee shirt or sneaker businesses. The first time, he was only slapped on the wrist and his records were expunged given his father's pull in the system. The second time, a 21-day stay in a country club kind of facility.

Harlem and I have had bad blood ever since back in the day when he was a hopeful and heavily sought after athlete showing pro potential. More importantly to me, he stole my girl Jasmine, and then there was his bullshit lying tactics in law school that almost compromised me as well. I tell you, that cat's bad news.

꩜

"Hey yourself, where are you?" I respond answering Torie's call.

"I've just left Doreen's ribbon cutting for her dress shop, and now I'm next door at your sister's bakery."

"Did her sign come in?" I ask.

"I'm looking at it as we speak—Charlie's Cupcake Factory—it's gorgeous!"

"That's alright!! Is she happy?"

"I'd say from the smile on her face and the long line of customers, she's very happy."

"Listen, grab me a few of the red velvets, okay?"

"Yup, I'll see you in a few."

"Torie," I call out before she hangs up.

"Yes?"

"I love you, girl!!"

THE BOULEVARD

One long continuous cobble-stoned street completely uniformed with mirrored images from left to right, looking backward or forward; street lanterns and planters, black wrought-iron benches, decorative street signs. The Boulevard—not the West Side or the East Side—simply The Boulevard; the main artery running through the heart of the City of Stamford, Connecticut. Busy with merchants and vendors, lofts and brownstones both residential and commercial, a location now displaying an amalgamated community that cohesively fused every resource to eliminate a past dichotomy.

"Hello everyone!!" I shouted over the incessant clapping, shouts and chants.

"Thank you . . . Thank you . . . Thank you!!"

I look over at Quinn, State Representative Hicks, Pastor Witherspoon, and Claudia Van Exel standing beside Joel Matheson and Liam Klein as they each take in this prideful moment. Speaking louder but patiently over the relentless excitement I began, "Tonight, we would like to welcome each and every one of you to The Boulevard." The crowd could no longer contain themselves; horns were blowing and children hanging on to their balloons jumping up and down obliviously screaming.

"Yes, welcome home . . . our home!!"

"Yes, each and every one of you should be proud. We've all worked so hard for this day. We knew that it would be a lot of work, but we also knew that once we pooled our resources we'd get here!!"

Strangers began hugging one another and feverishly jumping up and down as the children had. Looking around the gazebo at each familiar face made me whimsical and spiritually fulfilled, particularly when I saw Hollis and his lovely wife Angela waving and cheering me on as their twin boys danced in the crowd. I'm now a firm believer that with patience, a strong foundation and steadfast intentions, we can all make something out of second—and sometimes third—chances.

Quinn has shown me to take consideration when looking at life's many pictures and to be mindful of using the best suited lens, because clearly there are multiple views and depictions. He's also made me see that a foundation just has to be built or rebuilt in order to sustain in life. And that not all foundations are properly poured early on, but a house at any age can be rebuilt and soar with integrity.

"Who am I? I am only one out of the many proud and accomplished cultural social hybrids within our Black culture. I have used every experience that I've been given as an advantage to bridge gaps between a once-silent subculture and a very strong, proud, long-existing Black culture. Do I speak White? I say to you, 'I speak English!!' Do I act White? To that I say, 'I display remorseless human pride from a Black woman!!'"

One woman shouted over the positive mayhem, "That's alright sister . . . that's alright!!"

"So, who am I? I am Torie Harper-Matthews proudly standing here to oblige your request to introduce my husband, Quinn Matthews, as your Mayor of Stamford, Connecticut!"

My mind wondered how many people didn't realize that we'd married. Come on, no one could possibly believe that I'd let a catch like Quinn get by. Hell, I'm a woman first before belonging to any ethnicity! And as a woman, you just know!

It was last summer after our near-loss with Tishie. We both realized in that moment that it may have easily been our last; I'm still having some struggles today with those thoughts. Apparently Quinn felt the same way because after rekindling at Simone's and Nigel's wedding, he proposed within two months with a stunning 2.5-carat pear-shaped solitaire.

In August we decided to keep it "grown and sexy" and hosted a "fancy and quaint" wedding celebration. Seventy-five guests were seated in the stately ballroom aboard The Kennedy for an elegant surf and turf dinner while the boat traveled up and down the Hudson River for six hours.

Two months later, here we are. The crowd is roaring louder as Quinn kisses me and thanks me for a generous introduction.

"Thank you for accepting me as your messenger," he shouts humbly over the crowd. "Hey, I think I see my neighbors out here," joking and bringing about laughter as he reminded everyone of our recent move into a brownstone on The Boulevard. "I think you all are gonna have to make a little more noise at night. It's hard for a brother to get any sleep with all this quiet in our new neighborhood! You know, as a West Side youngster who'd moved up to the East Side, I've learned to fall asleep to the noise from the keg parties in this elite uptown building! Ha-ha . . . I'm just keeping it real." The crowd celebrated the block party as the official reopening and welcoming of the Boulevard being back.

As chairperson and mentor for a local minority organization, I'm often asked if I find the box identifying my race necessary or even offensive. In the past, I would have said yes because I personally felt that by choosing Black, it failed represent who I am. Now when asked where is the box for someone like me, I completely understand which box to select. It's the box that's been there all along, although it's changed its descriptions over the years. Black, Afro American, Negroid and Negro—a box that only identifies my race—certainly not who I am. Now that . . . well, that's all up to me!!

TRACEY FAGAN DANZEY was raised and educated in a woodsy Connecticut suburb. Following her attendance at Fairleigh Dickinson and Fairfield Universities, Tracey began to pursue her love of writing. To further her aspirations of becoming a published author, Tracey elevated her commitment by joining the Westport Writers' Workshop & Critique Group, as well as being a dedicated member of a local book club. *Jasper's Cafe On The Boulevard* is a rework of a project titled, *Where Is The Box For Someone Like Me?* This project advanced in the 2011 Amazon Breakthrough Novel Award.

Tracey currently lives in Connecticut with her beloved family and has begun working on her follow-up novel.

www.authortraceyfagandanzey.com

Photo courtesy of Mixali Media, LLC

Made in the USA
Columbia, SC
16 March 2018